"I dropped everything request, may I add. You s incredible finds in history anc it?" My voice was dangerous.., ...., and I rose to my feet, so we were face to face in the middle of the room. His eyes narrowed, and he took another step toward me, so we were only inches apart. We glared at each other, and for a split second, I thought he was going to kiss me. I could feel my heart thundering in my chest, and the atmosphere in the room was electric.

Suddenly, the door swung open, and we jumped apart in unison. Betty walked in carrying two cups of coffee and a collection of envelopes. She stopped abruptly, and her eyes widened. "Is everything okay?" she asked, looking from Marcus to me and back again to her employer.

"Everything's fine," Marcus responded, regaining his composure, and took another step back. "Ms. Clemonte will be leaving us sooner than expected. Please arrange for a flight for her today." He then gave me one last look and stalked out of the room. Betty stared after him, open-mouthed. I sat down heavily in the chair again, shaking slightly. What had just happened?

# The Slow Sip

## by

## Kirsten Abel

This is a work of fiction. Names, characters, places, and incidents are either the product of the author's imagination or are used fictitiously, and any resemblance to actual persons living or dead, business establishments, events, or locales, is entirely coincidental.

**The Slow Sip**

COPYRIGHT © 2022 by Kirsten Abel

All rights reserved. No part of this book may be used or reproduced in any manner whatsoever without written permission of the author or The Wild Rose Press, Inc. except in the case of brief quotations embodied in critical articles or reviews.
Contact Information: info@thewildrosepress.com

Cover Art by *Diana Carlile*

The Wild Rose Press, Inc.
PO Box 708
Adams Basin, NY 14410-0708
Visit us at www.thewildrosepress.com

Publishing History
First Edition, 2022
Trade Paperback ISBN 978-1-5092-4521-5
Digital ISBN 978-1-5092-4522-2


Published in the United States of America

## Dedication

For the man who makes sure that life is not boring

Chapter One

I pressed the phone closer to my ear, certain I had misheard. "You've found what?"

"We've found the Whiting Whisky," the voice said confidently.

"The Whiting Whisky," I repeated, tapping a pen on my teeth in irritation. "Of course, I have heard of it, but that story is largely discredited, Mr. McClean. Why do you think it's the Whiting Whisky?"

"There's a 'W' on the crate."

I bit my tongue. Was the man an idiot? "Yes, you can email me the photos, and I'll take a look at them." I hung up the phone with relief.

After another exhausting day at the conference, the last thing I wanted to do was entertain a disillusioned old man who had solved Scotch whisky's biggest mystery. The endless networking and round table forums had taken their toll on me, and not even the two glasses of Pinot Noir I drank at the happy hour social did anything to rejuvenate my waning energy. I headed to my hotel room, relishing the thought of taking off my shoes, watching a bad movie, and talking to no one. I was more than ready to leave on my morning flight back to my base of operations in Boston.

I dumped my swag on the floor and debated whether to perform my check-in to headquarters now or in the morning. Talking to Angus was the last thing I felt like doing, but I didn't want the call with my boss hanging over me.

"How's it going, lassie?" boomed his cheerful voice down the line.

"Well, I just had a call from a man who's found the Whiting Whisky."

He snorted. "Not bad. Solved one of the biggest Scotch mysteries and still had time to hit happy hour."

I clicked on my inbox of orders idly as he talked, flicking through the pending requests and inventory. A notification popped up in the inbox. Mr. McClean. And, of course, he had attached images to the email. I groaned inwardly, anticipating another conversation where I explained why he had *not* found the Whiting Whisky. My mouse hovered over one of the images, and I clicked. Click. Click.

"Shit." I dropped the phone.

"Emily? Emily, are you all right?" Angus's voice sounded very far away.

I could not speak for a moment. Then, retrieving the phone, I managed to stutter, "The Whiting, the Whiting Whisky, the missing…" I trailed off, eyes still glued to the image on the screen.

"What?"

"It looks like he's found it. Or something, anyway."

"What are you talking about, Emily?" Angus was beginning to sound annoyed.

"I'm going to Montana."

"What on earth is in Montana?!"

The Whiting Whisky. Until he had sent the photographs, I thought the call might be a hoax, but when I opened the first image, I immediately knew this was something I had to see with my own eyes. The legend of the Whiting Whisky was one of those stories that all Whisky aficionados had heard, and while a fun anecdote, it was never really taken seriously by anyone.

In the early 1920s, Samuel Whiting, an enterprising Scottish distiller, built up an organized import system for high-end contraband booze to satisfy the appetites of his thirsty American customers. Legend had it that law officials were moving in on Whiting's operation, so he devised a final large-scale shipping operation to Atlantic City, disguised as legitimate goods.

Rumor had it that a 'special reserve case' housed not only a one-of-a-kind blend but also a priceless painting, gifted to his daughter and son-in-law as a wedding present. There were various descriptions of the contents, each more exaggerated than the last, and thus, the actual contents of the Whiting shipment were pure speculation.

The story had various versions, including an accidental fire, but some claimed Whiting's men had purposely blown up the ship to avoid seizure. The result was the same. Whiting's entire shipment of high-end Scotch, fine Madeiras, and rare spirits had been lost to the blaze. If that hadn't been fodder enough for the tabloids, Whiting's own daughter, a beautiful socialite, had drowned trying to escape the fire.

The intrigue had come about when one of the patrolling customs agents claimed to have seen a smaller vessel leave the harbor, and debris revealed no remains of the shipment nor of a priceless painting. After the disaster, the heavily trafficked East Coast had seen even more activity with whisky hunters patrolling the waves for remains of Whiting's illicit booze or valuable artwork.

I pulled up the photos on my laptop again. He had

sent five separate images, and even though they were taken with a cellphone, the quality and light were good. The first image showed a large hole in a stone wall. In the opening was a collection of bottles of various shapes and sizes, any markings obscured by a thick layer of dust and cobwebs. The second attachment showed a small-sized crate—again, covered by the dusty layers of time. The third image had taken my breath away. Someone, presumably Mr. McClean, had wiped away the dust from the top of the crate and revealed a faint letter 'W' with the remains of what looked like an emblem depicting a horse. More likely, a unicorn, I thought, dredging my mind for my scant knowledge of the coats of arms. A "W' for Whiting. Experience told me not to jump to conclusions, but I found it hard to take my own advice.

The last two images were both bottles. A vatted Glenlivet and a cognac Jacquet, nothing remarkable, but in keeping with the times. The question, of course, was why were they hidden? Likely prohibition. Someone had hidden them and been unable, or perhaps forgot, to go back and retrieve them after the repeal of the Volstead Act. Possible. The problem was, if this was the remains of the Whiting Whisky, how on earth had it ended up in rural Montana?

I debated, lying on the bed motionless. Time for action. I swung my legs down and pulled out my cellphone. I pressed the contact for Danny, our researcher extraordinaire.

"Hi, Danny, this is Emily Clemonte."

"How's it going, Emily?" he said in a bright voice. Despite his crippling shyness, we had persevered with our conversations, and I found him to have a sarcastic sense of humor not unlike my own.

"Odd question." I cut straight to the chase. "How quickly can you date some bottles that might be the Whiting Whisky?"

He laughed, then registered I wasn't joining in. "Are you serious?"

After I hung up the phone from Danny, I sent Mr. McClean's photos to him as an encrypted file. I then began to raid my luggage to check the equipment I had with me. It was a lucky coincidence Mr. McClean had called while I was at the symposium, as I had various tools of the trade with me. Whatever awaited me was not a job for the bottle blue book. I looked at my open suitcase on the bed. Within an hour, I was in a cab heading to the airport. If any of the Whiting shipment had survived and somehow made it to the Western state of Montana, I was going to be there to see it.

I stared out the window on takeoff. My fellow passengers soon busied themselves with their laptops and phones, but I watched the clouds go by and thought about what awaited me. Work had kept me busy for the last few months, but the solitary peace of the airplane made my disciplined mind wander. Him. I shook off the thought and grabbed the airline magazine from the pocket in front of me. I flicked through the pages to the maps. Where exactly was Montana?

After Chicago, I had one more connection and boarded a much smaller plane with only four other passengers. The impression of my client had not been overwhelmingly positive. I was therefore surprised when I received an email with tickets and a hotel confirmation from his highly organized assistant Betty. She said someone would meet me at the airport, but I had no other information and wondered idly if I should look for a sign

5

with my name.

I needn't have worried. As I walked down the rickety steps to what passed as a terminal, I saw only two people waiting for the plane's arrival. One lady was hugging a short man who had sat in the seat in front of me, and the other was, presumably, my ride.

"Marcus McClean," he introduced himself with a slight drawl and an outstretched hand. "You must be Miss Clemonte. We spoke on the phone." He was a lot younger than I had expected and a lot more handsome. Sun-bleached brown hair and tanned skin evidenced much time outside, and his tall form was clothed in jeans and a light gray shirt, the epitome of the laid-back cowboy. I didn't know what color his eyes were behind the sunglasses and was annoyed at myself for the thought. I took a breath and caught a faint wisp of his cologne.

"Hi," I managed in return, wishing I had worn more makeup and my hair wasn't so windblown from standing on the tarmac. We stood looking at each other for a moment longer than was necessary, and without waiting for permission, he grabbed my bag and, with a look of amusement, gestured I should accompany him. He opened the door to a waiting pickup, and I climbed up into the passenger seat. I waited while he exchanged a joke with the airport's sole employee and watched him saunter toward the vehicle. He jumped into the cab, and I felt inexplicably nervous at his presence. We drove in silence that wasn't exactly the comfortable kind until I broke it by asking how the discovery had been made.

"We were doing some construction, knocked out a wall to extend one of the rooms, and that's what they found."

"I bet that caused some excitement," I offered.

"Yeah." A one-word response. The silence continued until he asked, "Ever been to Montana before?"

I shook my head. "This is my first time. I haven't been to the Western part of the country at all. I'm based on the East Coast."

"That figures."

So this was how it was going to be. I vowed not to care. This was going to be a short trip, whatever the findings. I had enough faith in my knowledge of the market to offer some pricing, but with such a legend attached, it would be uncharted territory, and bidding could set a new precedent.

"I think I might be able to manage a few nights in a hotel," I said, giving him a condescending smile and hoping he would pick up on the sarcasm in my response. I saw the side of his mouth curve upward slightly and took that to mean I had hit my mark.

"Can you tell me what happened when the wall came down?" I attempted again.

"We found a room full of old whisky bottles."

"Right." He was not going to make this easy for me. It appeared he was deliberately trying to annoy me, and I couldn't figure out why. "Mr. McClean," I addressed him in what I intended to be a stern voice, but even to my own ears sounded pompous, "you brought me here to authenticate these bottles. The more information you can give me, the quicker the process will be." And the sooner I can leave, I thought.

"Well, you're the expert. Not sure what you expect me to tell you." He was looking at the road with the same amused expression. Damn handsome. And apparently, a damn asshole too.

I looked out the window as the fields rolled by. I wanted to know how long this excruciating drive would take, but it seemed as though our small talk was exhausted. We sat in silence for another twenty minutes until he pulled the truck into a long drive, lined on each side with the tallest pine trees I had ever seen. The drive was winding and the trees so dense that I couldn't immediately see our destination. Finally, the road revealed a house so perfectly situated my jaw dropped open. An enormous chalet made of thick beams and rugged stones. The setting was a postcard. The place was enormous and screamed luxury. I couldn't wait to see inside.

"Is this your house?"

He didn't respond but shifted in the seat to face me. An uncomfortable moment passed as we just sat looking at each other, and then he finally gave an imperceptible nod.

"I don't know much about mountain retreats, Mr. McClean, but this house looks pretty new."

"It is."

I put my hand on the door, but he said, "Allow me." He jumped down and extended a strong arm to help me to the ground. I willed myself not to blush as he hoisted me down from the cab with his hands around my waist.

"This is the house where I live. This isn't where we found the booze."

"Right. So…"

"So you want to get straight down to business?"

"I'm that kind of girl."

"I can see that." He captured me in the same expression that made me want to jump into his arms and slap him across the face at the same time.

"Can you help me reach my bag?" I asked pointedly.

"I'll leave your stuff in the vehicle and take you to the hotel when you're ready. We can take a look now, as you're so impatient."

He swung open the imposing front door, and though I had planned to appear unimpressed, I instead said, "Wow."

I gazed upon a huge common room with enormous, vaulted ceilings from which hung several large wrought iron light fixtures. A dome in the center was held up by thick wooden beams arranged in a semicircle. Looking through this central feature, I could see floor-to-ceiling windows, tumbled rock walls, and two fireplaces. There was a collection of leather sofas strewn with luxe throws and pillows in the western theme. I had never thought this to be my taste, but the house was beautiful. I heard footsteps on the hardwood floor, and a lady I assumed to be in her early seventies approached us. She smiled and held out her hand in greeting. "I'm Betty Foster, Mr. McClean's estate manager."

"Nice to meet you. I'm Emily Clemonte."

"Well, we've had some excitement with this discovery. We're happy you could come so quickly." She had a warm, welcoming manner, and her voice was refined and soothing. I warmed to her immediately and was struck by the contrast to the rude and monosyllabic Marcus McClean, who stood next to her.

She led me away to a large kitchen off the main room and offered me various things to drink. Another man around the same age as Betty walked in and affixed me with a smile. "This is my husband, Ron," Betty introduced him. "He's probably sniffing around for some snacks." She tapped him playfully on the belly, and he beamed at his wife. I liked them both already.

"How long have you worked for Mr. McClean?" I asked, looking back through the door where he stood looking down at his cell phone, by a large arrangement of fresh flowers.

"A long time, honey." She smiled and shook her head. "The years pass in the blink of an eye."

"Is there a Mrs. McClean?" I inquired, not entirely innocently.

Betty faced me with a sly smile on her face. "Not anymore."

We moved back to where Marcus waited, and I followed him through the main room to an exit at the other side of the house. We emerged onto a large deck with one of the most wondrous views I had ever seen. "This is incredible," I breathed, spellbound by the natural beauty.

"Wouldn't have thought it was your taste." He sounded a little surprised.

"It isn't wise to make judgments about people you've just met, Mr. McClean," I snapped.

"Fair enough. And call me Marcus." He set off across the deck and walked down a set of stairs that led to the ground below. Asshole, I thought for the second time.

I followed him along a narrow stone path that snaked through the trees. After the short walk, we came to a small clearing, and I saw our destination. Happily nestled among the trees was a small cabin straight from the pages of a fairytale. Large rough-cut stones had been lovingly assembled and gave the structure a romantic appearance, yet it appeared sturdy, designed to weather the test of time. I paused for a moment to admire it, and Marcus slowed his own step. "This was one of the original buildings put up by my family when they bought the land. We tore down the main house but never messed with this."

"It's beautiful. It looks as though different people created it."

"What do you mean?" He looked puzzled.

"It has charm and romance, but at the same time, it's hardy and reliable."

"Can't one person have all those qualities?" Marcus asked thoughtfully.

"I suppose they can." We looked at each other, and an odd atmosphere settled between us. I turned hastily back to the business at hand. "And this is where you found it?" A nod.

The cabin was not furnished in such opulence as the main house, but the interior was still tastefully decorated with carefully chosen items. "It's back here." He started into one of the bedrooms. The floor was covered in plastic sheeting, and I stepped carefully to avoid the tools. There was a large hole in the wall, and peeking through, I could just make out the shadowy outline of bottles. He explained they had tried not to touch it but had taken a few photos, which had subsequently been sent to me.

Any initial foreboding I had that the bottles might be fakes disappeared when I set foot inside the cabin. I knew I was stepping into history, and hidden behind the wall was the proof, quite literally. Marcus pulled out a flashlight, explaining that the wiring was not yet finished. He offered me the light, which I snatched and used to peer inside the wall. The light found its target, and I gasped. It was the most incredible thing I had ever seen in my life. I pulled on a pair of forensic gloves I'd brought with me and gingerly reached out for the closest bottle.

After carefully wiping a little dust, I saw it to be a Macallan Valerio. I exhaled slowly and set it to the side to be cleaned. I wanted to cherish the first touch of every single bottle, but my impatience got the better of me. I moved the light around, searching for the object I had come to see. I reached for the crate.

Chapter Two

The crate didn't open. I tried again, a little more forcefully this time, but the lid didn't want to budge. I gave the flashlight back to Marcus, who stood beside me and made an impatient clicking noise. I shot him a withering look. "It's stuck."

He scanned the floor for an appropriate tool, but I shook my head. "We have to be careful. The crate is part of the packaging and is an important clue to the origin." He wasn't listening and motioned for me to move aside. Against my better judgment, I moved away. "Be gentle," I warned unnecessarily.

Marcus felt around the opening carefully, his slender fingers touching the grooves of the rim to find a weakness he could exploit. Unconsciously, I leaned in a little too close, and our heads almost touched. I smelled his cologne again and pulled away abruptly, disliking his effect on me.

"It's getting looser." A click.

Suddenly the lid began to slide from its long resting place. We both drew in breath simultaneously. Packing paper. Marcus began to rummage, tentatively at first, then with more urgency. "Careful," I hissed again. "You should be wearing gloves."

He ignored me; he had found something. Another box, this one designed to hold a bottle. "More liquor. I was kind of hoping we were going to find that priceless painting."

He opened the smaller box, and we both peered down at the bottle inside. It was a masterpiece; every inch of it was perfect. But it wasn't the contents of the bottle that interested me the most, it was the label. An exquisite caricature of two lovers etched with precision into the glass. It took me a moment to process my thoughts. Could it be?

"John Duncan," I finally stated triumphantly.

"What?"

I ran my gloved fingers carefully over the label. The surface was uneven where the paint had been applied to the etched grooves with greater thickness. The image was beautiful, classic early Duncan style. I made another exclamation when I found the date and signature. It was perfect in every way.

"Well? Is it worth something? Even if we didn't find any expensive art?"

"On the contrary." I turned to him, my face flushed with excitement. "That's exactly what we have found."

Marcus was waiting for me to explain myself, but it was time to take charge. "We have to get all the bottles out of here, but not in direct sunlight. Don't let anyone touch them without gloves. Or at all," I added as an afterthought. "We have to get things sent to the lab for testing."

He looked at me as if I had lost my mind. "This isn't a crime scene. We're not CSI."

I was fully alert now and ready to stand my ground. "Mr. McClean, Marcus," I corrected, "you might have the rarest bottle of Scotch in the world sitting here in your guest cabin. We need to do things properly."

"Let's not get ahead of ourselves." He addressed me

slowly as if talking to a small child. "I'm assuming the bottles are genuine?"

"I can't say for certain without more information, but yes, these bottles do appear genuine."

"I told you we had found the Whiting Whisky."

"That's not what I said at all." I frowned, and he opened his arms in a gesture that asked me to explain myself. "The age of the bottles, at least the three I have looked at here near the opening, coincides with that timeline. The glass, stoppers, and labels fit with the late nineteenth- and early twentieth-century manufacturing. The whisky is Scottish in origin, to be sure, and the brands are all consistent with that period of history. And this original label could be worth more than everything else put together." I focused again on the bottle with the caricature; I still couldn't believe it was real.

"But…" Marcus interrupted.

"But," I repeated, "we have nothing to say that this is the missing Whiting Whisky."

"Where did it come from, then?"

"It could have come from anywhere. I don't remember seeing anything in the archives linking Samuel Whiting to Montana. This is a long way from Atlantic City where everything happened," I reminded him, "and"—I paused for effect—"all historical accounts of the Whiting Whisky indicate that the whole shipment was destroyed. It's a great story but without any facts to back it up."

"I see." He was leaning against the wall now with his arms folded.

I suddenly felt a little nervous in his presence and continued hurriedly, "This is still an incredible find. If these bottles check out as I suspect they will, and we have an original label by John Duncan…" I trailed off, not sure what that would even mean for the value. "There's not ever been a find like this before that just appeared from nowhere. There's no telling how much this would fetch when you auction it off."

"Aha."

"I can start on the removal after I've made some calls. We need to arrange the transport, and I have to get everything photographed as soon as possible." Betty and Ron chose that moment to appear in the doorway, their faces eager for information.

"She says it's genuine but not the Whiting Whisky." Marcus gestured rudely in my direction, and I felt an immense flash of annoyance.

"That's actually *not* what I said." I glared at Marcus. I explained again to Betty and Ron that, essentially, we were at the beginning of the process. The crate would need to be analyzed more extensively to establish a clear connection with Whiting.

I spent the next few hours sitting on the floor of the cabin, meticulously removing the remaining bottles from their hiding place behind the wall. With every touch, it was as though a piece of the past was coming back to life. I surmised the hidey-hole had been built intentionally, after checking the angles of the adjoining rooms. It had been crudely constructed but very cleverly designed, and I was not surprised that the cache had remained undiscovered for almost a hundred years. Marcus had hung around for about twenty minutes after our terse discussion, then excused himself to deal with more pressing matters. I was wholly absorbed in my task and lost all track of time until I finally stood up to rub my aching joints. I stepped outside to stretch and saw the sun was already low in the sky. When I pulled out my phone, it was a surprise to see it was almost seven o'clock. On cue, I saw Betty walking through the trees along the stone path, and I held up my hand in a wave.

"Hi, hon. How's it going here?"

"Great. Amazing. Incredible," I said with a huge grin on my face.

She returned my smile and then told me I needed to take a break and get something to eat. I enjoyed her motherly fussing, being unused to such attention, and allowed myself to be led back to the main house. My small suitcase had been moved to her vehicle, and she was happy to take me to the hotel whenever I was ready, but I would be most welcome to join her and Ron for dinner at the house.

"Is Marcus gone?" I asked, looking around.

"He had to go into town."

I sat at the kitchen counter with Ron and Betty and devoured a delicious meal of pasta and bison meatballs. The couple were delightful company, and I enjoyed their affectionate banter. Full and appeased, I yawned and realized how tired I was.

"Someone needs to get to bed," Betty said, looking at Ron.

"And that's my cue to drive Emily to her hotel." Ron gcsturcd for me to follow him out to his truck.

At the hotel, I immediately washed the cabin dust from my body in the steaming shower and fell gratefully onto the clean bed. There was so much for my mind to process, but my body decided otherwise, and within a minute, I was fast asleep.

I slept for longer than intended, so exhausted by the events of the day that I hadn't even reached for the container of sleeping pills I normally needed to welcome sleep. My cellphone signaled a morning message from Betty, and I sent a quick reply to confirm that I would be ready to head back to the cabin in an hour. I stood in front of the mirror, holding up a couple of outfits to my reflection as I berated myself for the vanity. Did it matter what I was wearing to scrabble around a dirty cabin? My thoughts returned unbidden to Marcus McClean, and I scowled in the mirror. Why was he so rude and arrogant?

A slightly stale blueberry muffin greeted me in the lobby downstairs, and I picked unenthusiastically through the breakfast, reasoning that I would work better with something on my stomach. Coffee was the most important fuel of the day, and I was on my second cup when I saw Betty's truck pull in.

"How did you sleep, hon?" she asked as we drove in the direction of the McClean property.

"Well. I was tired."

"Strange being by yourself?" She inquired, looking not very surreptitiously at the naked finger on my left hand.

"I live alone," I responded, staring at the road ahead to signal an end to her line of inquiry.

She seemed not to notice my discomfort and cheerfully began to tell me all about life in Montana and the one time she had visited Seattle, which only reinforced that she could never live in a city.

"It certainly is beautiful out here," I told her wistfully. "I can understand that it would be difficult to leave all this behind."

"We couldn't leave Marcus either. He wouldn't know what to do without us," she said, laughing.

"He seems a little…" I broke off, searching for the

right word to say to her, which probably wasn't "asshole."

She smiled fondly. "I know how he can be. He's a little rough around the edges, but that's just hiding a heart of gold. He's getting better now that ex-wife of his is finally gone for good."

"Was his divorce recent?"

She sighed. "He filed a few years ago, but she dragged it out for as long as she could. He's well rid of that one. Gold-digger," she told me conspiratorially. I murmured in agreement, hoping she would continue. "But I'm not one to talk about other people's business," she concluded briskly.

We arrived at the ranch after the short drive, and despite being there only a few hours before, I looked on the beautiful land with a renewed appreciation. I took a breath of the fresh air, tinged with a hint of manure, and agreed that this was a beautiful place to wake up to every morning. Betty ushered me into the main house and told me Marcus wanted to check in before I headed back to the cabin again. She showed me into a large study off the main foyer, and I sank into an oversized leather chair to wait. Despite my two cups of coffee, I agreed to Betty's offer of another small one, enticed by the delicious aroma wafting from the kitchen. Footsteps approached, and Marcus strode into the room. I moved to stand and greet him, but he motioned to stay where I was sitting.

"Good morning, Ms. Clemonte," he said in his low voice, taking a seat opposite me.

"Call me Emily," I said, mimicking our conversation of the afternoon before.

The side of his mouth twitched, but then he fixed me with a hard stare. "I think there may have been a misunderstanding about what you are doing here." I said nothing, deciding it would be more prudent to let him continue. The phrase "know your enemies" flashed into my mind. "You were brought here to authenticate my bottles, and that's what you've done."

"Hardly," I responded indignantly. "We're only at the beginning of the process. We need to send things for testing. I know enough of the current market conditions to place a value of about twenty-seven thousand on the Scotch, if you add up the bottles independently, but there's no precedent for the collection together, and as for the bottle with the Duncan label…if it's genuine, you have a one-of-a-kind."

I opened my mouth to continue, but he put up a hand to silence me. "I know you said more tests were needed, but, in your opinion, the bottles were real."

"Yes," I ventured cautiously, "but that's one person's opinion. To get them properly valued, we need to send them for testing. If you plan to sell, you need to do that and get them on the books, probably at Sotheby's, as soon as possible."

"I didn't contract you to sell them. I contracted you to authenticate them." That tone again. He articulated his words slowly and deliberately as if I had not mastered language very well, and he sought to make it as easy as possible for me to understand.

"Correct. But to properly *au-then-ti-cate*"—I stretched out the syllables to the point of rudeness—"I have to be able to do my job. And that includes running those tests and getting a secondary agreement."

"Aha."

I rolled my eyes dramatically, patience wearing thin. "Mr. McClean, I don't understand why you don't seem to want me to do the job you called me here to do."

He nodded slowly, then rose to his feet. He leaned across the desk and stretched out his hand. "It's been a pleasure, Emily."

"What?" I burst out. "Are you hiring someone else?"

"No, no, I'm not. And I remind you that you signed a non-disclosure agreement when you agreed to the terms and conditions in our contract."

"I dropped everything and came here—at your request, may I add. You show me one of the most incredible finds in history and then tell me to forget about it?" My voice was dangerously shrill, and I rose to my feet, so we were face to face in the middle of the room. His eyes narrowed, and he took another step toward me, so we were only inches apart. We glared at each other, and for a split second, I thought he was going to kiss me. I could feel my heart thundering in my chest, and the atmosphere in the room was electric.

Suddenly, the door swung open, and we jumped apart in unison. Betty walked in carrying two cups of coffee and a collection of envelopes. She stopped abruptly, and her eyes widened. "Is everything okay?" she asked, looking from Marcus to me and back again to her employer.

"Everything's fine," Marcus responded, regaining his composure, and took another step back. "Ms. Clemonte will be leaving us sooner than expected. Please arrange for a flight for her today." He then gave me one last look and stalked out of the room. Betty stared after him, open-mouthed. I sat down heavily in the chair again, shaking slightly. What had just happened?

"Are you okay, hon?" Betty was looking at me with concern. "Was Marcus being his usual self? Don't take it personally. He has a lot on his mind, but I know he can come off as rude." She patted me on the shoulder consolingly.

I suddenly felt defeated. I couldn't believe I had been dismissed so quickly and without explanation but couldn't immediately think of anything I could do about it. On the plus side, I would now be able to leave and go as far away as possible from this obnoxious man.

"Would you be able to drive me to the hotel?" I asked Betty.

She looked crestfallen. "Are you sure you need to leave right now?"

"Yes, I'm sure. Mr. McClean has made it very clear that I should leave as soon as possible."

"Of course. I'll just grab my keys."

I waited for Betty in front of the house and admired the beautiful property again. It was a shame I wouldn't get to spend more time there. My cellphone buzzed, and I saw it was Angus. Impeccable timing, as always.

"What's the news?" he barked, no time for pleasantries.

"Well, it could certainly be the Whiting Whisky, but unfortunately, I'm not going to be able to stay and find out."

"What? Why not?" his voice was unusually high and panicked.

"The owner is a real piece of work. I'm not sure why he even got me out here in the first place."

"Well, I'm sure you can make peace with him for something like this," he cast around for a platitude.

I snorted. "Not likely. We haven't got off to a very good start."

"Emily, there's something you should know…" He

faltered, and I suddenly had a sinking feeling. "You see, the business…"

"What about the business?"

"I'm not quite sure how to tell you this, Emily…"

"What?" I practically screamed.

"Well, the finances are a little shaky right now."

"Shaky?"

"Do you remember the Macallan?"

Of course I remembered it. We had leveraged a huge amount to procure the bottle, but there seemed little risk as Angus already had two buyers lined up. "Yes, so?"

"So it's not quite what we thought. It's a copy. It was made close to the time of the original but is significantly less valuable."

I cursed. "So what exactly are you telling me?"

"Unless something else comes our way, we'll be up the creek without a paddle."

I cursed again. 'But," Angus continued, a little brighter this time, "if you've just found the Whiting Whisky, I imagine that would be very good for business."

"Dammit, Angus," I said and concluded the call as I saw Marcus striding toward me. I pulled my sunglasses out of my bag and put them on, feeling better equipped to deal with the confrontation. The news I had just learned made the situation even more complicated. He stopped in front of me, and several seconds passed until he finally spoke.

"Are you just blowing smoke about this whisky?"

"Blowing smoke? I'm not going to tell you things you want to hear unless they're true."

He nodded sagely. "I believe that we may be able to come to some sort of agreement." A pause. "If you are willing to agree to some terms and conditions." I wanted to tell him he could shove his terms and conditions where the sun didn't shine but bit my tongue in the hope that we might find a way forward. We were back to business.

"I'm willing to discuss your terms and conditions."

"I don't know how that whisky got there. But the fact that someone buried it behind a secret wall leads me to conclude that it probably wasn't acquired by legitimate means."

"Sure, but it was during Prohibition, most likely, and besides, that just adds to the value. Everyone loves a good story." I shrugged.

"But what if it's the Whiting Whisky?"

"Even better. If we can make a connection like that, it would add untold value to the collection, and it would take its rightful place in history."

He wasn't nodding in agreement. "I've heard several versions of that story, and none of them end with a lot of people getting out alive. From what I've read, a young girl and some innocent sailors all lost their lives. If some of the missing whisky shows up in my ancestor's house, what conclusions would you draw from that?"

My face fell. I hadn't considered these implications. "But we don't know anything yet. Maybe we should save those kinds of questions until we can find out more information. Right now, we don't have any link to the Whiting Whisky except the rarity of the collection. The Duncan label is the key. There must be historical records we can find. It must have been commissioned, and we might be able to find a link with Whiting that way."

He nodded his head thoughtfully. "But you can see why I don't want to broadcast this just yet."

"I do. And I can offer discretion if you give me a

chance to find out the story."

"Then I will choose to trust you. Please don't make me regret it."

We walked back to the cabin, an uncomfortable atmosphere between us, and upon arriving, he left me alone immediately to begin the challenging task of cleaning the bottles. I surveyed them, laid them out neatly, and felt a protective nervousness. I wasn't comfortable with them sitting unsecured in the cabin where anyone could conceivably take them.

"Where did you come from?" I said it out loud. Without an answer, I began the arduous task of wrapping and labeling them individually. I followed a meticulous process, glad that I'd had the foresight to ask Ron to collect appropriate packing supplies the day before. The cabin had been retrofitted with air conditioning, but the air still felt stifled and musty, and I was glad when I finally finished and stood outside on the deck to stretch my aching muscles. Realizing the time again, I walked back into the main house.

"Hello?" I looked around, not hearing anyone else. "It's Emily," I called out, a little louder this time. I felt like an interloper and knowing I had the right to be there did nothing to assuage the feeling that I was a voyeur of someone else's life. Despite the uncomfortable feeling, my curiosity about Marcus was piqued. He was very successful, judging by the scale of his house and business, and I sensed there was a definite sense of humor under the rough demeanor, but it certainly couldn't make up for his rudeness. I was beginning to think I had imagined the chemistry between us earlier and was relieved at the possibility that might mean we could ignore it altogether.

I prowled through the main room in the direction of the kitchen where I thought I might find Betty. Upon inspection, the furnishings were even more beautiful than I'd thought, and I noted more antiques and rare art than modern furniture. The result was an interior designer's dream and looked to have jumped off the page of a "rich cowboy" weekly, I thought wryly. My nosiness was interrupted when I heard Betty's voice behind me, making me jump. "I didn't mean to scare you, hon," she said with a tinkling laugh.

"It was you I was looking for."

"Hungry? Thirsty?"

"Both," I told her with a grateful smile. We talked of nothing in particular as she fixed me a sandwich and homemade chips, and I relaxed for the first time that day in her easy company. Her staunch defense of Marcus and his unwelcoming behavior demonstrated a strong loyalty and affection for her employer, and I felt a little more generous toward him, hearing her talk. I confided to her my misgivings about having the bottles unsecured in the cabin, but she waved away my concerns. "The ranch is secure, and we know all the folk around here. It's different from the city."

"Will Marcus be back soon?"

"Probably. He just went into Fairview to pick up a few things."

"I need to ask him some questions about his grandparents, or great-grandparents, maybe. I'm trying to figure out the timeline from the twenties. It's our best starting point to find out how the whisky got there and where it came from."

"It's a mystery," she said brightly.

"But one I'd like to solve."

Chapter Three

*1920, Inverness, Scotland*

James Macleary hurried down Argyle Street. He wasn't late for his interview at Whitings, but he remembered what his mam always said about the early bird and the worm. The world was changing, and he was determined to be on the side of the future and not the past. After the end of the Great War, so many people had been abandoned, rejected by the society for which they had fought so bravely. James knew he was one of the lucky ones. In the Royal Navy, he had seen his share of action but had never been hit by bombardments and received a good meal almost every day of his enlistment. It was a relief when the war was over, a great cost paid by so many, but he was left uncertain of his next move.

He had celebrated with a generous dram of Balvenie and, despite his thirst, held it in his hand and inhaled for a long moment before bringing the golden liquid to his lips. The smell of Scotland.

There were worse things for an ex-sailor to do than spend his time working at a distillery and one of the best in the Highlands at that, so he waited with nervous anticipation for his meeting with Benjamin Greer, Mr. Whiting's second in command.

"Macleary?" said a voice belonging to a small, portly man with a crumpled suit and thinning hair.

James jumped to his feet and was ushered through the door to where Benjamin Greer motioned absentmindedly for him to sit. He waited in uncomfortable silence as Greer positioned his monocle and busied himself with an enormous pile of papers on his desk.

Minutes passed, and neither said a word. James tentatively cleared his throat, and Benjamin Greer seemed suddenly alerted to the person sitting in his office as though he himself had not shown him in minutes earlier.

"Aha. What's your name again, son?" he demanded. James repeated his introductions, wondering if the man was half-mad.

"And to which station are you applying?" he said, removing the monocle and peering intently at the uncomfortable young man opposite him.

James cleared his throat. "Well, sir, my father worked for Mr. Whiting on the floor many years ago, so I had a mind to follow in his footsteps."

"I see." Greer picked up his papers again and began to read once more. James sat in the uneasy silence, wondering if he had said something wrong. Suddenly, Greer slapped the papers back down on the table and barked, "Experience?"

"I haven't worked directly with bottling before," James stammered, "but I'm a quick study, sir. My captain always said so." A touch of pride.

"Navy?"

"Yes, sir, five years active. I started as a steward but worked my way up."

Greer peered at him curiously. "Enlisted?"

"Yes, sir." James fingered the hat in his hands,

unsure where the line of questioning was going.

"Tell me about your experience with ships. Are you acquainted with smaller craft?"

"Yes, sir, actually I prefer to navigate smaller craft. The captain always said I was a natural." James swallowed.

Greer continued to stare at him, and James looked down at the table, unclear what information he was supposed to impart, when the line of questioning changed abruptly. "What do you know about whisky? Apart from how to drink it?"

James responded with a nervous chuckle. "My father taught me a lot about casks and strength and the best methods of distilling. I have a good nose, too."

"I see. You'll start on Monday. Report to Smithson in the warehouse."

James scrambled to his feet. "Thank you for the opportunity, sir." Greer was no longer listening and waved his hand in the direction of the door, indicating dismissal.

James was euphoric as he walked outside to the street. He knew he was a lucky one, and this just proved it. He had been born to a lowly station in life but was blessed with loving parents and a close brood of siblings. He'd realized early in life that he had a sharp mind, and his mother was always telling him that he needed to put it to use. The onset of the Great War had provided such an opportunity, and despite the horrors of those four years, he experienced rapid upward mobility that had whet his appetite with ambition. He knew if he could just get a foot in the door, he would be able to prove himself and climb the ranks. His captain had credited him with "thinking in a different way," and after a few strategic suggestions, he had often found himself called to the stateroom to help the higher-ups plot their moves.

His mother had been livid when he told her he had resigned his position and would no longer be in uniform. Her anger had been further compounded by his refusal to take a wife and settle down. His father, as usual, had sat in his chair, smoking his pipe, and cast an amused glance at his son. "What are you going to do with yourself, then, lad?" he asked, and that had been the question.

One of his childhood friends tried to persuade him to join a group of "chancers" as his Mam would have called them, working every job they could find to save for passage to America. James was intrigued by the idea, attracted by the prospect of adventure in the land of opportunity, but he had heard enough stories from the chancers that had gone before to know there were more poor Scots and Irish lads than there were opportunities. At least here he knew the lay of the land.

His lowly beginnings meant that he did not have any means or connections, so James knew he had to rely on his agile mind and quick wiles to make his way in the world. His natural charm and cheeky demeanor only abetted the swagger that the twenty-three-year-old had in abundance and made for a potent combination. He sauntered down the high street, raising his hand to shout a greeting to the traders he knew and to ruffle the hair of one or two of the grubby young boys that circled him as he walked along. He was well-liked among the working men of the borough and even more so by the lasses. He had quickly developed a reputation, since his return to Scotland, as a ladies' man and was never short of willing company when the sun went down. That evening it was going to be Flora Hamilton, and he grinned in anticipation of her generous bosom and round behind.

"Jimmy boy!" he was hailed by his friend Billy Wilson, who fell in beside him as he made his way down the cobblestones. Together they dodged the flurry of activity from bicycles, horses, and even a motor vehicle. They both stopped for a moment to admire it as it glided past them.

"One day, Billy, that's going to be me," James told his friend as he lifted his hat slightly to the suited gentleman in the shining new Argyll.

"Do you not know who that is?" Billy spluttered with laughter. "That's Samuel Whiting. As in Whiting Whisky. Even if you found all the riches in Scotland, I can't imagine you'd be as rich as him."

"You never know what the future might hold, Billy lad. Maybe I'll marry a rich lass who'll keep me in style." James smirked at his grandiose ambition.

"She'd have to have a face like a sow to go with the likes of a pauper like you."

"Does old Sammy Whiting there have a daughter? Is she ugly enough?" They both guffawed as they strolled along.

****

Five miles away, at Baliforth House, Sarah Whiting was not in a good mood. The fact that she was in Scotland was not a good beginning to the day. She found her ancestral home dark, depressing, and lonely and wanted nothing more than to return to her life in England.

Aunt Kitty was the perfect guardian for her there. Preoccupied with her own social engagements, she was more than happy to let her niece dictate her own schedule. Sarah had quickly amassed many like-minded acquaintances in both the town of Bath, where they officially resided, and in London, where she spent most of her time, among the newly powerful women of London's social scene. With title, wealth, and beauty, many doors opened, and Sarah's quick wit and penchant for salacious gossip ensured that she was a favorite and frequented all the best parties, where she would converse with an ear to the ground for interesting tidbits to add to her arsenal.

Sarah had a mild interest in fashion, a keen interest in politics, but her chief concern, as always, was her freedom. As a child, she had devoured books with tales of danger and adventure and spent many of her lonely nights dreaming of escape from her privileged and predictable existence. Her father had sought to check her "wild" temperament and had always selected similar caretakers for her. Dull, unimaginative women whom he had personally instructed regarding the need to instill in his daughter a sense of propriety and respect for the order of things. The outbreak of war in 1914 had barely affected the day-to-day life of twelve-year-old Miss Sarah Rose Violet Whiting, and she had romanticized the conflict and even felt envy for the boys who got to travel to the continent.

As the years had passed and she had turned from child to young woman, she had seen the shattered souls returning from the front and realized how small her closeted existence was in relation to the big wide world beyond. She vowed to stay in ignorance no longer and resolved that however unpleasant life was, she would nevertheless experience it. Life in London had afforded her many such opportunities, and the circles in which she mixed had given her windows into many ideas that her father would have deemed wholly unsuitable for an eighteen-year-old girl.

Politics is not a place for women, she had been taught, but her recent sojourns to the capital had left her questioning this wisdom. According to her more cosmopolitan friends, London was one of the most progressive cities in the world, and they, as young women, were the face of the future. Sarah had initially been scandalized by the behavior of some of her more worldly counterparts but quickly acclimated herself to the widening role of women. While the predominant social expectations of her gender would most likely never change, she reflected ruefully, she had glimpsed the possibility of a future where she had a chance to be something other than a pretty wallflower.

When her father had summoned her back to Scotland, she had tried various tactics to forestall the trip, but he had been firm in his insistence, and his demands were not be ignored. So there she was, sullen and uncooperative in her rooms at the Baliforth estate, waiting for the chance to escape. She heard activity in the rooms below and surmised he had probably returned from town. Moments later, the manservant informed her that her father was waiting for her downstairs in one of the drawing rooms. She believed she knew the reason for the summons, and as she headed down the stairs to join him for breakfast, she felt a definite sense of foreboding. She would have to bring all her powers of persuasion to the forefront to direct the course of events to her satisfaction. Her father might well be her most challenging adversary yet.

"Good morning, Father, how lovely to see you." She landed a quick kiss on his cheek before seating herself opposite him and pouring tea for them both from the silver serving set that had been laid meticulously on the table.

After a few minutes of requisite pleasantries, her father skillfully diverted the subject toward its intended target. "Did you see the Campbells at all on your visits to London?"

"No, Father," Sarah responded, shooting him a dazzling smile, on high alert now with the unwelcome mention of the Campbells.

"Their son Archie spends some time there, I am told." he continued mildly, stirring his teacup.

Sarah's eyes narrowed; her suspicions were now confirmed. "I don't think we move in the same circles, Father, and I thought the Campbells were business rivals of yours?" she said sweetly with an innocent tilt of her head.

Samuel Whiting surveyed his daughter with wry amusement. He had felt disappointment, naturally, that she had not been born a boy, but aside from the need to produce an heir, he had not had any interest in children at all. When his wife died, he had toyed with the idea of remarrying with a view to producing an heir but had not found anyone he could tolerate enough. Besides, he was more than content with the attentions of his mistress, Belle, to spend much time on the matter. The result was that his only child had grown up away from his ideas of discipline and been allowed mostly free rein over her own affairs under the tutelage of his younger sister Kitty.

She had obviously inherited his manipulation skills, and he thought momentarily that it was a shame he would not have time to get to know her better before she moved on to her matrimonial home. It was not an opportunity to be missed, though, as her marriage to Archibald would provide him with a long-desired treaty with the Campbells, whose political and economic aspirations were second only to his own. He watched his daughter for a moment longer as they sipped their tea and hoped she wouldn't cause any disruption to his plans. He had already made arrangements with Campbell Senior and wanted to have the matter concluded as soon as possible. He had mentioned the Campbell boy, and if he had assessed his daughter's intelligence accurately, she would understand his meaning. He would allow her a little time to get used to the idea before discussing more detailed arrangements about the union. He mused that it might be a good opportunity to bring in some other investors. The nouveau riche always enjoyed a lavish affair, and there was nothing better than a wedding.

\*\*\*\*

Sarah was pulling on her fur-trimmed coat in a hurry. She was desperate to leave the confines of her father's house and venture out to town, even if that only meant to Inverness. She summoned the chauffeur and sat sullenly in the back of the Argyll as they drove the short distance to the smog of the city. Pratt's was her destination, being the only passable clothing store in what she considered this northern backwater, and she thought a few indulgences on her father's account might improve her mood. Archie Campbell! She tossed her red hair over her shoulder in a gesture of impatience. She had only met him in passing on a couple of occasions and could scarcely remember him, which meant he was probably an uninteresting meek little character.

The car moved at a snail's pace and slowed to a complete stop. The chauffeur struggled to manage the engine and prevent a stall. "Why are we going so slowly?" she demanded, disliking the stares of the people in the streets, attracted by the novelty of the motor vehicle and the captivating figure of Sarah herself.

"There's a lot of people around here, Miss. Lots of children play in these streets, and they don't always move that quickly."

She rolled her eyes at the explanation. "They shouldn't be in the street, then. These roads were paved for horses and motor vehicles. Can't you go just a bit faster?"

The beleaguered driver stepped cautiously on the pedal, increasing the speed a fraction, and gripped the steering wheel tightly. A toy whip-and-top spun directly into his path, followed by a small boy who froze, paralyzed by the shock of seeing the motor heading straight for him. The driver slammed on the brakes, and the tires screeched across the wet cobblestones.

James Macleary had been absorbed in his thoughts and unaware of the commotion behind him until it was too late. Instinctively he hurled himself to push the child out of the path of danger but, in doing so, placed himself to take the brunt of the impact. The car knocked him off balance, and his muscled frame was thrown into the air to plummet with great force back down on the bonnet. The car finally skidded to a stop, and his motionless body slumped to the ground.

The whole event had happened within a few seconds, and for another one, it seemed as though time was suspended as all the players struggled to act. Sarah began to scream as she witnessed the scene before her. The driver jumped out of his seat and ran to the aid of the crumpled body. The mother of the child who had narrowly escaped grabbed her son hysterically. The crowd swelled as passersby began to cluster around the victim.

James was aware of noise and a throbbing pain behind his ear as he slowly moved his appendages. His quick brain pieced together the sequence of events, and when he tried to sit up, aided by a worried man in a chauffeur's jacket, he was relieved that his body, although a little sore, was able to respond to his intended movements.

"Are you all right, son?" the man asked him loudly.

James shook his head to regain clarity in his hearing and managed a weak smile. "I'm a little banged up but no worse than I've had from a night out at Gellions." The driver helped him to his feet and retrieved his cap from the ground nearby. James dusted himself off and turned to reassure the anxious driver once more.

Sarah, having regained her composure, climbed out of the car. "Are you quite well?" she asked the injured man. James turned at the sound of a women's voice, and his eyes flew open in surprise at the sight of the loveliest creature he had ever seen. Their eyes locked.

Sarah stood transfixed in his gaze until the sound of her driver's voice jolted her back to the crowded street. "He's going to be all right, Miss Sarah. Lucky escape for all of us there," he said with a nervous laugh.

The man was still appraising her with his eyes, and his face creased into a handsome grin. She bristled under his spell. "I'm glad that you are so well recovered," she addressed him haughtily, "although perhaps you might take better care in future on a street with motors."

"My lady, please accept my apologies for preventing you from colliding with a small child," he said with a mock bow.

"That's not what I meant, and you know it," she said, her voice becoming raised.

"Well, then, my lady, must I apologize again?" A few titters of laughter came from the small crowd on the street that the commotion had attracted.

"We're leaving. *Now*." Sarah told the driver.

"I'm not sure I can get her going again right now, Miss Sarah." He was examining the vehicle, which had sustained obvious damage to the bonnet and one of the wheels. "Pratts is not very far away…" he ventured cautiously.

"We can walk, then." She departed with a final glare at James but was aware the driver had not matched her step. He looked nervously at Sarah and back to the motor, clearly in a dilemma without an obvious solution.

"If I may," James interjected, "I can escort the lady to Pratts while you attend to the motor car. She can spend her time shopping and then request a concierge at Pratts to take her home."

"I am perfectly able to walk by myself." Sarah glowered at both the men. James raised his cap to the driver as he fell into step beside Sarah's slim frame. She strode off, giving a surreptitious side glance to check he was walking with her.

"I suppose you have a name," she said.

"I suppose I do."

"It's of no consequence to me."

"Then why did you ask me?"

"I didn't," she responded with an exaggerated sigh meant to convey boredom.

James was grinning at her once more. "You're something."

"Something?"

"Take it to mean what you will. People like you generally have a pretty high opinion of themselves."

Sarah gaped at the audacity of the comment and stopped walking, vaguely aware they had almost reached their destination. "You don't seem to have any manners, even for someone of your station in life."

"You seem to be proof that the higher the station, the worse the behavior," James responded.

They stood barely inches apart, and Sarah was all too aware of how intoxicating she found his presence. They continued to stand and look at each other. Neither said a single word. It was as if they were both participants in an unspoken game, and whoever broke the gaze first would be the one to admit defeat.

Almost imperceptibly, James ran his tongue along his bottom lip.

Sarah's eyes widened at the disrespect, and impulsively she slapped him hard across the face and stalked through the door of Pratts.

James stood on the street, rubbing his smarting cheek, and watched the door close slowly behind her. He swore under his breath as he realized that he was in love for the first time in his life.

Chapter Four

"Well done, lad," said Benjamin Greer and slapped James on the back. James beamed from ear to ear in response. His work was going well. Greer had taken a shine to him from the start, and that had opened the door on a few more opportunities for James to reveal his quick mind. He had started small by recommending some minimal changes to the production line. He had seen some minor flaws in the operating chain and realized that little changes could improve efficiency and reduce waste without a major overhaul, both things that Benjamin Greer liked to hear.

In just a couple of months, James had found himself with vastly increased responsibility and slightly better wages. His easy charm and self-deprecating humor had made him popular with the employees of Whitings, and he had been fortunate to encounter very little animosity toward his climbing stature. Benjamin Greer had noticed this and remarked that he had "a way with people that could be very useful." James had never been all that close to his own father, whom he had shared with his siblings and with his father's long hours as a laborer. He quickly realized that Benjamin Greer had given him the encouragement and praise he had never received from his own dear Da, and he regarded him in high esteem and with great affection. James worked even longer hours at the distillery than required, liking the satisfaction of work well done and the distraction from thinking about the girl he had met on the street. His heart told him that she was the one, but his head—and his friend Billy, doubled over with mirth—had told him she was most certainly not. He was young; there would be someone else soon, his mother had said with a shrewd but kindly tone. James had not told her about the events of that day, but somehow, with motherly intuition, she had known her son had fallen for a girl.

His work had overtaken almost everything in his life, and he preferred the certainty of the day-to-day grind over his previous frivolities with Billy and the boys. "Just for a quick pint," Billy had implored him the day before, but James resolutely shook his head. "Flora Hamilton might be there," Billy teased. "Whatever happened with you two?"

James was disinterested. "I'm working, Billy, going to make something of myself. Can't sit around here drinking all day."

"What else are you going to do? That's what everyone in Inverness does." Billy laughed but left him be. He could see his friend was not in the mood for merriment.

****

"You've been making an impression, son," Benjamin Greer told him. "The master's pretty taken with you and wants a word about a special assignment."

James had been taken by surprise that, after only five short months into his employ at Whitings, he was being summoned to Mr. Whiting's private residence at Baliforth House, and he was even more surprised by the strange welcome he received.

Samuel Whiting was standing alone by the window

with his back to the visitors as James and Benjamin Greer were ushered into an opulent sitting room by the manservant. Whiting turned to greet them, and James took in the immense presence of a man who surpassed his own tall but slight stature. He was immaculately dressed in a dark gray suit and blue pinstriped waistcoat, and his handsome face with its aquiline features showed clear intelligence, but his smile upon greeting lacked any genuine warmth. When James shook hands with him, he took in his gaze behind his spectacles and instinctively knew this was a man you did not want to cross.

"Good afternoon, gentlemen. Please have a seat."

James sat, on one of the expensively upholstered chairs, feeling uncomfortable and out of his depth. He had a panicked moment of terror when he wondered if Greer had got him mixed up with someone else and he had been summoned in error, but his fears were soon assuaged when Whiting addressed him by his full name. "I've heard some impressive things about you." He looked down at James from his elevated vantage point. "You made some improvements which have increased production. Very good. Now tell me about your time in the navy."

James swallowed and was, for the second time, unsure what his previous career had to do with his current one but readily supplied Whiting with a short synopsis of his naval highlights until the end of the war. Whiting nodded a few times and interjected with a couple of questions about his ability to navigate smaller craft—the same line of questioning Greer had employed when he interviewed for the position, James noted with mounting curiosity.

"And what do you know about the market for Scotch

in America?" Whiting asked, changing the subject of the conversation so abruptly that, for a moment, James was at a loss for words.

"Er, I'm not sure in what sense you mean, sir," he said hesitantly. Whiting did not answer but affixed him with a disdainful look. James wished the ground would swallow him up to escape from the gaze. "The Volstead Act will change things, I would imagine, for the market, er, from an import perspective," he offered, wanting to look down at the floor but willing himself to find the courage to meet Whiting's piercing gaze once more.

"Exactly," Whiting said simply. "Do you know anything about the logistics of alcohol in North America?"

"Do you mean bootleggers?" James shifted uncomfortably.

"I've heard them called 'rumrunners,' " Whiting mused.

"It seems as though there's a couple of ways the people are getting their drink. I read in the newspaper that many people are making their own nasty stuff in their bathtubs. The paper reported that a lot of people are dying from badly made liquor."

"That's interesting," came Whiting's response in a tone that indicated otherwise. "Do you have any information about quality alcohol coming from, say, Europe?"

"It's still getting there somehow. A mate of mine said boys are making a lot of money in the smuggling business again."

"Precisely. There is money to be made. There is a lot of money in the United States, even now with the state of the world, and people want something to spend it on.

There is a market which we can fill."

"Yes, Mr. Whiting." James was again lost in the conversation and what it could possibly have to do with him.

"I need someone I can trust. And Greer told me you might be just the person."

"James is a true patriot," Greer said, patting him on the shoulder.

"Anything I can do to help, sir," James ventured cautiously.

"I want to build up an operation to import alcohol. Not just ours but other brands too."

"Of course. But I imagine it would be…" James trailed off, trying to find a substitute for the word "illegal."

Whiting fixed him under his gaze once more. "Now, I am first and foremost a businessman. I would never undertake any operation that was not within the confines of the law."

"Of course not, sir. I didn't mean to imply anything. I was just trying to figure out how the, er…product would reach an American audience with it being prohibited…so to speak."

"St. Pierre and Miquelon are small islands off the coast of Newfoundland. Around Canada," he added condescendingly, "these islands are fast becoming a base for the arrival of high-end spirits. It seems as though the appetites of the islands' residents far outweigh what one would expect of such a small population, but there it is. As a businessman, my job is to supply where there is demand."

"I thought most imports passed through the Bahamas," James puzzled, wishing he had a better grasp of geography on the American continent. Whiting looked impressed at the comment, and Greer nodded at him as if to affirm James' worth.

"St. Pierre and Miquelon are cheaper. Import tax is but a fraction of what the Bahamas charge, and it makes more sense for us. We already have contacts with the Canadians who are planning to import there once this Volstead nonsense goes into full effect. We can't afford to have them take over the whole market."

"So where do I fit in?" This time, James gave Samuel Whiting a direct stare.

"I need boots on the ground. Someone resourceful to handle the transaction from point A to point B. We have some contacts in the area but not enough knowledge to get this operation up and running without someone to oversee things. The shipping from here to Canada is already organized. It's all aboveboard and documented. Officially, we will deliver to our customers in St. Pierre and Miquelon. After that…" He trailed off with a wave of his hand.

"So it seems pretty easy," James surmised.

"It is easy. It's getting it out again that is going to be the hard part."

James understood his meaning. "That's where I come in."

"Greer will fill you in on some details, and you will both come back next week to get things finalized." He nodded at Greer, and the latter stood up hurriedly, grabbing James by the arm and dragging him out of the room.

As soon as they were on the other side of the door, James stopped and looked at Benjamin Greer with a quizzical look. "Not here," said Greer urgently and continued to pull him in the direction of the door. James had a hundred questions whirling through his mind. America. He might find his fortune. He also might end up in jail or dead. He assessed that everything in life carried a certain amount of risk, and before they even stepped through the door, he had already made up his mind that Whiting's proposition was too enticing to pass up.

Standing outside Baliforth House, Greer was starting his automobile with difficulty. When finally the engine roared into life, he shouted to James, "I still have some business I need to attend to today. Can you make your own way back? Come to my office tomorrow morning, and we'll discuss the plans."

James nodded, unsure what else to do as Greer's motor disappeared down the drive in a cloud of dust. He was beginning to follow when he stopped in his tracks. A young woman emerged from the trees, guiding a large mare by its bridle. She, too, came to an abrupt halt when she saw him.

"You!" She gaped.

He removed his hat and gave her a slight bow. "Pleasure to see you again, Miss…"

"Sarah," she supplied, flushed. "And what is your name?"

"James Macleary. It's a pleasure to meet you, formally." His face broke into a grin.

Sarah, too, started to laugh at the absurdity of the situation. "I think we're going to be extremely polite and pretend we haven't met before. That I didn't almost run you over. That you didn't insult me and that I didn't slap you across the face."

"I think you are right," James replied in mock

seriousness. "I certainly don't recall any of those events at all." They both stood regarding each other until the horse snorted, breaking the spell.

"What are you doing here at my father's house?" she asked.

"Your father?"

"Samuel Whiting. My name is Sarah Whiting."

"I'm…I'm a business associate."

"You mean you work for my father." She smirked.

"Yes. That is exactly what I mean." They both laughed again.

"Are you walking in the direction of town?" Sarah asked.

James nodded. "At least, I think so."

"I can take you to the main track. You can't go wrong from there. I mean…only if you would like," Sarah was suddenly overcome with uncharacteristic shyness.

"I would like that very much," James replied.

"I just need to take her to the stable." Sarah indicated the patient mare. "Can you wait just a moment?"

"Certainly."

He was nervous. He had never been nervous around women before. They always responded to his charm, which was as effortless and natural to him as breathing, until now. He fidgctcd with his hat as he waited for her to return. Sarah Whiting. Of all the girls in all of Scotland, he had to fall for someone so completely out of his reach.

Sarah handed the reins over to the stable boy and saw her hands were shaking slightly. She smoothed down her hair and straightened her riding blazer. What was wrong with her? She was never nervous in situations like this. Why did she care what this man thought of her?

She returned to where he was standing, and they walked together slowly in the direction of the town. He sneaked a sideways look at her and was, as before, overcome with her beauty. Sarah knew he was watching her but didn't trust herself to look back. A few more steps. She stopped as they neared the lane. He stopped too. They finally faced each other. "If you just continue down there…" Sarah motioned in the general direction of the town.

"Do you think it's fate that we are meeting again?" asked James, his eyes not leaving her face.

"I don't believe in fate," she lied.

"I think we have been brought together for a reason."

They walked side by side on the rutted track and turned a sharp corner so the looming outline of Baliforth House was no longer visible behind them. They walked in silence, and James's mind raced as he struggled to find something intelligent to say to the angel beside him. He stumbled slightly on the uneven terrain, and his hand brushed hers.

Sarah grabbed his arm and pulled him into the small grove of woodland lining the track. "I'm sorry…I don't know what…"

James pulled her into his arms and brought her lips to his; together, they surrendered to the kiss. Soft at first, then more and more urgently. They were wholly absorbed by each other when the snap of a twig cut through the magic. Sarah hastily rearranged her riding coat and tried to smooth down her hair. "I have to go."

James shook his head. "I can't. I can't be without you."

"Meet me tomorrow. No, Saturday. I'll go to Pratts. Meet me there at ten o'clock in the morning."

She hurriedly started to move in the direction of the house. He grabbed her arm to stop her. "Wait."

"I have to go. But I will see you on Saturday." She broke away and suddenly was gone.

James stood motionless and watched her until her figure disappeared beyond the trees. He found his way back to the main path and walked along, dazed and bewildered. He had had his fair share of women, but it had never been like this. He didn't know what was happening. It was exquisite torture.

\*\*\*\*

The next day he was waiting outside the office when Greer emerged. "Ah, James. Give me just a minute, will you? I'll be right back."

James stared unseeing at the clock on the wall opposite. How had nobody noticed? He was not the same man he had been the day before. He was now the man in love with Sarah Whiting, and nothing else mattered. The events of yesterday already seemed so very far away, yet it caused him almost physical pain to know he would not see her again until tomorrow. He put his head in his hands.

Benjamin Greer reappeared and ushered James into his office. By now, James was accustomed to his fluster and disorganization and waited, uncaring how long it took, while Greer shuffled around in his piles of papers. "Here." He thrust a large map in front of James and jabbed his finger at a collection of small shapes surrounded by blue. "St. Pierre and Miquelon. This is where you'll be by September."

"September?"

"Yes. You'll leave in two months on the boat for New York."

"In two months," he repeated dully, unable to register the significance of what he was being told.

"Are you all right, son?" Greer was looking at him with concern. "You seem a little out of sorts today."

"I'll be fine, sir. Sorry, sir." James straightened his shoulders and tried to concentrate on what Greer was telling him. His life was about to change. Again.

"Things are organized…somewhat," said Greer, and James had a surge of affection for this man whose disheveled appearance was anything but organized. "Once in New York, you will head to the docks where you will meet our contact. He will brief you on the transport to the islands, but your real job will be what happens after that, if…you get my meaning."

Not for the first time, James felt a slight sense of foreboding at what the future might hold.

****

He looked at himself in the mirror for the last time and headed out the door. He had never been so anxious in his life, and despite his best efforts, he was still early. He rolled a cigarette as he waited across the street from the main doors of Pratts but had no desire to smoke it. He checked the time on the street clock. It was ten. Minutes passed, and he waited in excruciating anticipation for a glimpse of her. Nothing. He shook his head; obviously, she wasn't coming. She had changed her mind, and was it surprising? Why would someone like her show up for someone like him?

Ten more minutes passed, and he remained in place, despondent but not defeated. Suddenly, there she was. James simply stared, entranced, and watched her as she walked through the door of Pratt's, leaving her chauffeur outside. James saw the man open a newspaper and stop the engine, evidently under the impression that he would be there for some time. "It's now or never," he muttered to himself and, removing his hat, walked in the door after her.

Sarah felt his presence before she saw him. She whirled around and spoke in low measured tones that disguised the butterflies in her stomach. "There are people here that know me. We can't be seen together. I am going to leave by the side entrance on Crown Street. About five doors down, there is a cobbler. I will meet you there."

He waited for what seemed like an eternity but was only a few minutes, trying to feign interest in the cobbler's wares, until she appeared in the doorway. They looked at each other, and at that moment, they both knew their lives would be forever entwined.

Chapter Five

*Present Day, Montana*

It had been a productive morning, and I was glad to immerse myself in work after the tumultuous events of the previous day. We had sent off the crate and its precious contents to Danny at the lab for testing, along with a few of the other rarer bottles I had chosen from the exquisite collection on the floor in Mr. McClean's musty cabin. I was knee deep in the dust when I heard someone clear his throat behind me. I whirled around and was face to face with Marcus.

"Have you made any progress?" he snapped. My eyes narrowed at his tone, and a four-letter word flashed in my mind. I brought him up to speed with events, taking care to keep my voice and body language as neutral as possible. We were standing farther apart from each other than two people typically would to have a conversation, and I was irrationally disappointed that he was being as careful around me as I was around him.

"What about these others?" Marcus indicated the rest of my neatly cataloged row.

"That's up to you. I can list them if you'd like, but these aren't as rare as the bottles I sent away."

"So they're worthless."

"I wouldn't say worthless."

"I thought that's exactly what you just said." I took

a deep breath, determined not to take the bait. He was trying to goad me for some inexplicable reason, and I rewarded him with a fake smile that I hoped would irritate him.

"Let me try and explain myself a little better, then. These bottles wouldn't have been uncommon in the twenties, so you aren't looking at a great monetary value, but they have great historical value."

"Historical value. Are you serious?"

"There's a story here, and that's what makes them valuable. But you're right," I conceded. "That's more my sentimental opinion instead of a professional one."

He looked intrigued. "What would you do with them if they were yours?"

"I would keep them. I would put them up on my mantelpiece and look at them with wonder, and everyone who came to my house would probably think I was an alcoholic."

He laughed, and I thought how good-natured he looked when his eyes creased with laughter lines.

"Can we drink them? I mean, are they still good?"

I grabbed the nearest bottle, which was a weathered port. "Essentially, the alcohol acts as a preservative, and this port, in theory, should be just fine, as it's built for aging." He was looking at me again, very intently, and we had inched closer to each other.

"You're going to tell me there's a 'but' again, aren't you?"

"But…if the wine isn't stored properly, the fruit will taste acidy and nutty."

"Sounds a bit like my ex-wife." It was now my turn to laugh. Marcus grinned back at me, and I saw his charm and wit for the first time. "So what you're saying is these aren't exactly optimal conditions."

"It could have been worse. It's quite cool and protected in the cavity. There's a chance."

"There's only one way to find out." He grabbed the bottle from my hands and set off up the path. "Come on."

I hurried behind him, voicing a litany of reasons why he shouldn't open the bottle, but he ignored my protests and grabbed some glasses from the kitchen, where Betty was working on some ledgers.

"Bit early for that," she said reproachfully.

"It's from the cabin."

Marcus walked back out onto the deck and motioned for me to follow him. He poured a small measure into each of our glasses and held it out for me to take. I took a deep sniff of the liquid and fought the urge to sneeze. "I can't believe you opened the bottle."

"What else are we going to do with it? Doesn't this count as research?"

"I suppose you could call it that."

"Cheers." He touched his glass to mine but didn't drink. He looked like he was going to say something else but decided against it; he then downed the contents of his glass in one go and spluttered violently.

"That doesn't inspire much confidence." I laughed and set my glass down untouched.

"Maybe it's better to sip it slowly."

"That's certainly the case with Scotch."

"And many things in life," he said lightly. Again, I felt the unspoken atmosphere between us and wanted to pull myself away from a situation that could only signal trouble.

To my relief, Betty chose that moment to join us on the deck. "I assume you haven't solved the mystery."

"Tastes like crap."

"Where do we go from here?" She directed the question to me.

"I plan to work both angles. Find out what we can about the Whiting Whisky and see if any clues might have been overlooked, and then see what we can find from this side. Mr. McClean's family."

"My family?" Marcus looked surprised.

"Your ancestors built the cabin and presumably erected the wall. We need to find out as much about them as possible. Their connections, their origins, anything that could connect them to the Whisky or perhaps to John Duncan, the artist I think painted the label."

Ron popped his head around the door, catching the end of the conversation. "Can I help?"

"What help could you be?" Betty joked affectionately.

"The love of my life thinks I'm useless," he told me.

"They're always flirting," said Marcus, and Betty smacked him on the arm.

"You could do with a little flirting yourself," she told Marcus. "It's been long enough."

An uncomfortable silence descended, and then I said, "Let's get to work, then. Are there any family records or anything like that?"

"There arc," said Betty delightedly. "And I know where to find them. Give me a moment." She returned a few minutes later with several battered boxes. "This was something I was looking at a few months ago. Old photos and memorabilia of the McCleans."

"I'll let you get on with it, then. I have other things to deal with today," Marcus growled, the joker gone, and he stalked out without a backward glance. I turned to them quizzically, but Ron had busied himself with the boxes of papers on the table, and Betty wouldn't meet my gaze. Time to get to work, then.

After finishing university with a degree in hospitality management, I hadn't been inundated with exciting job prospects and so had taken a job as a bartender at the exclusive Embassy Club, where I made more in tips than I would have as an intern in the hotel industry. Angus Balfour was an "infrequent regular." He didn't visit the club as often as some more devoted patrons, but I knew his face well and knew better than to guess his order. After a few months of pleasantries, he began to quiz me about the spirit selection and sharp-shoot me with a series of questions about rare wines and even rarer blends. I was not often wrong, having amassed extensive knowledge from the job and my passion for Scotch, devouring articles and even historical volumes about the elixir of life.

One afternoon, our dynamic changed forever when Angus walked to the edge of the bar and offered me a job. It was quite literally a dream come true. Not only would I be able to make my student loan payments, but I would be able to work with something I was passionate about. Angus did not believe in learning feet to the fire and sent me on an extensive three-year course, on full salary, to learn all the intricacies of the spirit. Only when I had been schooled to his satisfaction had he let me loose on the business of authenticating Scotch.

The years had passed quickly, and now, in my early thirties, I was just beginning to take stock of all the doors he had opened for me. I was the director of his American arm of the business and had come to love my adopted country, with no intention of moving back across the ocean. Boston was, for now, the place I would call home.

I had thrown myself into the business and was slowly building a reputation for myself, at least judging by my burgeoning client list, as one of the leading experts of Scotch in the country. Angus was proud of my accomplishments and pleased at the revenue my consulting arm had brought to the business. "Just remember," he cautioned, "we do not cater to the needs of the many…"

"But to the wants of the discerning few," I finished. The mantra was one I had heard before.

I initially had misgivings about being so specialized in the niche market of Scotch whisky, but in recent years, the industry had experienced a boom, and interest in the rare, the exquisite, and the expensive had soared. Angus trusted me and my judgment but still demanded a weekly call, at the very least, so he could be in the know. Angus had been blessed with a raucous personality and penchant for storytelling, so our phone calls were, more often than not, a little one-sided. I turned on my laptop and put my cellphone on speaker. "We need to talk about the Whiting Whisky," I told him as the call connected.

"About bloody time!" he screamed back at me. "I've been sitting here wondering what could be going on over there. What the hell is the Whiting Whisky doing in Montana, of all places?"

"I'm hoping you can help me find out."

"What do you want me to do?"

"Find out what you can from the Scotch circles." The world of high-end Scotch on either side of the Atlantic was a small one, and while we needed to keep our cards close to our chest, we also needed the collective knowledge of the Scotch hive mind. Angus would never have been my candidate of choice for a mission requiring discretion, but right now, he was the only one I trusted with Marcus's discovery.

I relayed the events of my time in Montana so far and had to move the phone away from my ear when I got to the part about the John Duncan engraving. "Do you know what that could mean for the value of that bottle?" he bellowed down the line. "Priceless, that's what. I mean, who knew it even actually existed?" Angus was right. The legend of the Whiting Whisky had always been exactly that—a legend. It was going to be a serious undertaking to separate the facts from the fiction, but that was the job I was there to do.

"I'm hoping Danny can give us some definite information from the lab on the crate with what I suspect are the Whiting markings."

"Is that all we have to go on?" Angus sounded doubtful.

"Well, I suppose so. That and the legend of the artwork which turned out to be one and the same."

"Seems pretty slim, Emily. We better be a hundred percent before anything is released. Otherwise, we're going to lose a lot of credibility, and that means—"

"Money," I interrupted. "Don't worry, I understand what's at stake. It's just going to be challenging to be certain about anything. As it stands right now, we have absolutely no connection to Whiting or anything else, and zero explanation of how that whisky got to the cabin."

"Maybe it's not the Whiting Whisky."

"True. I have a feeling, though, Angus. I'm sure it's the real deal."

"Are you getting on any better with that MacCarter

fellow?"

"McClean," I corrected, "and not really, but I won't be staying long."

"Well, you better get on with it," he responded cheerfully.

"No pressure on me, then."

"Do your best, lass. That's all you can do."

"I will. And you can help me." I instructed Angus to put out the feelers in the Scotch circles for all the information we could find out about the accident that led to the supposed demise of the Whiting Whisky. There was a reason why the story remained, and perhaps we could glean some clues from the past.

I was ready to close the call when Angus passed a parting warning down the line. "You'd better watch out for you-know-who." I swallowed, not wanting to talk or think about members of the Whiting-Dahlberg conglomerate.

"I will."

I then busied myself with Betty's boxes on the table. She had brought out what appeared to be a library of photo albums of the McClean clan. "You can go backward; start with the most recent ones." She plopped down beside me on one of the oversized leather sofas.

The first one I looked at was only a couple of years old, judging by the image of Marcus. There were pages of him doing various activities. Shaking hands with a group of men in front of a construction site, a ribbon-cutting, riding a horse, more horses in spectacular settings. I leafed through the pages slowly, for some reason not tiring of looking at him. "Who put all these together?"

"Mostly me," Betty replied with a smile. "When his

folks passed away, he was still a young man, and Ron and I helped him figure out a few things. He doesn't need us anymore, but he still keeps us around anyway—we're part of the furniture at this point." She laughed.

"I can't imagine he would have it any other way. He looks up to you both and clearly adores you."

She patted my hand affectionately. "You're just trying to make an old lady feel useful."

We flicked through the pages together until I came to a picture of Marcus with his arm around a breathtaking blonde.

"Is that…?"

"The ex. Justine. We don't like to say her name."

"She's beautiful."

"She was a looker. All her beauty was on the outside, though, with that one. Cold and heartless. I never understood what he saw in her."

"I have an idea."

"Men can be simple creatures," Betty said, and we both giggled.

"What about you, hon? No one special in your life?"

I smiled at her thinly veiled attempt to get me to open up about myself. "There was, but not anymore. I don't…I don't like to talk about it."

She squeezed my hand reassuringly, and the small gesture, for some reason, caused tears to well up in my eyes. "I'm sorry," I said, blinking back the tears quickly. "I'm not usually like this. I'm not one of those people who cry and tell everyone their life story." I wiped my face, embarrassed.

"I can see that." Betty looked at me kindly. "You and Marcus are the same in that way. Keep everything to yourself and don't need any help from anybody." I opened my mouth to say something but closed it again when I realized she was right. "I'm just saying it can help to open up once in a while."

"I know. I'm fine, though," I answered brusquely, closing the conversation.

Betty and I spent the next few hours looking through the photo albums, talking and laughing about things that weren't related to the task at hand. She told me stories of the colorful characters who lived in Fairview, and then the conversation turned, inevitably, to Marcus, and it was again obvious she loved him like her own child. "What can you tell me about the family?" I pulled out my laptop to try and capture any details that might help, and Betty looked a little startled. "I'm just trying to recreate a timeline," I reassured her. "Let's start with Marcus's parents."

"They were nice people, good values, and always treated others well, but they weren't fools, if you get my meaning. His father was as shrewd a businessman as you'd find, and obviously, his son takes after him."

"So it was his grandparents who emigrated here? Or would it have been great-grandparents?"

"You're an impatient one." She chuckled, picking up the photo albums again. "I think it was great-grandparents. Wait, I remember…" She shuffled some of the albums around, and I waited as patiently as I could.

"This one here." She passed me a heavy book, and I took the album and studied the grainy image intently. It had been taken when they were breaking ground for what was now the McClean ranch. A couple of horses and what looked like a plow were standing in a field. The clue to the location was the spectacular backdrop of Montana's peaks, and the contours matched precisely with the view I currently beheld from Marcus's bespoke windows. The couple themselves were a good-looking pair, probably in their twenties, and though their expressions were serious, in fitting with the required demeanor for photography in those times, they looked as though they were about to burst into laughter.

Betty removed the image from the protective plastic and turned it over. Very faintly penciled in were the words "Jim and Rose MacClean, Fairview, Montana, 1924."

"That's odd; look how they've spelled 'MacClean'; it's like the traditional Scottish. Many Irish names contracted to 'Mc,' but it was less common for the Scots. Marcus spells his name with just 'Mc,' right?"

"Yes, but why would that matter? Wouldn't it just have changed over time?"

"Possibly," I conceded, "but that happened more often when people entered the United States, not after they were already established here. Perhaps someone else captioned the photo and just spelled it wrong. Were the McCleans a classic 'rags to riches' story?"

"We always thought so. They came from Canada to settle here, and we just assumed they were from Scotland or Ireland or something before then. You should ask Marcus to take one of those ancestor DNA tests you see on commercials."

"I can't imagine that going down too well." I laughed.

"You're right about that." Betty laughed too. "He's got a mind of his own, that's for sure. That was the problem with his marriage, I think. Justine wanted to be in control."

"Oh, yes?" I was trying to appear nonchalant but

desperately wanted Betty to continue.

"Marcus is attracted to strong women. He's never had time for those types that fade into the background. I suppose that's what attracted him in the first place, but she took it too far. Marcus wanted them to make decisions together, and she wanted to make them herself."

"Sounds like they were both a bit unyielding."

"Both their families were institutions in this part of the country, and they were used to getting their own way. There were land feuds and things like that—well, still are—but the founders were good friends. Look, here." Betty had been leafing through the books as she talked and indicated another picture of two men smiling, with cigars hanging out the sides of their mouths. I recognized one as the Jim McClean from the earlier photograph. Betty pulled the photo out from the sleeve and turned it over. The words "Liam Farley and Jim MacClean" were faintly visible.

"It's funny how things change over time," I mused.

"Well, I was relieved when his divorce finally came through from that horrible woman. In the end, she just wanted him for his money." Betty pursed her lips in an expression of distaste. "She wasn't exactly the loyal type, either. I'm not sure she ever was." I was beginning to think of Marcus in a different way.

"I can't imagine Marcus falling for somebody like that."

"Like what?" came a low voice from across the room.

"Nothing," I stammered, embarrassed he had caught us talking about him.

"Do you always talk about your clients' personal

lives?" he asked mildly.

I blushed. "It's not like that. I'm sorry if our conversation wasn't professional. It won't happen again."

He shrugged as if it didn't matter. "I was just surprised you thought it was any of your business."

"I can assure you, anything you do is *not* any of my business...or interest." I fumed. We stood glaring at each other until Betty jumped up from her chair.

"Now, then, let's keep our tempers in check." She looked at Marcus imploringly. "What we have here is just a misunderstanding."

"I understand gossip," he responded, still looking at me.

"Betty, I'm going to get some air." I turned on my heel and stomped outside. I was fuming but also embarrassed that he had overheard us. The worst part was that I was not, by nature, a gossiper. I had made enough missteps in my own life not to point fingers, and it turned out that perhaps Marcus and I weren't that dissimilar after all. We had both made some poor choices in our love lives and had suffered the consequences. But I thought uncharitably that a broken heart didn't give him the excuse to act like such an obnoxious jerk. It was unfortunate that he kept seeing me at my worst, I thought mournfully, and the damage was probably irreversible at this point. I walked back into the house, vowing to behave more like a grown-up, and saw Betty struggling to arrange some bottles over the fireplace. "What are you doing?"

"Marcus told me to put the rest of the bottles from the cabin on the mantelpiece. Something about looking at them in wonder, and stories. I have no idea what he was talking about."

I remembered our conversation from earlier and smiled. "Do you know where he is? I think I should probably apologize."

"He's in his office. But I think he's the one who should be apologizing," Betty said indignantly.

I knocked lightly on the door and waited until he barked at me to come in.

"Hi." I pushed open the door and stood on the threshold, unwilling to go back into his office in case it had the same unfortunate effect on me as the previous time.

"Hi," he responded, and I felt the chemistry between us again.

I continued in what I hoped was a businesslike tone. "I just wanted to apologize for our misunderstanding earlier."

"It doesn't matter." He shrugged. "Do you eat meat?"

"Do I *eat meat*?" I repeated blankly.

"Yes, meat. As in from an animal." He was smiling at me in a way that was undeniably sexy.

"Yes, I eat meat, as in from an animal." I smiled back despite myself. "Why?"

"Because I am going to eat meat for dinner, and I wanted to know if you would like to join me."

"Well, I don't think…" I struggled for an excuse but instead said, "Yes, I would like to join you."

Chapter Six

It was a pleasant surprise when I met Marcus for dinner to find myself walking in the doors of a beautiful turn-of-the-century hotel. The historic building was seated in the center of Fairview's old Main Street storefronts and had all the charm and decadence of the era. The mosaic-tiled floor and elegant chandeliers giving off a subdued light conspired to create the impression of an upscale speakeasy. Tufted leather wingback chairs were positioned thoughtfully in small clusters, and the long mahogany bar gave way to a beautiful dining room. I worried I was overdressed in a tan shift dress and low-heeled boots, but it seemed that casual yet classy was the vibe of this place. I was greeted by the maître de, who used my full name and was clearly expecting me.

"Mr. McClean is running a couple of minutes late," she told me, smiling to reveal blindingly white teeth. "He wanted me to show you to the bar." She gestured to an empty seat, and I sat down and looked over the extensive wine list. A baby-faced man in a smart vest and bowtie greeted me from behind the bar.

"What do you recommend?" I engaged him.

"Well, we have a good selection of reds right now. I'm brushing up on all the blends. Mr. McClean is going to send me on a sommelier course in Billings so I'll be able to impress his clients," he joked.

"Mr. McClean is *sending* you?"

"Sorry to keep you waiting," came a voice behind me, and I turned to see Marcus. He looked gorgeous in slacks and a white shirt, and an impure thought ran through my head.

"You didn't," I replied. "I just got here and was about to learn something about red wine."

Marcus shook hands with the soon-to-be sommelier and complimented him on his progress. The young man beamed from ear to ear, and it was evident that a compliment from Marcus McClean went a long way in this town. We were shown to an intimate table at the back of the dining room, and our white-toothed maître de lit a candle and made a show of excusing herself to leave us alone.

"This is a beautiful restaurant."

"It used to be an old hotel. It's one of the oldest buildings in Fairview. The Farley family built it. They were the law around here—until my family moved in, of course."

The server's arrival stalled my questions momentarily, and I raised an eyebrow as Marcus ordered a premium bourbon.

"Of course you're a bourbon man," I stated after the server departed.

"Why am I not surprised that you have a problem with bourbon?"

"I don't have a problem with it. It's fine for people who've never tasted Scotch."

The server returned quickly with our drinks and took our orders for entrees. Marcus raised his glass, and I reached for mine, thinking he would make a toast, but instead, he brought the glass to his nose and inhaled appreciatively. "This is what it smells like when the Americans take something they like and improve upon it." His eyes twinkled mischievously, clearly trying to get a rise from me.

"It seems your sense of smell has been severely compromised by the smell of cow shit," I responded, giving him a wink.

"Well, you are just charming company, Miss Emily." He laughed.

"I aim to please. Do you come here a lot?" I kept looking around appreciatively.

"It's one of my favorites."

"Everyone seems to know you."

"I try to keep a low profile. I don't want them to think I'm checking up on them."

"Checking up on them? You mean this is *your* restaurant?"

He shrugged, seeming a little embarrassed. "It's a nice place. We have to try to preserve things. Nowadays, people don't appreciate elegance and a slower pace to life. And it makes money," he added.

"It sounds like it's not really the money you're interested in," I said lightly.

"I have enough. Well, more than enough. I know how lucky I am. I just think people with means have a responsibility to do what they can to help those around them."

"So you want to use your powers for good and not evil."

"Something like that."

"How did the McCleans acquire the property if it was built by the Farleys?"

"A game of poker."

"Poker! It must have been pretty high stakes if someone ended up with a hotel."

"That's the legend, but you never really know," he said thoughtfully. "Most stories get embellished over time."

"Exactly like the Whiting Whisky," I said, my mind returning to the reason I was there. "What are you going to do with it? Preserve that too?"

"Maybe. I mean, it's just liquor."

"I couldn't disagree more, Marcus," I replied, liking the way his name sounded when I said it.

"You think it's art."

"You have unearthed a piece of history in that cabin. It's the creation of a master of his time. But it's even more than that--it's a story. A story we don't know yet."

"You're showing your sentimental side, Emily." I also liked the way my name sounded when it came from his lips.

"Perhaps. Aren't you curious, though? It's linked to your family somehow."

"Maybe not. It could have been someone else who hid the bottles there. Someone who helped build the cabin. I don't know. I'm trying to keep an open mind."

"An open mind is always good," I said, and we clinked glasses in agreement.

The evening passed in a blur. It was one of those perfect nights when everything falls into place as if by some grand design. Marcus had recommended the steak as "one of the best in the whole state," and I had not been disappointed. After our aperitifs, we moved on to a delicious cabernet sauvignon. Marcus had instructed our server to bring the bottle from the special cellar, enjoying my look of impressed amusement.

The conversation flowed easily. He was naturally charismatic and an excellent storyteller, and I found myself laughing out loud more than I had in a very long time. We finally moved on from the trials and tribulations of livestock sales to matters a little closer to home.

"You don't have any children?" I confirmed cautiously. I had noticed a moment of fleeting sadness when a girl of about six had run through the lobby wearing a pretty party dress.

He shook his head. "My wife Justine—ex-wife," he corrected, smiling ruefully. "She never wanted kids, and in the end, that was a good thing." A shadow crossed his face, and he cleared his throat. "I always thought I would have them someday, but it just wasn't meant to be."

"Never say never." We locked eyes for a moment. Then I abruptly changed the subject, not wanting to pry further. He was just a client, I reminded myself again, aware I was beginning to think of our relationship on a much more personal level than I should.

"Do you invite all your business associates out to dinner?"

"Montana hospitality. But, truthfully, only if they're good-looking." He twinkled at me mischievously. "What about you? You haven't said much about yourself. Is there someone in your life, or do you have a Justine too?"

"No, I've never been married." I took another quick sip of wine and decided not to elaborate. Marcus seemed to sense my reluctance and was too much of a gentleman to press me on the subject, and the conversation moved to safer territory. I noticed we were attracting a few furtive glances from other patrons, and I asked him if he minded the attention.

"Yes. But you've got to expect that in a small place. Besides, I don't think they're looking at me."

"I am." The words came out of my mouth before I could stop them, and I wondered how I had become so intoxicated. The hours had flown by, and I was shocked when I saw the staff remove the tablecloths from what was now an empty restaurant. I looked at my watch and saw it was almost midnight.

"It got late on us," said Marcus and gestured in the direction of the doors. "Shall we?"

As we walked out, I felt a mix of nervous emotions. I knew it was not smart to get involved with a client, but I didn't want to say goodbye to him. We both stood awkwardly on the sidewalk facing each other.

"I don't do relationships," he suddenly said.

"Right, well, thanks for telling me," I reverted to sarcasm.

"I just didn't want you to get the wrong idea."

"I think *you* might have the wrong idea. I am a consultant you have hired. I am here to do a job. That's all there is to it."

"Right."

"Can you drop me back at the hotel now, please?" I asked pointedly, suddenly feeling stone-cold sober.

\*\*\*\*

The next day I woke up with a slight headache and lay in bed wondering whether I should have drunk less or perhaps more. I looked over at the empty bed next to me and felt a mixture of disappointment and relief. Romance was the last thing I needed in my life right now.

Feeling revived after a hot shower, I waited in the lobby for Betty to pick me up. "Did you have a nice evening?" she asked slyly as soon as I got in the truck.

"I did, indeed. Marcus is good company, and I'm sure he treats all his employees well."

She snorted. "Just don't go hurting his feelings now."

"Me? He's being polite and probably didn't want me to spend the evening by myself."

"Okay, you carry on telling yourself that." She was shaking her head with a knowing smile on her face.

"I bet Marcus takes a lot of people out to dinner," I continued, unable to drop the subject.

"Do you?" She chuckled again. Apparently, Betty wasn't going to be loose-lipped when it came to Marcus's love life. I groaned inwardly.

As I walked into the house, I marveled again at how gorgeous the property was. Marcus was lucky to live here, I decided, an image of my cramped apartment in Boston coming to mind. I opened the door to the deck and spotted Marcus below, instantly spellbound by the scene. Marcus was stroking the flank of a beautiful gray horse. Even though I couldn't discern his words, he spoke in soothing tones that had the desired effect on the distressed animal. I watched them for a while, then finally crept down the steps, hoping to pass by without attracting his attention.

Marcus heard my footsteps and looked up.

"I'm sorry, I didn't want to disturb you. It looks like you have your hands full."

He continued to run his hand up and down the horse, stopping to pat her reassuringly. "I had a good time last night," he said.

"You have a very nice restaurant," I responded neutrally.

"I think of it more as belonging to the town."

"Well, then the town is lucky to have such a beautiful place." I smiled and then took a step down the path, away from this seductive man.

"Wait," Marcus said forcefully, making both myself and the horse jump slightly, "I didn't mean for the night to end like that."

I shrugged as if I didn't know what he was talking about. "It was time for bed. I appreciate you keeping me company. When you travel as much as I do, you get used to eating alone."

"I know." The charged atmosphere was back. There was something between us that words were not going to say. I didn't trust myself to meet his gaze and raised my hand slightly as I turned and walked hastily down the path.

So he didn't mean for the night to end like that—what was that supposed to mean? I kept turning the phrase over in my mind, getting more enraged by the minute. What was he insinuating? He probably thought he was so irresistible that women were lining up to throw themselves at him. Although that might not be too far from the truth, I realized ruefully as his handsome face flashed in my mind. I shook my head to dispel the image, and it was instead replaced by my ex-fiancé, Leo. I wasn't sure which was the lesser evil.

The hours passed, and fortunately, thoughts of everything but the beautiful bottles in my hands faded away. I loved my work and smiled as I carefully brushed the dust from another long-forgotten bottle, covered by time and someone's secret. What if I was unable to solve this mystery? What would it mean for the business? For Angus and me? If we could definitively say we had discovered the Whiting Whisky, our fortunes would look a lot brighter. However, I thought morosely, many things would depend on Marcus, and he was not a predictable customer.

****

"Oh, there you are," said Betty as I opened the door to the main house. "Would you like a sugar cookie?"

"Is that a trick question?" I smiled and grabbed the biggest one I could see. Marcus walked into the room and washed his hands in the sink behind Betty.

"I thought I could smell cookies."

"He's always had a sweet tooth," Betty said to me.

"That's not fair," Marcus interjected. "I never eat the pies at the county fair."

Betty continued talking to me. "He's supposed to judge the pie competition and has sometimes been a little too honest for his own good."

Marcus pulled a what-can-I-do face. "One time. I spat it out one time, and they'll never let me forget it."

"You spat it out?" I laughed. "In front of the baker?"

"In my defense, it was really bad. Not like Betty's sugar cookies." He winked and grabbed another from the plate.

I followed suit, and Betty slapped our hands mockingly. "You little sugar fiends," she scolded. We heard the doorbell ring, and she pointed at Marcus and then me. "You'd better not eat them all."

Betty answered the door and returned almost immediately, stony-faced. "It's for you," she said to Marcus. "You'd better take care of this once and for all," she commanded in a terse tone I hadn't heard her use before.

Marcus cursed softly and took a deep breath, then strode to the front door where the mystery visitor awaited. I looked at Betty quizzically. "Misty Farley." Betty's tone indicated that she wasn't impressed. "She hasn't been around here in a while, and I hoped we wouldn't see her again anytime soon. Marcus is useless when it comes to her."

"Useless?"

"Can't say no."

"Oh." I felt crushed and berated myself for being so stupid. Of course, Marcus had a girlfriend. He was rich and single and probably held the title of Montana's most eligible bachelor. Back to asshole for the time being, then.

Betty opened her mouth to say something more, but we were interrupted by the sound of raised voices drifting in through the front door. "Haven't you got anything else to say?" a woman's voice screamed. I could hear Marcus respond, but his voice was too low to make out the words. More shouting and the slam of a car door. "This isn't over," came the woman's voice again, followed by the sound of an engine starting.

"Come on, Misty, wait," Marcus's voice came again, coaxing this time.

We heard his footsteps come back into the house, and Betty and I both jumped, unsure what we were supposed to do. Marcus slammed the door and looked in our direction. "Don't you say anything," this was directed toward Betty, who just shook her head mutely. I didn't look up until I heard his footsteps retreat across the floor, followed by a loud bang as he slammed the front door. Betty gave a low whistle and asked me if I wanted more coffee. I desperately wanted to ask more questions about this Misty person but reminded myself, not for the first time, that it was absolutely none of my business. This turn of events made things easier. Whatever odd attraction to Marcus that had been forming in my mind could firmly be put to rest. I had my work, and he had Misty, whoever she was.

****

Angus had done his homework. Spread out on the table in front of me were copies of about a dozen newspaper articles from the *Inverness Herald*, the *Times*, and another lowland periodical I had never heard of before. He had also got his hands on a copy of the claim that Samuel Whiting filed for the missing shipment. I had not thought about the legalities of the import of Scotch during the time of prohibition, but it seemed as though Whiting had been an astute businessman. Reading on, I learned that most of his whisky was imported to islands off the coast of Newfoundland, St. Pierre and Miquelon.

Not being governed by the stringent laws of the United States, Whiting could run a legal and aboveboard operation. Therefore, why would you not have an inventory and insurance? He had done business by the book...up to a point. That was why I was holding a certificate of assets issued by the Union of Scotland National Insurance Company in my hands. I did not know the outcome of the claim, but given that the certificate explicitly mentioned "accident" and "marine," I imagined Whiting had been able to recoup at least some of his financial losses. I pulled up a map on my phone and saw the distance between St. Pierre and Atlantic City. There couldn't possibly be a connection. Nothing made sense.

I scanned the next article in the pile. "The price of America's war on whisky," screamed the headline framing a picture of two women, one standing slightly behind, but the main focus was a young woman in a black beaded evening gown and feathered headband, captured on what looked to be the deck of a ship. The picture was a little blurred, but the outline was enough that I could see in her face she had been a beauty. She had light hair, possibly strawberry blonde, and I looked at her eyes for a long moment as if that would help her reveal her secrets. After scanning the text, I realized that the beautiful woman pictured had been Samuel Whiting's daughter Sarah. The article told of the disappearance of this innocent girl who had traveled to America with her future husband and had ended up an unintentional victim of disorganized crime-ridden colonies and their war on alcohol and civility. What could you expect, the article questioned, from a country that had taken away a gentleman's basic right to a drink?

I set the paper copy to the side and moved to the next piece, but then I picked up the first one again. Even when you cut through the sensationalist propaganda, some things didn't make sense. Why would Whiting's daughter have been anywhere near a cargo ship? I supposed the connection was with her father's business, but it was very unlikely that a young twenty-something or even teenage girl would have any business responsibilities at that time. I set the paper aside again. I'd had the beginnings of a thought, an intuition, but it had gone. I looked at the papers on the table, and a feeling of futility washed over me. Time for more coffee.

How much do we actually know about our own families? That was the question that kept coming to me as I dug around in someone else's family history. The McCleans were a Fairview institution. That much was evident to anyone in the small town for more than five minutes. Several of the buildings on the main street bore the name, and I had already heard enough of Betty and Ron's tidbits to know the family's influence and reach extended far beyond this small enclave in Montana. It was a little puzzling, then, that I could find relatively scant mention of the McCleans until the late 1920s. From Ron's retelling of history, they had arrived in Canada at the end of the first world war and spent several years working as hired hands before moving West and eventually finding their fortune. It was all frustratingly vague.

So how had they made their money? You had to speculate to accumulate, or so the saying goes, and even if Marcus's great-grandfather had been as canny as his great-grandson was, he would still have needed some means to acquire so much land in the first place.

In the roaring twenties, this had certainly been thought of as the land of opportunity, and it was no surprise that the refugees fleeing war-torn Europe had landed on these shores in droves. But, even with my poor grasp of the era's history, I knew that the great depression and the interwar years had not been kind to many. Perhaps they had been successful con artists rather than entrepreneurs, I mused. It was looking more and more likely I would never find out.

Chapter Seven

"This just arrived. I had to sign for it." Betty waved an envelope toward Marcus. "It's from London."

I held my breath, hoping against hope that it wasn't what I thought it was. Marcus ripped it open and then looked at me with a face like thunder. Apparently, it was.

"It's from a representative of Whiting-Dahlberg Inc. They have been informed of a finding...yada yada, legal stuff...and look forward to our continuing cooperation to determine the authenticity." Marcus was looking at me, and I couldn't bring myself to meet his eyes. "Discretion," he said softly.

I opened my mouth to offer a defense but had nothing to give. It was probably down to Angus and his big mouth, but I knew the real fault lay squarely with me.

"Come on, now, let's not start fighting among ourselves." Betty started fussing around us and poured some more coffee. "There's probably a bright side to all this."

"That son of a bitch can't just demand to take our property because of some family claim from a hundred years ago," Marcus fumed.

"Is it that valuable, then?" Ron asked with raised eyebrows. "Must be worth a fair bit if they got onto the story so quick." They all looked in my direction.

"The collection of bottles without the Duncan bottle is worth a bit by itself. But we're talking fifty thousand

U.S. dollars max. The bottle with the John Duncan label..." I gave a low whistle. "Nobody even knew that existed, and if we can show a connection to the legendary Whiting Whisky, there's honestly no telling how much it could fetch. Certainly, worth the Whiting company staking a claim."

Ron looked impressed. Marcus looked angry. Betty looked confused.

"But explain this to us," she said hesitantly. "The bottles were found here on McClean property, so how does this Whiting-Dahlberg company even have a claim to them?"

I sighed. "They might not, but that will be a job for the lawyers, if it gets that far." Marcus looked pained at the mention of lawyers. "I'm sure you've all read about discoveries of gold and art and things that were taken by the Nazis in the second world war. Well, when they were discovered years later, the courts mostly decided they should be returned to their rightful owners. If the trend were to continue that way, the rightful owner of the whisky would most likely be the Whiting company."

"So is it better if it's *not* the Whiting Whisky?" asked Betty.

"If you ever want to sell it or insure it or even know what you have, you need to have it authenticated." I pointed at myself. "That process includes finding the origin. The John Duncan is the key, and with some digging, we should be able to find out something."

"Let's say it is the Whiting Whisky. How do we know it wasn't bought by Marcus's grandfather or great-grandfather or whatever?" Betty pushed.

"That's going to be a tough sell," I said reluctantly. "First, we're talking the era of prohibition. If it were bought in the United States, it would have been an illegal sale, and there's unlikely to be any record of that. Second, it was hidden behind a secret wall." I gave a quick laugh. "Nothing says, 'I don't want this to be public,' like erecting a wall to hide it. Then, we have the problem of how it was procured. Someone set a fire and stole it? I hate to say it, but the Whiting company has a pretty good claim unless we can show something else."

"Let's just forget about it, then," Marcus said abruptly.

I looked at him in horror. "We can't just forget about it! This is probably the biggest discovery in the history of Scotch whisky!"

"And, obviously, you felt the need to tell everyone."

"It's not like that." My voice was getting higher. "My boss, Angus--he's not the most discreet person."

"So it's his fault we received a summons from this, this Whiting Dahlberg company?" he was brandishing the letter, still furious.

"No, the fault lies with me, and I apologize, but we need to find additional information if we are to say, with certainty, that it has a link to Whiting. As I said, I'm sorry." I swallowed and forced myself to meet his angry gaze. "I should have explained better to Angus that we had to keep this under wraps for now."

"You promised me discretion, and you haven't kept your promise."

"Now, just a minute," Betty jumped to my defense. "How else do you expect her to find anything? Isn't that part of your job?" She directed the last question to me.

"We spend a lot of time on research," I responded in a quiet voice.

Betty spread her arms and looked at Marcus

pointedly. "You hired her to find out the truth. How do you expect her to do that without asking questions?"

I was gratified to see that Marcus was looking a little uncomfortable. "Well, I suppose we would've had this conversation sooner or later." He indicated the letter again. "I just didn't think we'd be dealing with legal stuff before we even know what we have."

"Why don't you let Emily get back to work so she can *find out* what you have?"

"Fine, whatever." Marcus stalked out of the room after pausing to give me one last venomous glare.

Betty let out a loud sigh. "I'm sorry, hon." She squeezed my arm reassuringly. "Don't pay any attention to his temper. He can be a bit hot-headed, especially if he thinks someone isn't being completely honest with him."

I fought the urge to leave the McClean ranch immediately, but there wasn't room for more than one of us to be so hot-headed. Marcus had overreacted a little to the letter, but he had a point. I was also acutely aware that I hadn't explained everything to Marcus about my association with the Whiting-Dahlberg company, and he wasn't likely to be very understanding if I raised the subject now.

"Perhaps I should head back to Boston," I concluded reluctantly.

"You just carry on doing what you were doing and leave Marcus to me." Betty wore a look of grim determination that I wasn't going to question. "What else do you know about this Whiting company?" she asked, deftly changing the subject.

"Enough. The company is old. It has clout. One of the Dahlberg shareholders is supposed to be a direct descendant of the original Whiting."

"The Whiting from the Whisky?"

I was studiously avoiding Betty's eyes, afraid my expression would give me away, but she seemed to accept my feigned nonchalance. "Yes. I've heard he's not a good person. He has a bad reputation around London, and he and my boss hate each other's guts. I did research the relationship, though, and there's an undisputable family lineage."

"Amazing everything you can find out at the touch of a button," Betty commented wistfully.

"I have no idea what we did before we could find everything just by looking at a phone."

"We spent more time looking at each other than down at our phones," she replied.

"Talking of phones, I need to use mine to take a few more pictures of the whisky in the cabin, in case Marcus decides to sell. Do you think he will?"

"No idea. Honestly, I think he's more interested in how it got there in the first place. The mystery of it all, and having something to do with his ancestors."

I scribbled on my tablet, listing various hypotheses to link the McCleans to Samuel Whiting, until I heard someone clear his throat behind me. "Hi, Marcus," I said without turning around.

"How did you know it was me?"

"Women's intuition."

"I just wanted to see if you needed anything."

"No, I'm doing fine. Making less progress than I would like, but I hope to be finished up as soon as possible, and then I'll be out of your hair and back to the East Coast." I gave him an insincere smile and pretended to study my tablet intently.

"I probably overreacted about the letter."

"Probably. But I am partly to blame." I turned around, and we looked at each other, neither knowing what to say. The chemistry was back.

"You're very loyal to your boss," he observed.

"He's more than a boss, really." I thought of Angus and unconsciously broke into a smile.

"Aha, I see."

"No, nothing like that." I laughed at the thought. "I mean, he's more like family. Besides, his romantic inclination doesn't go in my direction."

He looked momentarily relieved, then suddenly blurted out, "She's not my girlfriend."

"Who?"

"Misty. The woman you saw earlier."

"I didn't see anyone, and it's none of my business. You're my client, and whoever you decide to spend your time with has absolutely nothing to do with me."

"Okay. I just don't want any more misunderstandings."

"There won't be," I said, looking him square in the face, and he flinched at my expression. "As I said, I haven't made too much progress." Turning the conversation back to the work at hand was a safer road to travel. "I can't find any connection between Whiting or the Whiting Whisky and Montana or the McCleans. Perhaps we just need to conclude that this isn't anything to do with the Whiting Whisky?"

"Is that what you think?" he asked with raised eyebrows.

"It's just too big a coincidence." I groaned in exasperation. "That's a rare and elite collection you have, and it would have been at the time too. There wouldn't have been that many bottles like this imported, and the John Duncan label..." I trailed off, having no explanation.

"You're saying that it's unlikely they came from somewhere else," he surmised.

"Perhaps we'll learn something more from the newspaper archives. There might be a mention of Duncan specifically."

Marcus shifted uncomfortably from one foot to the other. "Let me know if you find anything else."

"Wait. Was there anything about your ancestors that was *strange*?"

"Strange how?"

"I don't know, just something that didn't add up. They were self-made, right? They came from nothing?"

"I guess. I mean they had nothing when they arrived here in the 1920s." His brow furrowed.

"Nothing except a hoard of illicit whisky and a bottle designed by John Duncan." I laughed.

"Right." Marcus turned to leave but then stopped. "Actually, there was one thing. She had a necklace, my great-grandmother. When they were kids, my dad said they used to joke about it being a ruby, but then they had it appraised, and it *was* a real ruby. I guess that's weird, if they had nothing."

"Can I see it?"

"Sure, ask Betty. She'll probably know where it is."

"Thanks."

"Okay, I'll be going, then." He made no intent to move.

"Okay."

"Fine," he said and then slowly turned and walked away. I wanted to scream in exasperation but contented myself with putting my head in my hands. It appeared we had an unfortunate effect on each other that made us both behave like children.

When it was beyond time for a morning break, I set off in the direction of the main house, hoping to find Betty and one of her tantalizing treats to tide me over until lunchtime. I was nearing the back entrance when I heard Marcus on the deck below me shouting furiously into his phone.

"I understand that, Misty, but it's not going to happen. I would say that love has *everything* to do with it. I just don't want things to get ugly."

I banged the door loudly on my way inside to avoid another misunderstanding about me poking my nose into his business. Love. He had said the word "love." Nothing could have signaled the end of my attraction to Marcus McClean more than the fact that he was in love with someone else, whether he called her his girlfriend or not.

"Hi, hon," Betty greeted me. "What's the matter?" she asked when she saw my face.

"Nothing. Nothing at all." I feigned surprise, embarrassed my expression told a different tale.

The door slammed again, and Marcus appeared, finishing his phone call. "She is just so unreasonable!" he flustered to Betty and then stopped when he caught sight of me.

"Sorry, I just came to grab something to drink," I said haughtily. "I'll head straight back to the cabin."

"It's not that—" Marcus started.

"You don't owe me an explanation," I said snippily. "You are my client, nothing more, and if I can't make any further progress by tomorrow, I plan to leave tomorrow evening." I walked back to the cabin with haste, ignoring the sickening feeling in the pit of my stomach.

Betty appeared a short time later with a plate of gingerbread cookies and a pitcher of iced water. "Are you okay?" she asked with sympathy.

"I'm fine. Why wouldn't I be?"

"I don't know what's gone on with you and Marcus," she began.

"Nothing. Nothing has *gone on* with Marcus and me," I interrupted.

"You're both your own worst enemy." She sighed.

"I think you're barking up the wrong tree here, Betty. Marcus is my client, and we have a business relationship. There's nothing personal between us, and he's obviously involved with someone else."

"Who?" She looked astounded.

"Misty."

"Misty? I think you're the one *barking up the wrong tree* here, Emily."

"Maybe they've split up right now, but it's obvious there's still something between them."

"I mean, they'll always be connected in a way, I suppose, but right now, they're talking about business."

"Betty, I know that you mean well, and I don't want to be rude, but I have a lot to do here, and talking about Marcus's love life isn't one of them." I firmly closed the conversation.

"Have it your way, hon, but I'm telling you that you're wrong."

"Do you know anything about a ruby necklace?" I changed the subject. "Marcus mentioned his great-grandmother had an unusual necklace. He said I could take a look at it."

"Of course, but why? Does it have something to do with the Whiting Whisky?"

"Probably not, but it's another piece of the puzzle that doesn't seem to make sense."

After Betty left, promising to look for the necklace, I reflected on what she had said about Marcus and Misty. *They would always be connected.* Another red flag on Marcus, and I cursed myself for even subconsciously entertaining the thought of something more happening between us. The last thing I needed right now was another man who was going to break my heart. My thoughts turned involuntarily to my ex-fiancé Leo, and I shuddered at the memory of that day. The worst day of my life.

****

I was engrossed in my task when Betty appeared at the door. "Time for a break, and no if's or but's from you, missy."

"I don't need any convincing. I'm stuck anyway."

"A break and some iced tea might clear your head."

"I prefer my tea hot."

"Then you haven't had good iced tea."

Betty set a mason jar down beside me, and I took a deep glug of tea and had to agree that I had not tasted the good stuff before now. Betty pointed us to a couple of rocking Adirondack chairs that were thoughtfully positioned overlooking the lake. I sat down gratefully and savored a moment to drink in the mountain air and feel the warmth of the sunlight on my face. We sat in companionable silence, rocking back and forth and sipping our tea.

"Oh, I found it." Betty slid a weathered box toward me.

I opened it and gasped at the contents.

"Isn't it beautiful?" She chuckled at my reaction.

The necklace was exquisite. A ring of small diamonds was attached to the chain and a link dropped down to house a shimmering red stone. The teardrop shape was unusual and, combined with the clasp, made it truly a one-of-a-kind piece. "It's a real ruby?" I confirmed.

"According to Marcus, or at least that's what his father had said."

I sat holding the remarkable pendant, trying to process a chain of events that had no explanation. Poor immigrants, originally from Europe, by way of Canada, arrived to settle in the Montana wilderness, bringing a necklace worth a small fortune and the priceless picking of the Whiting Whisky. How had these things come to be in their possession? Who were Jim and Rose McClean?

"What do you make of it, then?" Betty interrupted my thoughts.

"I have no idea."

"I wish Ron would give me a necklace that beautiful." She chuckled again, rocking back and forth comfortably.

"I was engaged," I blurted out, suddenly, surprising myself. Why was I talking about this? Betty gave a slight nod to signal she had heard me, and I surrendered to the urge to unburden myself.

I had dated Leo for about three years when he proposed. We had both just turned thirty, and my career and his were on the upward ascent. We were both in the same business, so we had everything in common; we talked about the kind of house we would buy and the personalities our children would have, and I believed that life, for the two of us together, was nothing short of perfect.

I threw myself into the business of planning the wedding and was out with Leo's sister when she fell and twisted her ankle. Cake tasting abandoned, we returned to the apartment far earlier than planned and had evidently not been expected.

What happened next would be forever etched on my memory. I helped Leo's sister up the steps and headed straight to the bedroom. My hand was on the door handle, and I heard a familiar female voice from within and the sound of Leo's deep-throated laugh. I stopped outside the door, paralyzed by shock. I could walk away now, and my life would still be intact. Leo could offer me a reasonable explanation for the woman in our bedroom. Alas, that wasn't my nature, and I had pushed open the door. They were in our bed together. My future husband Leo, and my best friend, Melissa.

I was unaware that a tear had rolled down my cheek until Betty passed me a tissue. I took it from her and smiled at her kindly face; I already felt better for some reason. She said nothing but patted my hand, and we lapsed back to silence for a moment, sipping our tea while she gave me time to collect my thoughts.

"That day…when I caught them, I ran out of the apartment. I haven't seen either of them since."

"And what now?"

"Now?"

"Yes, now." Betty was wearing a determined expression.

"I packed up my things when he was gone, and his sister took care of canceling all the wedding arrangements."

"It sounds like you might have some unfinished business."

"Like telling him to jump off a cliff?" I laughed.

"Exactly. Look at you. You're smart, you're beautiful, and you've got the perfect opportunity for a second chance. I know you've been hurt, Emily. In the blink of an eye, you lost two people in your life who were supposed to love you the most. But this is no way to live. What's a headstrong girl like you doing, letting a pathetic excuse for a man treat you like that?"

Betty was right, and instead of feeling sorry for myself, I felt a little stronger. "You and Marcus are both too young to be moping about like this," she concluded and then stood up. "I'd better let you get back to it." She turned to go but stopped to squeeze my arm affectionately. "I'm here if you need me."

As I watched her walk away, I thought how lucky Marcus was to have this good-natured lady in his life every day. Her soothing words and kick in the pants were exactly what I needed. Refreshed, I turned my attention back to the task at hand and picked up another article, this time with the headline "Smugglers and victims off the coast." The pictures below were mostly mugshots captioned with the names of suspected rumrunners.

But one picture stood out from the others. A young man who had perished in the disaster. He was not holding a number in a police cell or dressed in civilian clothes like the others but instead wore a British naval uniform. Despite the stiff dress, he had a look of roguish amusement on his handsome face, as though he could come to life and charm the world. There was also something familiar about him that I couldn't quite put my finger on. The picture was captioned with his name below. James Macleary.

Chapter Eight

*1920, Inverness, Scotland*

James was seeing time run through his fingers like grains of sand. Weeks before, he would have wanted nothing more than to embark on an adventure on the other side of the world, courtesy of someone else's pocketbook, but now, the last place he wanted to be was anywhere other than with Sarah.

The past weeks had been heaven. They had, by way of a friend with connections, found a hidey-hole in Balifeary where they could be together without too much fear of prying eyes. The hours disappeared when they were in each other's company, and they both felt as though they were looking at the world anew. Mostly they talked, and sometimes they argued.

James had not spoken much about the war since returning home, but he was an open book with Sarah. Several times he saw her eyes glisten with tears as he recounted the horrors he had seen. Friends he had lost to enemy weapons or even their own hand. He was ashamed and regretful to talk of such things, but Sarah forcefully insisted he carry on. She knew nothing of the real world, and she had a chance to experience reality through him. However brutal it was.

They talked of politics often, and James was amazed to discover her passionate and knowledgeable opinions about everything from the Spartacist Manifesto to Calvin Coolidge. Sarah had a belief that they were standing on the precipice of great change in society, in technology, and in governance. She told him they must choose whether to be the face of a gilded past or of the untold future.

James was an avid devourer of the daily paper but had been conditioned to distrust any ideas outside the realm of his own experience. He had dismissed some of her thoughts as childish naivety but found himself, in quieter moments, pondering the possibilities. Sarah opened up a world of new principles, revolutionary thought, and philosophy that he had never before encountered, and they became both the teacher and the student to one another.

They disagreed more than they agreed, and James lamented on more than one occasion that he had the bad luck to fall in love with someone so fearless and high-spirited. Although, as he sat nursing a bruised ego from a whipping by her sharp tongue, he acknowledged ruefully that this was probably what had attracted him in the first place. Meeting Sarah had made James realize what had been missing in his life. It was someone whose mind worked as quickly as his own. Time with Sarah was his addiction. Alcohol and opium had no allure that could compare to the spell she had cast.

Sarah had the same realization about James and felt as though a veil had been lifted from in front of her eyes to reveal a bright but savage new world. As a member of the fortunate class, she had been raised to believe the wealthy had earned that right by being more intelligent and noble than those below them. With a lurch of self-revulsion, she realized she had always accepted this repugnant wisdom. If her lover, one of the most intelligent men she had ever met, was representative of the lower classes, then the world was, in her opinion, decidedly upside down.

They talked, and they played cards, and they made love. "So where do we go from here?" Sarah lay contentedly in his arms and wished she could stay in their safety forever.

"Marry me," he said impulsively.

Her eyes widened, but then she shook her head sadly. "He would never allow it. Besides, I'm already engaged to Archie Campbell."

"Archie Campbell!" James exclaimed. "You've only met him a couple of times, if that. And are you telling me you're going to let your father determine every part of your life? Besides, your father likes me."

Sarah looked at him with pity. "My father doesn't *like* anyone. He surrounds himself with people who are useful to him and can help him get what he wants."

"He might come around to the idea of us. I'm sure he wants you to be happy."

"He could not care less if I am happy or not. He sees people as possessions, in a way, especially his daughter. He would never allow anything that would affect him or his reputation to get in the way." She gave a bitter laugh.

"We'll figure something out," James said with a confidence he didn't feel. They had to; the idea of a world without Sarah was inconceivable.

Sarah tossed and turned in her four-poster bed, willing sleep to come and give her some relief from her thoughts. Her feelings for James had gone beyond the point of no return, and she knew she would do whatever it took for them to prevail. Her days revolved around whether she was able to meet James. The days they were apart were long and unforgivably cruel stretches of time where she felt exhausted by the need to continue her daily routine. She sat for meals, barely touching her plate, and conversed with the visitors to Baliforth House with an absentminded detachment.

One of the servants had remarked on her change in demeanor, and Samuel Whiting had taken note and began to pay a little more attention to his daughter than she typically commanded. He observed that she went into town with surprising frequency and saw a brief look of fear flash across her flawless face when he questioned her about the errands. Whiting had not become a master of industry by distrusting his instincts and summoned his trusty servant to verify his suspicions.

Sarah was out of the motor before the chauffeur had a chance to open the door. She bid him goodbye and promised to bring him some toffee from the confectionary counter. Spending so much time with James was affecting her, she thought with amusement. She had begun to take more interest in some of her father's household staff. She found that the groundskeeper had a witty sense of humor, the cook was a talented artist, and her chauffeur was one of the kindest men in the world, with a penchant for expensive toffee. She practically skipped along the route to meet her lover and failed to notice a man lurking in the shadows, watching her every move.

****

Samuel Whiting was not pleased. "And you are certain that is who she has been meeting?"

The manservant nodded and explained she had been followed on several occasions. There was no mistake.

Whiting dismissed the man and sat back in his chair to contemplate what would happen next. He needed leverage and knew where to get it. He rang the bell and summoned his only child.

"Yes, Father, I was told you wanted to see me?" Sarah entered her father's study cautiously.

"I would prefer to avoid any pretense."

"Pretense?" Sarah inquired with a wide-eyed innocence plastered on her beautiful face.

Whiting slapped the table in front of him, making her jump. "Don't play with me," he commanded. "I know you've been spending time with that commoner."

Sarah was shocked at the revelation, but then her mind unfurled the jumble of events, and she sneered, "Oh, I see. You had that despicable manservant follow me, did you?"

"And it's a good thing I did. Do you have any idea what this could do to your reputation if this were revealed?"

"That's all you care about. *Reputation.*"

Samuel Whiting strode around the large mahogany table, separating him from his daughter. He grabbed her roughly by the wrists. "I will *not* be disobeyed. The consequences will be dire indeed, and I am not referring only to you," he said pointedly. "Put a stop to this immediately."

Sarah let out an exaggerated sigh as if the conversation was tiresome. "Father, there is nothing of concern. The commoner, as you put it, does not hold my interest, and I won't be seeing him again. I would so enjoy it if you let me return to London with Kitty."

Whiting settled back into his armchair and let out a bark of laughter. His daughter was audacious! Not unlike himself, he reflected with a rare touch of pride. "Out of the question. Although I imagine that once you become Mrs. Archibald Campbell, you will have quite a few opportunities to spend time in London."

He noted Sarah's thoughtful expression as she left the room and hoped that his point had been made successfully. He had found her spirited behavior quite amusing, although it was evident that the time had come to check it once and for all before there were any lasting repercussions. The Macleary boy! That presumptuous little upstart. Whiting couldn't believe he had the gall to even approach his daughter, let alone take it any further. This type of behavior would certainly not go unpunished.

Sarah left her father's study and ran straight to the safety of her rooms. She slammed the door behind her and sank to the floor. Her chest heaved uncontrollably, but she willed herself to stay calm and gulped down the rising panic. She hoped her father had believed her display of nonchalance, but she knew him well enough to understand that whatever he thought, there would not be any mercy for James. That night she tossed and turned, but sleep was more elusive than ever. She had been so caught up in the intoxication of James that she had not fully understood how dangerous a game they were playing. Her mind replayed moments from lavish parties when she had laughed at offhand remarks about her father's cutthroat business practices. Now she was the target of his wrath, it wasn't so funny anymore.

The following day she had made up her mind. She dressed with even more care than usual and checked herself in the mirror, noting with a frown at her reflection that however carefully she applied her cosmetics, they could not cover her exhaustion. She sat in the back of the motor and stared unseeing as the bright trees rolled past. The window rattled slightly as the vehicle negotiated some rough terrain and jolted her from her reverie. She smoothed down her skirts and took a deep breath to steel her nerves. She had to see her plan through; it was the only option.

She left her driver with the usual instructions and hastened to the house in Balifeary. She rattled the door handle to signal her arrival, and James opened the door immediately and ushered her inside.

"Every time I see you, I can never believe how beautiful you are." He was staring at her with wonder and took a step toward her to take her in his arms, but she held up her hand to stall him.

"We have to talk."

"I have a feeling this is not something I want to hear." His face clouded over.

"You have to leave. It's not safe for you here."

James' handsome face was a picture of shock. "What are you saying?"

"We can't be together anymore, you know that. This isn't real. We're too different."

"This is the 1920s." He tried to move toward her again. "The world is changing—you always say so," he tried to comfort her.

"Not for pcople like me."

"What do you mean?" His mouth felt very dry, and he unconsciously clenched his fists.

"You wouldn't understand," Sarah said patronizingly.

"The world is very hard for people like you," James responded sarcastically, "telling others what to do every day of your life, being waited on hand and foot and wanting for nothing. Yes, it's a hard life indeed."

"I'm happy that you're leaving!" Sarah burst out, finally naming the reason for their squabbling.

"You just told me to leave!" he burst out in exasperation. "I won't go. I can't leave you anyway."

"You have to go. I can't be the reason you stay."

"You're the reason for everything," he said simply.

Sarah swallowed as she regarded this man she loved more than anything in the world and realized he felt the same about her. She knew the world would not be kind to them, and she had to act to protect them both.

"I may not have to worry about where my next meal is coming from, but I still live in a cage."

"One with fur coats and expensive champagne."

"Well, I pity you so much being free to make all your own choices," Sarah sneered.

"My own choices! You have no idea of reality for regular people like me. We don't get to *choose* what we become; we take whatever job we can and work all hours of the day to survive. Every scrap of bread goes into the mouth of a hungry child, and there's never enough. And the reason for this? Your kind are keeping us where we belong, down in the gutter."

"I see," Sarah responded coldly. "I'm glad you've told me how you really feel, and it seems evident that we have come to an impasse. I shall take my leave and wish you well, James Macleary."

"Sarah, wait…" He tried to stop her, but she had already stalked out to the street and disappeared into the crowd of people. James searched vainly for her striking figure among the throng that had hastened their steps as the relentless rain began to pour from the gray Scottish sky.

****

Sarah sat down at the walnut writing desk and pulled out a piece of embossed paper and a monogrammed fountain pen. The letter was overdue, and she resolved to get it posted before the end of the day. "Dear Mr. Macleary," she began.

*I have enjoyed your company these past few weeks, but I regret to say that we must not see each other again. I am sure that you can see it is not only improper for us to maintain an acquaintance, but with my forthcoming engagement, it would not be an acceptable arrangement for my betrothed. I wish you health and happiness in the future. Sincerely, Mistress Sarah Rose Violet Whiting.*

She ran down the stairs lightly as she had done as a child and called out impatiently to her father's manservant. He appeared instantly as though he had been lurking nearby, and she told him of her errand. He offered to deliver the letter himself, and Sarah shrugged and handed him the envelope.

Moments later, Samuel Whiting opened a recently sealed letter in the privacy of his wood-paneled study, and the contents were much to his satisfaction. He handed the letter back to his servant; he would be able to make the post if he hurried.

****

Ma Macleary looked at her son James with concern. Gone were his carefree attitude and playful charm, and in its place was a skeleton with hollowed eyes and little interest in anything. She had told her husband to talk to their son, and he had looked at her as if she had grown two heads.

"What am I supposed to say to the lad? Some lass has probably broken his heart. He'll meet another one and get over it." He puffed on his pipe without concern.

As much as she didn't like this response, Ma thought he was probably right. James had gone from being the cheeky jokester she had always known to this morose, serious lad almost overnight. She hoped he would recover just as quickly and idly wondered which of the pretty girls in the borough were still looking for husbands. The most important thing was that nothing interfered with this opportunity he had for a new life. Fancy Samuel Whiting taking such a shine to her boy! He had always been smart as a whip, but still, she couldn't believe he had been lucky enough to be picked from the crowd like that and was being sent on his way to America!

James had been worried after Sarah stormed out, but it hadn't entered his mind that it was over between them. The idea was inconceivable, but James had the proof of the devastating reality in his breast pocket. He had received her letter a couple of days ago and had tried to send word immediately that he needed to see her. The gardener on the Baliforth estate, who had acted as a courier for the young lovers before, told him Sarah had refused to take a message from him and wouldn't give him the time of day. James was desperate, and as three days turned into four, he resolved that he would have to go to Baliforth House himself and wait in the trees until he could see a chance to speak to her when she was out riding or walking. The half-formed plan was on his mind when he walked through the doors of the distillery and was accosted by Benjamin Greer in his habitual fluster. He ushered James into the small office and looked him over with bright eyes. "Three days," he said excitedly.

"Three days for what?"

"They've moved up the date. We've got your tickets and a bed in steerage. All you need to do is say goodbye to your ma and pack your things."

"I can't. I can't leave now."

Benjamin Greer looked at his protégé in abject horror. "What are you talking about, boy? This is what you've been waiting for. It's a chance that most would jump at, and it's yours for the taking. You won't see another opportunity like this to make something of yourself. Don't get cold feet now. Besides, I wouldn't like to imagine what would happen to a boy that lets down Samuel Whiting. He's not the most forgiving of employers, mark my words."

"But he *does* reward good work?" James suddenly perked up as he saw a potential avenue to Sarah.

"If you make him money and don't cause any trouble, he can be a very good man to work for."

"I won't let you down," James told him sincerely. "You're right. I will make something of myself."

He left Benjamin Greer's office with a mind full of jumbled thoughts. He had not realized how restless he had become since returning from sea, and his thirst for both love and adventure was at an all-time high. Greer had spent the better part of the previous evening outlining the plan. James always found him easy company. Far from being hesitant to speak up, he found himself questioning and challenging some of the components of his itinerary and plan of operation once he arrived in St. Pierre.

The day before he was due to sail, Greer relayed that his proposed changes had been received with approval from Samuel Whiting. "His man on the inside," Whiting had called him, and that was music to James' ears.

He smirked at himself. Better not get above his station, as his old ma would have said. James was under no illusions that Mr. Whiting had not become so successful in business by having a good show for his confidants, but he made no mistake. James understood that despite his new heights in the company, he was as dispensable as the rest. But that was something he hoped to change.

Sarah was wrong. James knew he had a quick mind and wanted to impress that upon his employer, who he hoped one day, one day soon, he could convince to look upon him as something more than just an employee. Planning for his new adventure was a welcome distraction from what was ailing him—her. He shook his head, a refusal to dwell on thoughts that always returned to her. Now was the time for action. Now was the time for a new beginning.

Chapter Nine

Sarah looked apprehensively at the dirty red door and paused for a minute before knocking. She smoothed down her fur stole and wondered why she was so nervous. She checked the number again--this was the address she had been given. She raised her hand and knocked. Nothing. She knocked again and then heard a commotion from the other side of the door. It finally swung open, and a young girl of about ten stared in astonishment at Sarah.

"Who is it, Elsie?" came another voice from within.

"It's a gentry."

The first voice emerged from within the small house, and Sarah beheld the kindly face of Ma Macleary. "Can I help you, dear?"

"Yes, I'm a friend, a friend of James," Sarah stammered.

"Of course you are." James' mother smiled at Sarah, not seeing a well-dressed aristocrat but instead a nervous young girl come to say she was a friend of her son. "Come on in, dearie." Sarah followed her into the cramped room, which despite the sparse decoration alluded a sense of cheer. She sat on a proffered wooden stool and accepted the offer of tea. James' mother banished the other children outside with a cheerful scolding and closed the front door. "A little peace for us," she said kindly.

"Well, as I said, I'm a friend of your son James," Sarah began.

Ma said nothing but patted her hand and gave her a little smile.

"You're probably wondering what I'm doing here," Sarah said nervously. "In fact, I'm not sure why I'm here either." The words tumbled out. "I'm sorry, I should probably leave." Sarah looked around for somewhere to leave her cup and rose from the stool.

"Stay a little while, dearie. I don't get good company very much. Tell me about yourself."

Sarah sat down again, embarrassed. "Well, my name is Sarah. I've known your son for a while now. He's very smart."

"And he'll certainly tell you that himself." Ma snorted.

Sarah gave a little laugh. "Yes, he's not exactly the timid type."

"He'll get himself in big trouble one day, much too brave for his own good, and my goodness, he's never learned to respect authority, always questioning everything that's kept the world turning for this long." Ma was shaking her head with a smile. "But I suppose he wouldn't have met you otherwise," she concluded slyly.

"But he's gone now," Sarah said desperately. "I thought it was the right thing to do, but I'm not sure now, and maybe I'm just being selfish, because I want more than anything for him to be safe."

"We don't have control over things like that, and he loves you. I've never seen anything like it. Changed from one man to the next overnight."

"Really?" Sarah felt a spark of hope ignite. "I think

we're just too late."

"That's really up to you. Where there's a will, there's a way."

"I love him, I don't want us to be apart, but I worry that we're too different."

"My son isn't an easy one. He's given me no end of headaches." Ma shook her head. "He's as smart as they come, and he's an adventurer, always has been. He'll never be happy having a life that's the same every day."

"But that's what I think too!"

"Then are you really that different?"

****

James guided the schooner expertly into the harbor at St. Pierre. "Frenchy Island," as his men had come to call it, was now a place James knew well after his arrival several months before. The island off the coast of Newfoundland was the perfect point of origin and departure for precious cargo and offered proximity to the mainland and a well-organized base of operations. "The Ellis Island for alcohol," James had thought more than once. The passage for a bottle of Whitings was fairly simple. Upon arriving at the islands, things were unloaded and organized. James oversaw several warehouses and checked the inventory personally at least twice a week when he was there, to ensure that not too much was "lost" to the laborers.

The riskiest part of the operation was the handover. James and his small fleet would file a regular manifest to the Bahamas. En route, however, they were often caught in a squall that would force the craft to take a more westerly path. That path inadvertently took them just close enough to the shoreline of the United States, where they would be greeted by another silent army who took the cargo safely to shore under cover of darkness.

The waiting was the part that made James uneasy, the quiet lapping of the waves against the boat as they waited for their American counterparts to haul off the whisky and whatever else was in Whiting's shipment. When they were on their way back to the islands, they could finally breathe a sigh of relief. He and his small crew of six were disembarking on one of these occasions when another small craft hailed them, heading to shore with immense speed. His men looked in alarm toward him, waiting for direction.

"Macleary!" shouted O'Brien, prompting him to action. O'Brien was one of his most seasoned sailors and closest confidants, but the man was easily spooked, and James had often had misgivings about how well he would keep his counsel if they were ever apprehended. He held up his hand for calm, looked again at the approaching craft, and broke into a relieved grin. "It's only Bobby," he told the men.

The customs vessel slowed as it approached the harbor, and James raised a hand in greeting. "How're things, Bobby?" he asked the coast guard.

"Thirsty work, son," came the response.

James shook his head resignedly. If he could get rid of Bobby and the customs with one casket and perhaps a couple of cases of Madeira, then the shipment would still be in good shape. The question was "if."

Corrupt customs enforcers like Bobby and his crew were to be expected, and their now-established arrangement had significantly eased the perils of passage to the mainland. James didn't much like parting with a portion of the shipment every time but reasoned that you get what you pay for and, so far, had no complaints with how effective the arrangement had been. Nobody was in jail, and nobody was dead.

James had quickly mastered the codebook, which had become his new bible when sailing around the archipelago. He had underestimated the cunning of his boss but immediately realized upon his arrival that Whiting had got a foothold in the operation at the very beginning, and James, with his quick mind and easy charm, had been instrumental in no small part to smooth the way of the operations in the region. He quickly acquired a name for himself by avoiding a customs seizure that had ensnared some of the more seasoned runners and vowed with this near miss to devise an early warning system. It had started with a few greased hands and some radio equipment but had quickly burgeoned into a full-scale operation with eyes and ears covering almost every breach point out from the islands all the way to the coast near Philadelphia.

The passage of Whiting's Scotch from its homeland to the glasses of his discerning American customers was a well-trodden and highly efficient operation, thanks to James Macleary. The mothership arrived each week, and its giant bulk rested off the coast safely distanced from territorial waters. James and his crew then made several trips to transport the cargo between the vessel and the docking point. The trips were so routine that he had to constantly remind his crew to be alert and prepared. Too often, he had seen one or more of his men lolling on the deck or even playing cards when they were waiting in position.

James had been surprised at how many fellow Scots he had found in the area. Most were due to the intense migration of the 1850s, and he found that far from being the alien land he had been expecting, the North America he had found seemed in some ways to be exactly like the Scotland he had left behind. He much preferred his work on the open sea to the inside of the distillery and relished the feel of the wind whipping his hair when the weather was fair. Once a sailor, always a sailor, one of his crew had remarked.

He had not expected to find such good men, and O'Brien and Bisset, in particular, had become almost as dear to him as his own brothers back home in Scotland. He had fostered a camaraderie among the group and established himself as a reliable and fair overseer. His men had quickly come to realize that, regardless of their place of origin or native tongue, Macleary would take them on their merits and nothing else. He had no time for slackers, though as the pace of work in Whiting's operation was constant, James was relieved he had scant time to dwell on anything. Work had to be done, and his mind, when focused on the tasks in front of him, meant there was little time left for darker reflections.

The business was booming, and James could not have imagined how lucrative a business it could be. Every two weeks, James released his employees for a few days to reap the benefits of their labor. He was an astute leader and knew his men would perform their best when treated well and given certainties and routines. St. John's and occasionally Sydney were favorite places for a few days respite where the brothels and gaming houses were a little livelier than the offerings on St. Pierre. James enjoyed the taverns of St. John's, where the fishermen jostled comfortably alongside regulators and merchantmen. There was a cross of classes that hadn't been so rampant in his native Scotland, but James still saw the underhand deals, the tongues of politicians, and the honest man turned to an unsavory duty to make a living for his family. A new world indeed, but there was much of the old to be found there, he thought with a touch of sadness.

He worked hard, and he played hard on the rare occasions when his time was his own, and he actively sought any distraction that would take his mind off *her*. O'Brien and Jacques Bisset had ignored his protestations, and after enough liquor to tranquilize a small horse, they had tried to introduce him to Molly.

"She'll cure whatever's ailing you." O'Brien laughed, pushing his friend in the direction of his target. James had looked at the vivacious Molly and did not doubt Molly had cured more than one man's pining for another woman.

"Can I sit for a moment?" he asked her, removing his hat. He would play along and might earn himself a little peace from his well-meaning men.

She turned her bright blue eyes on James and liked what she saw. "You can sit a while," she replied in a strong Irish accent that James had become used to hearing in the ports.

"How long have you been over here?" he asked.

Molly gave him a long look and ran her hand along his cheek. Ignoring his question, "You have a sadness about you," she said gently. James tried to dismiss her with a laugh, but she continued, "You're missing someone."

"Everyone misses someone."

"But yours is a one in a lifetime, I'll wager."

He took a big slug of his drink. "She's gone."

"Do you want me to see?" Molly took his hand and

raised the palm upward.

"I don't believe in fortune-tellers." James laughed again, with a conviction he didn't quite believe. Molly gave him a knowing look and turned her attention to his palm. She carefully traced the lines with her finger, smiled slightly, and then furrowed her brow. James leaned in. "What is it? What do you see?"

"You're mighty interested, for one who doesn't believe in fortune-tellers." She twinkled up at him.

James shrugged as nonchalantly as he could and took another swig from his cup. "It matters not to me."

"She'll be on her way soon."

James laughed again but this time bitterly. "I doubt that."

Molly shrugged. "You'll see soon enough. You will be reunited."

"If there's a happy ending, why did you frown when you looked at my hand?"

"It's strange," Molly said slowly, "your story. I'm not the only one looking."

"What do you mean?" James wondered for a moment whether Molly had all her regular senses straight, let alone the supernatural ones.

"Someone else is looking from a long way away."

"Like back across the ocean?" he asked with a touch of sarcasm.

Molly shook her head. "That's not it. Maybe a faraway time, instead."

James snorted. "Great, the ghosts of the past are looking at me too."

"It might be the future." Molly smiled at him. "Now, if you'll excuse me, Mr. Macleary, I'll share my fortune with someone who might believe it." James raised his cup to her as she departed and chuckled to himself. It was only after they all left the tavern that James realized he had never told Molly his last name.

That night, he lay in his small bunk and listened to the waves lapping against the sides of the boat. The soothing sound was interrupted occasionally by the snores of O'Brien, who had been unable to make it back to his own bed and so graced the floor of his tight quarters. James lay propped up on his arm and stared unseeing at the blank ceiling. What if Molly was right? What if Sarah was going to come to him? His natural optimism was still alive and well, but James had seen enough Dear John letters during the war to know that absence does not always make the heart grow fonder. What if she had forgotten about him? What if she had been growing closer to her supposed fiancé? His fist clenched tightly at the thought of her in the company of another man. His work was relentless. That was exactly what he wanted. The exhaustion had, at least, provided a momentary distraction from the heartbreak. But she plagued his thoughts when he closed his eyes to sleep. He could see her sweeping her red hair absentmindedly from her shoulder, the curve of her face when she smiled up at him. And even with senses dulled from intoxication, her beautiful face was the last thing he would see. Damn Sarah Whiting.

Chapter Ten

*Present Day, Montana, USA*

I angled the photograph toward the light. Although her tragic fate had shown she was not blessed with good fortune, Samuel Whiting's daughter Sarah had certainly been blessed with beauty. The image of a hand, palm upward, suddenly flashed in my mind, and I had an odd feeling that a pair of bright blue eyes was looking at me from a place very far away. I put the photograph down and laughed at my folly; there was no such thing as ghosts. What I needed was a cup of coffee, and I followed the smell of freshly brewed beans.

"You haven't forgotten what day it is!" Betty admonished Marcus, who put his head in his hands and released a painful groan.

"What? What day is it?" I asked, filling my cup in a kitchen that was beginning to feel quite like home.

"The cattleman's ball!" She laughed at my quizzical face. "Anyone can tell you're not from around these parts."

"It's a big deal for the industry," Marcus tried to explain.

"Like the who's who of Montana and the surrounding states." Betty gave a short laugh. "It's not Marcus's favorite night of the year."

"What's so bad about it?"

"They all hit on him," Betty said mischievously, earning a withering look from Marcus. "I don't know why you're looking at me like that. You know it's true."

"It was bad enough when I was married to Justine. She loved all the attention and gossip about who had gotten divorced, who had what mistress, and all that kind of stuff."

"It sounds dreadful," I surmised.

"That's why we've become so fond of you." Betty put her arm around me.

"Anyway, I have to go," he concluded, "although I can think of many other things I would prefer to do with my evening." He gave me a look that moved from my eyes and lingered on my mouth a little too long.

"Why don't you go together?" Betty suggested lightly.

Marcus and I both opened our mouths to tell her what a terrible idea that was, but she held up her hand for silence. "You…" She pointed at Marcus. "…have to go, and you…" It was my turn for the finger. "…need to give yourself a night off from all this *working*."

"You can give me an update on things," Marcus said loftily. "I mean, if you want. I wouldn't mind talking about something other than Montana's gossip of the day."

"I don't have anything to wear," I protested feebly.

"Tsk." Betty made a scoffing noise. "That can soon be fixed."

"It would be my pleasure if you would accompany me," Marcus said formally, "if you don't have any other plans."

"I don't have any other plans."

"Okay, till tonight then." He held my gaze and then

stalked out of the kitchen. I sighed; the man was still an enigma.

After I'd spent less than an hour of halfhearted work on my laptop, Betty came to find me. "Come on," she instructed.

"Where are we going?"

"To see Mrs. Jensen."

Mrs. Jensen turned out to be the small-town equivalent of a celebrity wardrobe designer. We walked into a shop so crammed full of dresses and fabric that we could barely move. Betty and I finally made it to the desk in the middle of the room, and Betty, following the instructions on a small sign, rang a brass bell.

I stifled a giggle, but Betty turned and glared at me to be quiet. Mrs. Jensen emerged, and I understood why I had gotten the glare, as the formidable character made me think of a superior nun who had scared the convent into submission.

"This is Emily Clemonte," Betty introduced me. "She is going to the cattleman's ball this evening and has nothing to wear."

An eyebrow shot up on Mrs. Jensen's perfectly made-up face, although her other features didn't change at all. "I see. So we need to make you something on *the day* of the ball."

"Well, I don't think we need to *make* something," I started. "I mean, if you have something that will work in my size…" I lapsed into silence at the look she gave me.

She pointed to a tiny cubicle with a ragged shower curtain. "Go in there and disrobe, please, down to your underwear." I was more than a little uncomfortable but had no intention of disobeying this terrifying woman. She whipped into the cubicle moments later and measured me from every angle in a matter of seconds. "You can get dressed again now."

When I came back out of the cubicle, Betty stood alone beside the desk. "We have to come back at three o'clock," she whispered, pushing me in the direction of the door.

"Don't I get to choose my own dress?" I asked her incredulously when we were outside beyond the hearing of the formidable Mrs. Jensen.

Betty shook her head. "No one is allowed to choose, but I'm sure you'll like it."

"How can you be so sure?"

"Everyone always does. Coffee?"

Betty next took me to the cutest little coffee shop I had ever set foot in and exchanged pleasantries with the server, the owner, and almost all the patrons. "You know everyone around here," I observed.

"Small towns, hon, it's all part of the charm."

After our short stop for a latte, she took me to the local salon, and I was given the "cattleman's do" per Betty's instructions. After what seemed like an eternity of pulling and plucking and closing my eyes and pursing my lips, I was allowed to look at my reflection in the mirror.

"Wow!" I looked amazing. I kept staring at my reflection in awe as Betty and the beautician did a high five behind me. She had hit the perfect note between effortless glamor and fresh-faced, so my fears of looking like a garish clown were completely unfounded. My hair was in a half-up, half-down do with soft waves framing my face. I continued to stare at my reflection until Betty pulled me unceremoniously up out of the chair. It was time to go back to collect my dress from Mrs. Jensen.

I hoped that the frightening lady would live up to her reputation and give me something passable to wear, because I doubted that many other options for formalwear existed in Fairview. Once again, I was made to undress in the minuscule cubicle, and then an arm shot through the curtain, holding an exquisite gown. The color was a gray slate that almost seemed blue; it was floor length with off-the-shoulder straps and beautiful embroidery around the neckline.

"Put it on; I need to see whether the chest needs adjusting," Mrs. Jensen commanded. The gown fit me like a glove, and I couldn't believe how beautiful it was as I twirled as best I could around the tiny fitting room.

"Come out! The suspense is killing me," Betty shouted, and I emerged from behind the shower curtain to her gasp of delight. I saw the corners of Mrs. Jensen's mouth curve up for a split second, and then it was back to business.

"No adjustments are needed," she said briskly. "I'll get you a dress hanger, and you can be on your way."

"Mrs. Jensen, the dress is so beautiful," I began to compliment her, but her expression clouded in disapproval.

"You don't have too much time. Get dressed." She gave Betty the gown, now wrapped in its protective layer, and shoved a large box into my arms.

"What's in here?"

"Your accessories, of course." She rolled her eyes at Betty. "Dear heaven, where did you find this one?" She practically pushed us out the door, and the closed sign snapped up in the window.

"I don't know that I've ever met such a scary person…or such a good dressmaker."

Betty and I laughed as we headed to the truck to make our way back to the McClean ranch.

I was checking my reflection for a final time in the full-length mirror of one of Marcus's guest rooms when there was a knock at the door. Mrs. Jensen had equipped me with heels, an evening bag, and some beautiful crystal drop earrings that perfectly complemented the dress. I heard Marcus cough discreetly, and I told him to come in.

"Holy crap." He stopped dead in the doorway, and his jaw dropped, literally.

"Is that a good 'holy crap'?"

"Emily, you look absolutely beautiful." He was still staring at me in amazement.

"Well, you don't look half bad yourself." He was wearing a tux but hadn't shaved, and his nine o'clock shadow made him look like a slightly unkempt James Bond. I once again had to censor my thoughts.

He held out his arm for me to take. "Shall we?"

\*\*\*\*

I felt like Cinderella arriving at the ball when Marcus and I pulled up at the sprawling lodge. I had no idea Montana had so many luxury venues but had seen little else since my first meeting with Marcus McClean a few days earlier. He held the door open for me to get out of the car, and I took his arm a little shyly as we made our way up the steps. "Here we go," he said into my ear. "I'm glad you came tonight, although, in that dress, you're going to make us the talk of the whole state."

I was enjoying the evening immensely. Marcus had visibly relaxed when we were seated at the table of another couple, people he admired, who turned out to be some of the most hospitable and charming individuals I had ever met. They regaled me with amusing stories of transporting cattle, and we were all laughing when the atmosphere suddenly changed, and I saw Marcus's jaw harden into a grim expression. I followed his gaze and saw a striking figure heading toward our merry table. He stiffened as the slender form of an attractive blonde with heavy makeup stopped next to him.

"It's so good to see you all, hello, Marcus," she said insincerely, looking not at Marcus but me with an expression meant to convey "I don't like you."

"Misty, can I do something for you?" Marcus asked rudely.

"Yes, you can," she hissed at him, and he stood up, excused himself, and, taking her by the arm, steered them both outside the ballroom. My dinner companions gave me a momentary look of dismay and then resumed their witty banter to try and save me from embarrassment. Now I knew who Misty Farley was; it was obvious Marcus had a type, I thought, remembering the photograph of his ex-wife Justine, and I certainly didn't fit the mold.

Almost half an hour passed before Marcus finally returned with a face like thunder. He took his seat and muttered an apology to the table in general before leaning over to whisper in my ear, "I'm sorry for leaving you on your own. I was afraid she was going to make a scene and wanted to get her away, for everyone's sake." I had been going to make some sarcastic remark about his tumultuous relationship with Misty, but he looked so weary I didn't have the heart to reproach him at all.

"It's fine. I can take care of myself. I hope you got things sorted out, though?"

"Not really, but it's as good as it's going to get.

Anyway, let's not let her ruin our evening. Would you like to dance?"

"I didn't have you down as the dancing type." I looked at him in astonishment.

"I'm happy to hear you're keeping an open mind about me." He took me by the hand and walked us to the edge of the dance floor. There were quite a few couples already in motion, and I was glad when he guided us toward the middle, where I felt a little less conspicuous. His strong arm circled my waist, and I felt him pull me a little closer. I could smell his cologne again and briefly closed my eyes, savoring the moment. We danced slowly, moving perfectly together as if we had been practicing for many years.

"I think we're attracting some attention." He smiled down at me.

"I imagine Marcus McClean is one of the most eligible bachelors around here," I said flirtatiously.

"I don't know," he countered. "You're the one attracting most of the attention, in that dress. You've certainly got mine."

"You know all the right things to say," I teased. We held each other closely, and I couldn't remember a time a dance had been so perfect.

When the song finally finished, we pulled away from each other and joined in the applause as the band took a bow. We migrated back to the table and were just about to sit down when I saw Misty Farley heading toward the table again, obviously with Marcus the intended victim. I nudged him and nodded in her direction.

"Want to get some air?" he asked. We set off in the direction of the door, but Marcus guided me toward the bar and ordered a bottle of champagne and two glasses. As he pocketed the flutes, we headed outside.

"I have a secret spot where we can hide." Taking my hand, he led us off the path at the front of the resort and into a cluster of pines at the side of the road.

"Are you sure we won't get eaten by a bear? I'm not wearing the right shoes for hiking," I joked as he continued to lead us into the woods.

"It's not far, and I promise it's worth the wait."

He was right. We finally emerged from the trees, and he made a triumphant noise. The view rendered me speechless. The ripples of an enormous reservoir were reflected in the moonlight, and a thousand stars lit the sky, colored with vivid hues of pink and purple.

"I'm guessing by the look on your face that we can stop here for a while."

"Thank you for bringing me here. Having seen this view, I don't want to ever imagine going through life without it."

"There sure is something about this place," he agreed. "I've spent my whole life here, but it still catches me by surprise sometimes. Here, sit down." He indicated a dilapidated swing that was just big enough to accommodate the two of us. He pulled the glasses from his pockets with a flourish and topped them up with champagne. "I'm guessing it's not wild like this where you're from."

"Some parts are. Take Scotland, for example, the home of my parents and your priceless bottle of whisky. The highlands and the moorlands are wild and rugged but in a completely different way."

"What about the people?"

"Also just as wild." I smiled.

"Here's to you"—he proposed a toast—"for making this evening not just bearable but one of the best I've had in some time." We chinked glasses, and he held my eyes as we both took a sip of the bubbles.

"You know, I didn't like you very much when we first met," I told him, laughing.

"I'm an acquired taste."

"You can say that again!"

"I just don't go in for all the show. I believe a man is only as good as his word, or perhaps his actions."

"You're right," I replied thoughtfully. "You're a refreshing change from some of the people I meet in Boston...or London, before that. Everything about them is the show. It doesn't matter the substance, just how it might look."

"Who cares how things look?" Marcus frowned. "As long as the people who matter know the truth."

"That might be your world, but it isn't mine."

"We can choose what we want," he said lightly. "It's within our control."

"Well, some of us have to earn a living, and sometimes that means spending time in the company of people we might not choose."

"I didn't mean to offend you."

"No, I'm sorry. I shouldn't have been so thin-skinned."

Marcus put his arm around me and pulled me in to his chest. I smelled the aroma of the pines mixed with his cologne and thought that if someone could make that into a scented candle, I would be a lifetime buyer. Marcus looked down at my face and, after what seemed like an eternity, finally brought his lips to meet mine.

He held me close as we drove back to the ranch,

neither of us saying a word. When we arrived, he pulled me around to the back of the house and put a finger to his lips.

"Why are we hiding?" I stifled a giggle.

"Betty's probably waiting up for us," he said, looking around furtively.

"I was not waiting up," came a voice from inside, and a light snapped on over the deck.

"She always stays up this late," said Ron's voice with a chuckle.

"I feel like a kid again," I whispered, and we both laughed.

"So, as we're all here," Betty continued, "how was your evening?"

"Fine," Marcus gave his standard one-word response.

"No trouble from you-know-who?" Betty persisted.

Marcus let out a big sigh, and his shoulders visibly sagged. "She was there and tried to cause a scene, but I think I put an end to it for now." Misty. They were talking about Misty. I chastised myself for forgetting about the show-stopping blonde who seemed to be in the picture only to complicate things.

"Good. Oh, and some other guy came around this afternoon. Wants a meeting about the whisky."

Betty had our full attention now.

"What was his name?" I ventured, trying to fight the sinking feeling in the pit of my stomach.

"Let's see…" She was rummaging through a pile of magazines on the table. "I don't know where I put his card now."

"It doesn't matter," Marcus said curtly. "The vultures can call again if they want. I'm not going out of my way to help them."

"What did he look like?" I asked, feeling sick to my stomach.

"Dark hair, handsome, well dressed. Insincere, of course. About what you would expect."

Although the description could have applied to any number of people, I knew exactly who Betty was talking about. I pulled away from Marcus abruptly. I needed space and time to think, and this wasn't the place for either. "I'm pretty tired," I said. "Betty, is there a guest room I could use for this evening? I'll return to the hotel first thing tomorrow."

I followed her into the house, avoiding Marcus's quizzical look, trying to figure out the sudden change in my behavior. I refused to meet his eyes. Betty fussed around me until I finally held the door open, and she left me to my solitude. I took off my exquisite gown with a touch of regret, hanging it up carefully, and got ready for bed. My mind was whirling with a hundred thoughts. I would have to come clean to Marcus, but I was terrified of what he would say or do when he found out I hadn't been wholly truthful. I then thought of another man I might be letting down and pictured Angus's good-natured face, telling me not to worry. I had done my best, even though his life's work was now destroyed. If what he had said about the business was true, losing the find of a lifetime would be the last nail in the coffin for us. I tossed and turned for hours until the first orange rays of the sun finally broke through the darkness. I was up and out before I had a chance to run into Marcus, and I told Betty, as she drove me into town, that I would be back the following day. She looked as though she was going to say something else but decided against it and dismissed me with a wave. I walked into the lobby of my hotel and stopped dead. In front of me was the ominous sight of Leo Dahlberg.

Chapter Eleven

He hadn't seen me yet, which gave me a split second to compose myself. We had not spoken since that day, although I had heard his voice in the many voicemails he'd left on my phone. I had deleted the messages, but not before torturing myself by playing them over and over. He sat in a small booth by the window, drinking a cup of coffee, and somehow looked smaller and thinner than I remembered. He was wearing a pinstriped shirt and khakis, which looked out of place here in Montana. His black wavy hair was slightly unkempt, but nothing could disguise how handsome he was. The bastard. I desperately wanted my own cup of coffee but didn't trust my hands not to shake when I confronted him. Unbidden, I heard Betty's voice in the back of my head: *What's a headstrong girl like you doing, letting some pathetic excuse for a man treat you like that?* I silently thanked her and strode over to stand next to the booth. "Hello, Leo."

I had the satisfaction of seeing him jump, and a drop of coffee landed on the table. "Emily, I…I…didn't see you." We stared at each other.

"What are you doing here?" I finally asked.

"I wanted to see you. I know so much has happened, and you probably don't think a lot of me right now, but I just want to explain. I can't go on any longer without you letting me try and explain." He looked anguished, and for a split second, I almost felt sorry for him but then remembered the vision of him and someone else in our bed.

"No, I mean, what are you doing *here* exactly? In Fairview, Montana."

"As I said, I wanted to see you."

"So you suddenly decided to fly across the country even though we haven't seen each other in months," I said, sarcasm dripping from my voice.

"The timing worked out. I was coming anyway." He made a pathetic attempt at a chuckle.

"Coming anyway? To Fairview, Montana." I gave him a look which I hoped was the same I would give a dog turd on my shoe.

He spread his hands in a gesture of helplessness. "Emily, I just can't stand any of this. Can we talk properly? Please."

"Leo, I don't have time for this right now."

"Okay, so later, then? Tonight? What are you doing tonight?"

I was saved by the buzzing of my cellphone and saw it was Danny, our researcher extraordinaire.

Leo gave me a "you're not going to answer that" look, and I ignored him, hurrying through the glass doors of the exit, where I would be beyond earshot of Leo.

"Hi, Danny, do you have any news for us?"

Danny started to speak, and I stopped pacing and clamped my hand over my mouth in disbelief. I frantically rooted in my pockets for a pen. "Wait, Danny! Wait!" I shouted and ran back into the lobby, straight past Leo, and took the stairs, two at a time, up to my room. "Wait a minute," I shouted down the phone again, breathing heavily.

"Are you running?" Danny sounded amused.

"Okay, okay, go ahead." I found the remains of the hotel's complimentary notebook paper and a half-chewed pen from my purse. I sat down heavily, poised to write.

*My darling,*
*You will always be with ____ even though we may*
*____ see each ___*
*This r____ ____ help with ex____*
*Cherished child ___ luck be with____*
*___ beloved nie__*
*K ___*

I sat back and exhaled deeply. "That's all you can get from the note?"

"I'm sorry, Em. We tried, but it looks as though it had got wet at some point, and those are the only words we can make out. The person's writing had lots of curls and stuff, not too easy to make out the letters."

"No, you did a great job, Danny," I told him encouragingly, "and this was in the lining of the crate?"

"It looks as if it was put in the back of the crate at some point, got wet, and stuck there. If it weren't for the technology we have today, we wouldn't have been able to make out there was ever ink on the paper."

"A love note?" I wondered, transfixed by the words on the paper in front of me.

Danny laughed down the phone. "That's not my realm of expertise."

"Hey, thanks a ton." I hung up and continued to stare at the message. What did it mean? I texted Betty saying, *I have news.* My cellphone rang almost immediately.

"Hi, Betty."

"It's me," came Marcus's low voice. "I thought you

were staying away today."

"There's been a development," I replied, unsure whether he had asked me a question.

"Are you ready now? Betty is in town."

I got my things together and wondered if Leo was still in the lobby and if I could sneak past him without having to speak to him. Apparently not.

"Emily!" He pounced on me. "What was that all about?"

"I have to go right now." I saw Betty's truck outside the window and started walking away toward the doors. Leo jumped up and tried to bar my way through the lobby.

"Tonight? I'll be here, waiting."

"Fine."

I walked outside, trying to muster a composure I didn't feel, very much aware that Leo was still watching me through the window. I climbed up into the cab, amazed that my legs were still working when it felt they had turned to jelly. My stomach heaved, and I thought I might be sick.

"Are you okay?" Betty was looking at me doubtfully.

"I'm fine, just drive."

I rolled down the window and stuck my head out like a Labrador retriever. The slap of the wind in my face and ears had the desired effect, and I pulled back into the car, feeling a little less nauseous and a little more relieved as the miles between Leo and me grew.

"You look like you've just seen a ghost," Betty observed, still watching me with concern.

I gave a humorless laugh; she didn't realize how close she was to the truth. We didn't say much more until we arrived back at the ranch, and she turned to face me in her seat, evidently settling down for another of her fireside chats.

"Let's go inside. I've got news." I jumped down from the truck, stalling the conversation. I was not in the mood for motherly advice today.

I had been nervous about seeing Marcus again after my behavior the day before, but all thoughts of my messy love life were pushed to the side with this new development. "Danny found this note in the lining of the crate," I told them excitedly. "It's the best clue we've got so far." I pulled the crumpled paper from my pocket and tried to smooth it out on the kitchen table. We all stared down at my writing, trying to decipher the missing words.

"It's not a love note," Ron concluded.

"How do you know?" asked Marcus.

"Ron's an expert in that department," Betty ribbed her husband.

"Cherished child. Who calls their lover a 'child'?"

"They used to speak differently in those days," Betty interjected.

I shook my head. "I think Ron's right. This sounds more like a friend or family member than a lover."

"That's 'me' though." Marcus was pointing to the first line of the note as he read, "My darling, you will always be with *me* even though we may…something…see each…something."

"Now that *does* sound like a lover," Betty insisted again.

"Can't your guy get any more writing from it?" Marcus asked.

"No, the note had got wet and was compromised. It

sounds like we're lucky we got anything at all."

"What begins with 'r'?" Betty wondered, and we lapsed into silence, each running through the possibilities. "Ex what? You used to like puzzles when you were a kid," she said accusingly to Marcus.

"I'm sorry I can't figure out a hundred-year-old mystery note in under two minutes." He laughed.

"It's okay. It's another piece of the puzzle," I soothed. "We're a lot better off than when we started."

"Are we? It looks like another dead end," Ron said mournfully.

"Don't you go giving up so easily." His wife elbowed him gently. "How about we have some coffee and brainstorm a little together?"

Marcus and I both bent over the note again, simultaneously almost bumping heads. "Sorry," he said, not moving from his position. We were so close together, and I had the lustful urge to kiss him. I jerked away and saw that Betty had hustled Ron out of the room, leaving the two of us alone.

"I'm sorry about last night," I told him, embarrassed.

"I've been thinking. I'm not sure if I'm getting my money's worth," said Marcus, ignoring my apology.

"You mean with me? I've talked to Angus, and we won't charge you more than a consultation fee if we can't authenticate the bottles."

"That's not what I mean. I'm a bourbon man, always have been, but I try and be open-minded about things. I don't pretend to understand what's so great about Scotch, but as you're here…"

"There's a lot of things 'so great' about Scotch," I replied. He cocked an eyebrow, knowing I couldn't resist the temptation to talk about one of my favorite subjects. "The name comes from the old Gaelic word meaning 'water of life.' You can trace the origins of Scotch back to the fifth century when the monks distilled it, so when you sip whisky, you are not just having a drink but tasting a spirit steeped in history. Imagine all the people, stories, and traditions that came before you and conspired to make that golden liquid."

"Isn't it really the same as bourbon? It's all whisky."

"All Scotch is whisky but not all whisky is Scotch. They're both types of whisky but very different. Even the word 'whiskey' is spelled differently," I explained.

"Why?"

"There's a very long explanation to do with the use of grain in the production of blends. Basically, the Irish and the Scots were fighting over the market and what should be defined as 'whisky.' The difference in spelling and subsequent definitions came from that. The evolution of the industry is very interesting," I told him.

"Perhaps I should do some more sipping, then."

"But only if you will appreciate it," I answered, aware we might not be talking about Scotch anymore.

"Why don't you educate me?" he asked with a twinkle in his eye, breaking the tension.

"I already have a big job to do." I smiled back at him.

"I'll never be able to improve without a teacher." He spread his hands in a gesture of mock helplessness.

"Fine, I will take that challenge, but only if we do it properly."

"Yes, ma'am. How many bottles do we need for my education?"

"Five would be perfect, but three would do in a

pinch. Do you think they're going to have that much choice in Fairview?"

"Let me make a call." He tapped the side of his nose and disappeared into the house.

\*\*\*\*

We drove in the opposite direction of the town, and I didn't inquire where we were going. After almost an hour, we followed a sign for Hot Springs Golf Resort and Spa.

"Are you taking me on a luxury vacation?"

"Not today." He chuckled. "But I figured this was probably a better option than the liquor store in Fairview. Here they have more of a selection of the finer things."

"So they don't have any bourbon," I commented flippantly and was gratified when he shot me a look of amusement.

We took a detour at the front entrance down a smaller road that veered to the left of the main resort. A sign with a small arrow indicated we were headed toward the clubhouse. Marcus put the pickup in park, and we both jumped out. He knocked loudly, and a young man in a white polo shirt opened the door. "Hi, Mr. McClean. I've got those boxed up for you. Let me just go fetch them."

Marcus rested on the door as the young man ran off to collect the box, giving me a chance to admire his toned physique. Our courier returned moments later and handed Marcus a wine carrier with several bottles wrapped in paper. When it was safely stowed, we drove back in the direction of the McClean ranch.

"Do we need anything else while we're out?" Marcus asked.

"Dry bread and water."

"Sounds delicious," he replied, giving me a look that made me want to jump across the truck into his lap.

Arriving back with our supplies, he handed me the wine carrier and told me to meet him outside on the veranda. It was a beautiful day, and as I set the box down carefully on the table, I took a deep breath of fresh air and envied Marcus that such a beautiful setting would be where he would taste Scotch for the first time. Despite my short time in this beautiful state, it had earned a permanent place in my heart, and I thought morosely of my imminent return to the city and the smells of asphalt and street food to replace that of the pine trees.

Marcus reappeared a few minutes later with a tray of glasses, a pitcher of iced water, and a loaf of French bread. I assumed Betty had been enlisted to help.

"Perfect. Can we open the bottles now?"

He laughed at my eagerness. "Now, don't go getting too excited. Aren't you the one who always talks about the rewards of patience? I seem to remember being told that you should sip slowly."

"Do what I say, not as I do." I unwrapped the first bottle eagerly. Springbank 18. I nodded in approval. "Lowlands, vanilla, a little bit spicy." I set it to the side and reached for the next one, a Macallan 25. "Now, this is the classic masterpiece. Matured in sherry casks for…guess how long?" I teased, giving him a sideways glance. The third bottle was a Speymalt 1973, and my eyes widened in surprise. "And they had this just lying around?" I asked him incredulously.

"Is it that rare?"

"Well, it's not unheard of, like the booty you have sitting in your cabin. But it's not that common. Or that cheap."

He shrugged, and I felt a little silly realizing that Marcus and I probably had very different definitions of expensive and cheap. Next was a Dalmore cigar malt. "You'll probably like this one--this is the closest to bourbon. Cab sauvignon barrels—you can smell the bananas."

I unwrapped the final bottle slowly, savoring the anticipation. A Bowmore 25. "This is more nuanced, dark, and smoky. It's very seductive," I told him quietly. I sat back and surveyed the bottles. "This is an impressive collection, even more so to collect on a whim. You are a man of many talents, Mr. McClean."

"I aim to please." He rubbed his hands together. "Well, where do we begin?"

Prepare. Look. Nose. Taste. The four steps to appreciate Scotch whisky. "First, you have to prepare your palette. Hence the water and the bread."

"Why don't I step inside and rinse with mouthwash?"

"That will have the opposite effect. It will effectively render your palette useless because the chemicals will invade the tongue," I told him, enjoying the thought of his tongue.

"But I'll be minty fresh."

We both chewed on a piece of bread and sipped our glasses of water, saying nothing. I knew he was watching me, and I returned his attention. Damned handsome, I thought for the umpteenth time.

"Ready for the next step?"

"I'm just here to follow instructions," he responded huskily.

"Right, then next we will use our eyes." I dragged my own eyes reluctantly away from Marcus to concentrate on pouring us each a small measure of all five bottles. He reached for the Springbank and peered closely at the glass.

"Hold it up to the light," I instructed softly. "You are looking at both the color and the legs. When whisky is young, it is lighter, very pale. If it is yellowed or light gold, you are probably looking at something aged in a new cask, and the flavors are sweeter. Look at the different colors of them all." I indicated the glasses lined up on the table. "When the color is deeper, you can see it's a well-aged expression. Slightly red is usually from sherry or port casks, and a deep gold might be a bourbon barrel."

"I don't think I've ever paid so much attention to my liquor before." He looked surprised.

I walked him through the process of examining the whisky legs by angling the glasses correctly and watching the run of the drams. We then moved on to nosing, and he was amused when I told him he needed to put his nose as far into the glass as possible. "I should have got wider glasses."

I described the different smells to him and was impressed by his olfactory sense. He could easily identify the fruit and the peat, which was a skill that usually took some time to perfect. As we talked, I was aware that we had inched closer together, and our knees touched the chair. Neither of us moved away.

"It's time to taste," I told him, and our eyes locked. The atmosphere changed, and I held my breath with anticipation of what was to come. I picked up the Springmore again and held it out to him. He took the glass from my hand but didn't drink. Instead, he set it on the table, his eyes never leaving mine. Slowly, he leaned in toward me. I closed my eyes and surrendered to the kiss. It was soft. Soft at first as we explored each other, but then it became more urgent. I held his head in my hands and pulled him roughly towards me. I wanted him. And he wanted me.

We finally broke away, gasping, and stared in amazement at each other. A split second passed, and we were in each other's arms again, frantic now, our mouths engulfing each other, our bodies pressed together. He picked me up, grasping my buttocks in his hands. I coiled my legs around his waist and heard him groan with desire. Still holding me, he fumbled for the door handle and pushed it open, taking us both inside. He carried me into a bedroom off the hallway and put me down. He closed the door, and we faced each other, panting with desire.

"Emily," he croaked, but I pressed my mouth onto his once again. It was not a time to talk.

\*\*\*\*

"Pizza?"

"Yes, I think that would be the thing I would miss most, pizza delivery."

We lay wrapped in each other's arms in the oversized king bed and discussed the pros and cons of living in the middle of nowhere. I felt a sense of warm contentment wash over me as I snuggled into his broad chest. It had been a long time since I had experienced the pleasures of a man, and he had been well worth the wait.

"I would just hate all the schmooze of the city, all those fake people," Marcus reflected. "I'm not good at glad-handing."

"You're better than you think," I contradicted him. "The way you do it is just more genuine. I saw you at the cattleman's ball—Marcus McClean was the charmer of the room."

"I was thinking maybe I need to hire a city slicker for some lessons in etiquette," he said, sliding his hands under the covers again and making me shudder with pleasure. The hours passed by in a blur, and it was only when Marcus suggested a drink on the deck to watch the sunset did I realize the day was almost over.

"I'm not sure I've put in a good day's work today," I told him.

"I think you've done some very good work today," he responded, kissing me again.

We finally emerged from the sanctuary of the bedroom, to where Betty was bustling around the kitchen. She pretended not to know what we had been doing and casually inquired if we wanted some dinner.

"I'm ready to drive Emily back to the hotel." Ron appeared at the door.

"Don't worry about that." Betty took her husband's arm and dragged him behind her as she headed out of the kitchen.

"That was embarrassing," I said to Marcus.

He shrugged, and I suddenly had the unwelcome thought that perhaps it wasn't unusual for single women to spend time in the bedrooms at the McClean ranch. Perhaps one person, in particular—I remembered the attractive Misty Farley and shook my head at my stupidity. Was I never going to learn my lesson?

"I should probably get back, though," I said, remembering that another lothario would likely be waiting for me at the hotel.

"Do you have to go?" Marcus looked a little hurt, but I thought suspiciously that it was probably a well-perfected show.

"Yes, I'm afraid so. Thanks for a fun day, though." I tried to sound breezy and carefree.

My mood darkened further on the drive back to town. I couldn't believe Leo had shown up in Montana, but the strangest thing of all was that I hadn't given him a single thought all day.

Chapter Twelve

"Emily, we have to talk." Leo grabbed my arm as soon as I walked into the lobby, and he looked at me imploringly. I felt a surge of emotion wash over me at the sight of his face. An emotion I had not experienced before—extreme annoyance.

"I don't think we have anything to talk about," I snapped.

"I just want to explain."

"Fine. I'm all ears. Explain why you asked me to marry you and then cheated on me with my best friend, and goodness knows who else."

He stared at me open-mouthed, but I wasn't finished yet.

"Wait a minute. I want to grab a glass of wine before you begin. Would you like anything from the bar?"

Leo continued to ogle me in amazement.

"Is that a no, then?"

"Double Scotch," he growled. At least he was faithful to one thing, I thought uncharitably as I waited for our drinks. I had an urge to laugh at how ludicrous a situation we found ourselves in. Leo and I were about to have a drink together in an economy hotel in Fairview, Montana, because we had both answered the siren call of a bottle of hundred-year-old whisky. We were still no nearer to finding out the story behind the remarkable find, and it seemed there was a lot of unfinished business in the air.

I took a seat opposite my ex-fiancé, informing him with pleasure that Fairview only served bourbon. "It doesn't matter," he muttered. "What matters is *us*, Emily. I've been lost without you these months. I can't work properly... I can't do anything right without you in my life."

"It's a shame you didn't realize that before you started sleeping with my best friend." I took a large gulp of Pinot Noir.

"I felt as though our lives were all mapped out... I panicked and made a stupid decision... I'm going to regret it for the rest of my life... He waved his hands around as if that would be a substitute for words. "I've made a mess of things, haven't I? Is there any way we could ever...?" He looked downtrodden and pitiful.

As I looked at him, I had a moment of piercing clarity about the real culprit here. The person to blame was me, not Leo at all. "I think I may have made some missteps, too," I told him.

"I see," he said cautiously, fearing a trap.

"You have always been the same. You know that expression, 'Fool me once, shame on you, but fool me twice...'?"

"Shame on me," Leo finished, still wearing the same guarded look.

"Exactly. I should have had more self-respect."

"Maybe we can get through this." He looked at me, his handsome face a picture of sincerity.

"No, Leo. I'm sorry, but the thing is, I've moved on." As soon as the words were out of my mouth, I realized they were true. I *had* moved on, and I had no desire to be with the man sitting in front of me.

"What?" Leo looked astounded. "You've met someone else?"

"Well, yes, I mean no, well, not exactly."

"Which is it?" he asked with an edge to his voice.

I stood up and looked down at him, enjoying the elevated position. "You know, Leo, that's just none of your business."

"You're different," he told me accusingly.

"Yes, I am. But the problem is that you are still the same person you've always been." I finished the remainder of my wine in one very large gulp and began to walk away. I paused by the bar, set my glass down, and told the bartender to make sure to put our drinks on Leo's tab. I sashayed toward the elevator and pressed the button. While I waited for the doors to open, I allowed myself one last look at Leo's shocked face, just for the heck of it.

****

The next morning when I jumped into Betty's truck for our morning commute, she remarked that I looked refreshed. I thanked her and said that was exactly how I felt.

"I see, Miss 'pep in her step' Emily. Can I have some of whatever you had for breakfast?"

"I might need a ride or to borrow your truck today," I told her as we arrived at the house.

Marcus was coming out of the front door and overheard my request. He raised an eyebrow at me and asked, "Have you ever driven a truck before?"

I opened my mouth to say something witty back to him but couldn't think of anything and started to laugh. "Honestly, no. I don't think I've ever driven a vehicle that big, but the roads around here are pretty wide. I think

I can manage."

"I don't mind taking you somewhere, hon," Betty offered. "I find this detective business quite interesting. Where do you want to go?"

"Wherever the county records are kept. I've been thinking about this all from the perspective of the Scottish connection, but we might find something if we work backward, too. The McCleans seem pretty elusive until they arrived here, but there might be a county land record or something from when they purchased it."

"That sounds interesting," interjected Marcus. "I'll bring the truck around." He was gone before I could object.

I looked at Betty, who waved away my apologetic expression. "I've got too much to do around here anyway."

Marcus returned, and I jumped up into the cab next to him, sneaking a look at his well-formed figure in the seat next to me. "Do you know where we're going?"

"Nope. But you're going to look it up on your phone and tell me."

"I appreciate you giving me a ride," I said as I searched my phone for the local maps, "but don't you have more cowboy things to do?"

"Like making YouTube videos of myself roping cattle?" He sounded amused.

"Honestly, I don't know anything about life out here. All my stereotypes seem wrong, and I find myself having a wonderful time."

"That's the problem with stereotypes," he said, pushing his hat up slightly. "They can stop you from seeing what's actually in front of you."

"This, from the man who judged me for being a city

girl, the minute I stepped off the plane," I teased him.

His face broke into a self-deprecating grin. "You got me there, but I was still able to see what was in front of my face."

Our destination was a couple of hours' drive, and Marcus insisted on stopping at the Museum of the Rockies on the way.

We spent far too long in the museum, but I didn't tire of Marcus's passion for land conservation and found my own wonder at the area's remarkable history. He felt a responsibility for the atrocities committed over the centuries by the incoming settlers, and he was empowered to use his standing to encourage initiatives that would preserve the land.

"Isn't that a little ironic? I thought livestock was one of the worst things for the environment." We were back in the truck, and I was having trouble deciding what the better view was—the breathtaking landscape out the window or Marcus's side profile in the driver's seat.

"There isn't consensus from the scientific community."

I opened my mouth to respond and noticed that his mouth had curved upward slightly. "Are you trying to get a rise out of a liberal?" I laughed.

He smiled, then looked thoughtful. "I agree we should find more sustainable ways to do things. We have a regional consortium that does exactly that, and we work closely with the universities to fund that type of research." I was impressed and told him so. "But that doesn't mean I believe in ruining someone's livelihood in the process. I don't think Washington is very in tune with reality."

"Now, that is something we can both agree on." I

smiled.

When we reached our destination, I got to witness the full weight of Marcus's charm. Within no time, he had sweet-talked the elderly lady manning the records desk into letting us poke around the archival room. The musty smell of time-yellowed paper and dusty files made me think of my homeland, and I made a comment about it to Marcus.

"Do you think you will move back?"

"Hopefully not any time soon. I've grown to love my adopted country."

"There's a lot to love."

We were working our way inward from the farthest bookshelves and had almost met in the middle. We moved closer together, and he brushed a stray tendril of hair from my cheek. I reached up to pull him toward me, but just then I felt something run across my foot, and I let out a horrified scream.

Marcus doubled over with laughter. "It's only a field mouse. There are much worse rats in Boston."

I shuddered at the thought of rats, and again at the thought of field mice in the cramped room. "Let's be quick and get out of here." I wanted to finish up as soon as possible, but I knew from experience that old archives rarely yielded their treasures without some serious grunt work.

Several hours later, and with an aching back, I hadn't been wrong. A breakthrough had come when I found a copy of the original homestead certificate for a large tract of land to Liam Farley Senior in 1893. It was presumably from his son that Marcus's ancestors had acquired it, but I didn't hold out hope that we would find that document today.

"Come on, let's go." He held his hand out to pull me up from the dusty floor. I took his hand, reluctant to leave without finding what we came for, and he remarked on my perseverance. It was an idle comment, but I couldn't remember the last time Leo had ever complimented me on any aspect of my personality. Perhaps he never had.

Marcus brought me back to the hotel, and I was unsure how to interpret the situation. "Thanks for coming with me today," I said, unbuckling my seatbelt slowly. I had decided to ask him to join me for dinner when I noticed Leo's dark hair through one of the lobby windows. "I'll see you tomorrow," I blurted out and slammed the door of the truck before he had a chance to respond. I walked slowly into the hotel, waiting for him to drive away so he would not see me with Leo. I hated myself for deceiving him and realized that he probably thought I was a deranged lunatic because of my bizarre behavior. Job well done, I told myself sarcastically.

Leo saw me immediately and pulled out a chair to indicate I should join him. I checked out the window to ensure that Marcus had driven away, and Leo followed my gaze suspiciously. "Fine," I said lightly and sat down in one of the club chairs, feigning a composure I didn't feel.

"We could have dinner or go someone more private?" he suggested, seeming surprised I had agreed to talk with him.

"I assume you're here about the Whiting Whisky," I said bluntly.

Leo cast about as if weighing his options, then matched my directness. "That's one of the reasons."

"The discovery and investigation are ongoing, and I'm not at liberty, legally or otherwise, to reveal any details."

"It really has been found," he said incredulously, his eyes widening.

"As I said, it's ongoing," I ventured, more cautiously this time, aware I needed to tread very carefully when it came to Leo.

"But Emily, this is amazing! I mean, no one even thought it was real! Did you find the artwork? How do you know it's actually the Whiting Whisky? Was it hidden?" His questions spilled over each other, unable as he was to contain his excitement.

I simply stared at him and lifted my eyebrows slowly, hoping he would catch on to my meaning. "I know, I know." He patted my hand condescendingly. "You can't tell me right now, but it won't be long."

"What do you mean, 'it won't be long'?"

"As soon as you've done your part, the process will begin to send it back to the rightful owner."

"The rightful owner?"

"Yes." He gave a self-conceited smile, and I fought the urge to slap him across the face.

"I think we're done here." I stood up and took a step away from him.

"What?" He jumped to his feet. "I understand you're trying to keep it confidential, but soon it will be public knowledge. The lawyers have already sent a letter."

"Goodbye, Leo." I walked to the stairs, not wanting to wait for the elevator and, this time, not trusting myself to look back.

"Emily, we still have things to talk about," he shouted after me.

As soon as I got to my room, I called Angus and got his voicemail. I called again immediately and finally heard his sleepy voice growl down the line, "Do you know what damn time it is here?"

"Yes, sorry, but it's important."

His voice changed immediately to one of paternal concern. "Are you all right?"

"I'm fine," I reassured him and felt a surge of affection for this grumpy man. He was my protector, and I knew he loved me like a daughter. I had felt envious of Marcus with the love and wisdom of Betty and Ron in his life, but I suddenly realized I had my own version, albeit less diplomatic, as a steadfast rock.

"Leo Dahlberg is here."

"That piece of shit!" Angus roared, fully awake now. "If I get my hands around his—"

"I know," I cut him off, "but we have to tread lightly. Leo is certain that if the Whiting Whisky is discovered, then he, or rather the company, will be the rightful owners."

There was a long silence down the line. It appeared that Angus was at a loss for words for once in his life. "He might have a point," he finally uttered begrudgingly.

"I agree. That's why we need to figure this out as soon as possible. If there's even the tiniest chance that I can show Marcus has a claim to it, I have to try."

"It sounds like you and 'Marcus' have a good client relationship," Angus baited me.

"It's just business," I lied, "but they're good people here. I don't want to let them down."

"What can I do to help?"

"I have an idea. I've just been to the county archives here, and it occurred to me that you could do the same."

"Archives?"

"Yes, you're going to be looking for something very

specific."

\*\*\*\*

Betty pushed me in through the front door. "Wait till you see what I've done!" she crowed excitedly.

"Welcome to the command center," Marcus said in greeting.

I ogled the scene in front of me, at a loss for words. Betty had assembled an enormous easel in the center of the living room with photographs stuck on one side and a timeline on the other. It looked as though she had also categorized the newspapers and my notes in some type of system, likely understood only by her, stacked in piles on the coffee table.

"It looks like a murder mystery," I commented and rolled up my sleeves. "Let's see what we have."

"Exhibit A is the discovery of the century..." I tapped the first photograph with a pencil, but Betty shouted at me to wait. She rummaged in a drawer and passed me what looked like the handle of an adjustable duster, tapping it on the easel to indicate I should use it as a conductor's baton. I stifled a giggle and took the stick to continue the monologue. "A hundred-year-old bottle of Scotch whisky, with a label engraved by the world-famous artist, John Duncan. The bottle was found in a crate, with what we believe to be the markings of the Whiting company. Also discovered was a mysterious note, author unknown, and recipient unknown."

"That's a lot of unknowns," Ron said unhelpfully.

"Exhibit B," I continued, giving him a mock stern look, "a reputed ruby necklace."

"The necklace?" asked Marcus, "I don't think that has anything to do with it. That's a separate thing."

"There are no separate things. This is all connected

to your ancestors. Everything somehow revolves around them. What else do you know about Rose McClean?"

"Not much," he answered.

"She was a legend," Ron interrupted softly, "ahead of her time."

Not for the first time, we all stared at Ron in surprise, who cleared his throat importantly, clearly enjoying his newfound platform. "In Montana, women got the right to vote in 1924. The McCleans arrived here around that time, but that wasn't the end of the struggle. The anti-suffrage movement gained a lot of ground from both men and women who wanted everything to stay the same. Rose McClean was on the front lines for change. She led the call for elections to have oversight. She started fundraising efforts. The list goes on."

"I bet she wasn't very popular among those in power at the time," Betty remarked.

"That's the strange thing, she was. She was very charming, and several of the local newspapers claimed that was why she was so successful."

"Seems like something got passed down the family line," I remarked slyly, giving Marcus a side look.

One by one, they left me to work in my newly acquired command center. I couldn't explain how, but I knew I was right. Everything we had found was related somehow, and I just needed to connect the dots. I sat down on the leather couch, marveling again at how comfortable it was. As much as I wanted to figure out this great mystery, having the answers would also mean that my time in Montana would be over.

My cell phone interrupted this realization, and I picked up to Angus. "Please tell me you have some information."

"Indeed, I do, you impatient lass. I contacted the attorneys for the Whiting holdings. It turns out they retained the archives for the original Whiting company, and when the company went public, they tried to capitalize on the name with all the pompous historical stuff." He let out a booming laugh. "I bet you finding the Whiting Whisky would have helped—"

"Angus!" I interrupted impatiently, "You said you had some information."

"Fine, fine, I'll get to the point as you're so bad-tempered today. Well, the public can look through the archives up to the 1950s—for a fee, of course," he grumbled.

"That's good. Perhaps you'll find something useful."

"We already have."

"You've been there already?" I had trouble imagining Angus scrambling around dusty files or having the patience to undertake painstaking research in the digital archives.

"Not personally, of course."

"I see. So your poor assistant Julie found something is what you're telling me." I allowed myself a small smile.

"You'd better be a little more appreciative if you want to hear what we found."

"Just tell me!"

"There's a ledger entry for two hundred and twenty-seven pounds paid to a J. Duncan, artist."

"Oh, my goodness," I whispered, "it *is* the Whiting Whisky." We were both silent for a moment as the enormity of the discovery began to sink in. However, my ever-cynical mind quickly found a loophole. "How do we know it wasn't a separate painting they commissioned? The amount is what? Around five thousand pounds in today's money?"

"More like ten thousand," he corrected. Apparently rapid math was not my strength.

"That's a pretty price tag, even for Duncan. At that time, he had not reached the height of his fame. I wonder why it was so much?"

"Well, Emily, don't say I never give you anything…" Angus continued, dangling the carrot to infuriate me.

"What?" I fought the urge to smack the phone down repeatedly.

"There was a description column in the ledger. It said, 'etched on glass.' " I almost dropped the phone. We had our link to the Whiting Whisky.

I ran outside, barely able to contain my excitement, and found Ron and Betty sipping iced tea on the deck. I hopped from one foot to the other, unable to stand still. I looked around for the one person I really wanted to see but couldn't find him.

"Marcus has gone out," Betty told me, reading my mind, "but you can tell us. I think you have to tell someone!" I relayed the new information to my excited audience.

"When will Marcus be back?" I asked them desperately. "I can't wait to tell him!"

"I don't know, but he'll be pleased. How does this help his case?"

I stopped hopping. Betty had hit the nail on the head. While we could now say with certainty that we had discovered the legendary Whiting Whisky and the mysterious "artwork" in one beautiful package, we still had no explanation.

"It didn't all go up in flames," I stated the obvious, "but we still don't know how it got here. And unfortunately, that's now the question we have to answer."

Chapter Thirteen

*1921, Inverness, Scotland*

Benjamin Greer had a sinking feeling as he rang the servant's bell at Baliforth House. The Inverness distillery was doing well, and the American operation had exceeded their revenue projections, but Samuel Whiting was still not happy. Greer was shown into the opulent dining room and offered a drink by one of the servants. He declined, then regretted it as he waited for Whiting to appear. His feeling of foreboding was increasing as the minutes passed, and a cognac might have eased his anxiety.

"How are you, Benjamin, my good man?" said Samuel Whiting by way of introduction as he entered the room. He turned and dismissed the servant hovering close to the door. "Tell me, how are things going across the ocean? Are the residents of the islands still thirstier than ever?" he asked humorlessly. Greer opened his briefcase and pulled out some ledgers, but Whiting waved them away. "I don't need to look over the figures again. I've seen enough to know it's good news. I'm more interested in what has been happening on the ground, so to speak."

Benjamin Greer looked at his employer uncomprehendingly. "Is there anything specific in which you have an interest?"

"How's that Macleary boy doing?"

"James?" Greer relaxed momentarily. "He's bright and motivated, hungry for success, you might say. He's served us well over there. The operation is running very efficiently and, more to the point, he's not ruffled any feathers. Nothing unsavory, if you get my meaning."

There was a long pause, and Samuel Whiting drummed his long thin fingers on the mahogany table. Benjamin Greer suddenly felt very nervous again.

"That's interesting, as I've heard several reports to the contrary."

"Really?" asked Greer incredulously. "I would put money on it that Macleary is as straight as they come."

"So straight that he's running an illegal smuggling operation with my whisky," Whiting replied loftily.

"What…what reports have there been?"

"The boy's dishonest. He's been stealing from the company and selling to bootleggers for his own profit."

Benjamin Greer's face was the picture of confusion. "But I don't see how that can be right. I mean, the figures all add up, and we're making a sizable profit…" He trailed off as he saw that Whiting was shaking his head.

"I assure you, this news was very distressing to me, too. I had taken quite a shine to the boy, but the matter has been fully investigated."

"How? I mean, everything adds up," Greer blustered, opening one of the ledgers again.

Whiting removed some envelopes from his inner pocket and tossed them onto the table. "That's where you'll find the evidence."

Hesitantly, Greer reached for the envelopes and pulled out their contents. He made an involuntary gasp of dismay as he scanned the pages. "Can this be right?"

He removed his monocle and wiped it agitatedly on his shirt.

"As I said, I was as dismayed as you were when this was first brought to my attention, but as you can see, with three separate accounts that all corroborate his treachery, there is no other explanation." Whiting spread out his hands in a gesture of futility.

Greer was shuffling through the envelopes again. "This first account is from our partner in Nova Scotia. He's a reliable fellow, to be sure, but is it possible he could have been mistaken with the inventory?"

"On multiple occasions?" Whiting's sarcasm withered the question. "We have accounts from the captain who delivers to those waters every other week. The man is meticulous. He keeps excellent records, and there is a clear discrepancy every time Macleary takes receipt of the shipment."

"There must be some mistake." Greer was still shaking his head.

"There's no mistake," Whiting barked. "You've let your affection for this boy blind you to the fact that he is a dishonest rogue. He's taken advantage of you and needs to be dealt with accordingly."

"What do you think is appropriate?" Greer asked shakily.

"We could turn him over to the authorities, but that might not be the most prudent course of action. We don't want them tracing things back to you. I wouldn't like to see you behind bars, my good man."

"Me?"

"Of course. The authorities would no doubt ascertain that the boy was in your employ, and they might even deduce that you were involved in these

illegal activities together. Theft, extortion, bribery…"
He listed each one on his thin fingers and gave an
insincere sigh.

"There must be another option," Greer exclaimed
with mounting alarm.

"Well…I believe there are contacts on the mainland
who may be involved in his operation."

"The bootleggers?"

"Among other unsavory types. I'm sure someone
could be persuaded to help Macleary see the error of his
ways."

"Rough him up?" Greer whispered.

"Or they might get carried away…you know how
these types behave. That would be a pity, of course, but
it would also mean that Macleary would not pose any
threat. To anyone." He fixed Greer with a meaningful
stare. "Do we understand each other?"

Greer nodded mutely.

"You know the way out," said Whiting with a wave
of his hand.

Sarah held her breath as she heard Benjamin Greer's
footsteps retreating hurriedly. She watched his worried
expression as he left Baliforth House. She felt sorry for
him; he had been shocked at her father's ruthless plan to
neatly dispose of James. Samuel Whiting's family
obviously knew him better than that. After the heated
exchange with her father before, she had no such
illusions about what his next steps would be. If he could
be so callous and dismissive of his only daughter, her
lover could expect no mercy. Time had run out.

****

Benjamin Greer looked up in annoyance as the
insistent knocking on his office door continued.

Whoever was there would not be deterred. He had been unproductive all morning, unable to focus on any task as his mind kept returning to the problem of James Macleary and the realization that his employer had essentially ordered his death or he himself would pay the price. "Enter," he said resignedly.

"Good morning, Mr. Greer," said Sarah as she entered his office.

Greer did not immediately respond but blinked uncomprehendingly at the unlikely sight of Samuel Whiting's daughter Sarah in his messy office. "Please take a seat." He tried to recover from his surprise and began to shuffle one of his many piles of paper out of the way.

"Please, don't trouble yourself," Sarah commanded and sat down, indicating that he should do the same. "I'm sorry to arrive without an invitation, but I must speak to you about a rather important matter."

"Of course," Greer ventured cautiously.

"It's about James," Sarah said flatly. "James Macleary."

The color drained from Benjamin Greer's face. "He was, is…was an employee here," he spluttered.

Sarah bestowed a kindly smile on this portly little man who would not stand up well under interrogation. "I understand you hold James in high esteem." Greer inclined his head slightly without actually replying. "James is my lover," she concluded. The words hung in the air as Benjamin Greer's jaw slackened, and he beheld Samuel Whiting's daughter, having no idea how to respond to this revelation. Sarah continued, "I am also aware that my father does not look favorably on this and has directed you to resolve the matter."

"Perhaps you should discuss this with your father."

"I am discussing it with *you,* Mr. Greer, because I believe you are a much better man than my father."

"What can I do?" Greer whispered, the blood draining from his face. "James is a good lad. I don't want any harm to come to him. I mean, I wouldn't even consider such a thing." He shuddered at the thought. "I'm not a murderer! But, allegedly, he has been stealing, and your father won't be easily appeased."

"You know as well as I do that James hasn't stolen anything. My father is fabricating these charges because he found out I had a relationship with James, and he wants him dead," Sarah stated matter-of-factly.

"But why now? James has been doing well for all this time." Benjamin Greer's round face contorted in confusion.

"Father has probably concluded he can now be replaced by someone else, but I am glad to see that you don't share his ambition. Perhaps there is an alternative?"

"I have thought of nothing else," Greer responded desperately.

"I'm happy to hear it, but the question is, how far will you go to help him?"

\*\*\*\*

Many miles across a vast ocean, James held a telegram in his hands that he had read many times, but it still made no sense to him. A few weeks prior, he had received the message from Benjamin Greer to say that he, himself, would be taking a trip to New York in the upcoming month. James had been puzzled that he would be planning the journey himself and even more so with the onset of winter. His crew of seasoned sailors, much more familiar with North America than he, had told him many tales of winter on the continent and the perils of seafaring in the plummeting temperatures. Even Jacques Bisset, one of the St. Pierre natives James had been fortunate enough to employ, had refused to sail in the harrowing conditions that winter would bring to the islands. James took the warnings seriously and spent many hours creating a schedule that would increase activity before the season set in, to allow them to rest in place when the weather was so perilous. His devotion to his crew and investment in their lives over profit was another reason for the loyalty he inspired, and he easily maintained the manpower needed for his operation.

His mind returned to the impending arrival of Benjamin Greer, and he felt uneasy. "Is everything as it should be?" asked Bisset, noticing his expression as he joined James to smoke a cigarette.

"Of course." James slapped him on the back with a happy-go-lucky air he did not feel. "We're just going to be getting a visit from the boss."

"Samuel Whiting?" Bisset was impressed.

"No, but his second in command."

"This is not a good thing?"

"He's a good man. It's just the timing is a little strange." They both sat in quiet contemplation, exhaling plumes of smoke that drifted upward to the gray sky. James looked out over the foreboding mass of the Atlantic Ocean and felt the first heavy drops of rain land on his cheeks. The weather matched his mood.

****

Samuel Whiting allowed himself a very small glass of sherry while he waited for his daughter to make an appearance. He savored the taste of the strong wine and spared a thought for the Americans and their ridiculous law, which he hoped would endure, for his profits. Sarah had been uncharacteristically quiet and thoughtful since their conversation of marriage to Archie Campbell, but he supposed that was probably just a young girl preparing herself for the duties of matrimony.

She entered the room, and he was pleased to see that her mood had brightened a little. "Good afternoon, Father. Are you feeling well?" She, too, helped herself to a small glass of sherry, ignoring his look of disapproval. Whiting felt a moment of trepidation as he waited for what was to follow. His many years of negotiation and manipulation in the business world had finely tuned his senses, and intuition told him that matters with his daughter were far from settled.

"I've been thinking a little about the wedding of Archie and me."

"I'm glad that you seem to have had a change of heart about Archie."

"I thought about what you said, and to be honest, I can't think of anyone more suitable than Archie and I to run the business when you decide to relinquish control."

He had been poised to take another sip of sherry but froze before the glass reached his lips. His brow furrowed, and he fixed his daughter with a hard stare. "What are you talking about, Sarah?"

"Archie and I, of course, Father. As your sole heir, I assume you want me to be involved in the business, and I know, of course, I can't be much use in these matters, but I can help extend your influence. I have a lot of friends in London." She looked at him covertly from lowered lashes.

"What exactly do you want?"

"To go to America. For a short visit. It's becoming one of our biggest markets and obviously will be even more so after their prohibition ends."

"What exactly would you do there?" Whiting puzzled.

Sarah groaned in exasperation. "Make friends, of course, powerful friends. I don't know much about the business end of things, Father. I don't deny it, but I do know that many things in this world can be made a lot easier if you know the right people. And knowing people is something I am extremely good at."

It was an interesting proposition, and Whiting agreed that his daughter was indeed good at cultivating connections that she seemed able to exploit for her gain. However, the revelation of inheritance was something he had not given an undue amount of attention to before now. He knew he would not live forever but had not contemplated the succession of the business after his demise. Sarah and Archie. He would have to get to know the Campbell boy better and see if he had the mettle. He didn't have any doubts about Archie's future wife.

"I heard that Archie is planning to travel at that time too. I think it would be good for us to spend a little time in each other's company. I believe that he has quite an active role in the Campbells' operation, and it would be beneficial for us to know more."

Samuel Whiting sat back in his wingback chair and pondered his daughter's proposition. The tick of the enormous grandfather clock was the only sound in the room as he weighed up his options. He looked at his daughter again, her head bowed in deference, and decided that the proposal might have merit after all. He turned over various options in his mind and made a decision.

"If you are to go, you should go bearing gifts," he informed her cryptically. He rang the bell to summon the manservant and gave brisk instructions to bring his "special order." Giving a rare and expensive gift to the Campbell boy would serve the dual purposes of further recommending the union to Campbell Senior and would also obligate Campbell Junior to Sarah. The manservant brought in a wooden crate stamped with the Whiting emblem and positioned it carefully so the pair could examine its contents.

"You're going to give Archie some whisky?" Sarah asked sarcastically. "Don't you think the Campbells might already have enough?"

"This isn't just any whisky. This is rare and precious."

"I'm going to cart a bottle across the ocean?"

"I'll send it with the cargo, and it can be delivered to the hotel. It will be more impressive if you bequeath something like this. And this is an impressive gift." He removed the lid with a flourish and stood back to inspect the contents. Both were again silent as they scrutinized the bottle before them. Etched upon it was a classic image of two lovers entwined in each other's arms. It was in no way graphic, but the artist had skillfully depicted intense passion. Celtic elements were also very evident, and they combined the romantic with the traditional in an effortless symphony.

"What do you think?" asked Whiting, the sides of his mouth curving upward slightly as he observed her reaction.

"Father, I don't know what to say! It's beautiful." Sarah was overwhelmed by the artist's skill and touched by the thoughtfulness of the gesture.

"Good. I commissioned that John Duncan chap to create it. Everyone seems so taken by him. His work is already valuable, and I foresee it will only increase. It's quite a prudent investment—think Picasso about ten years ago, excellent recognition for our brand."

"Our brand," Sarah repeated dully, realizing her father's motivations, and with her mask on once more, gave him a pinched smile. "Of course, that is an excellent idea. I believe Archie's mother will also be there, and I will be delighted to spend some time with them both."

Whiting was pleased. They had the beginnings of a profitable plan, and he looked appraisingly at his daughter, who was still examining the bottle with care. Perhaps she could make a valuable contribution to the business after all. Sarah looked up and caught his gaze. "One more thing. I was wondering where mother's jewels are? I want to look my best, and I think this might be a perfect occasion." Whiting waved in the direction of his manservant, who had been waiting unobtrusively in the corner of the room.

****

Benjamin Greer was not an adventurous type. He had never been, and he much preferred the solitude of his office and the company of words and numbers over that of people. James Macleary had been one of the few exceptions to that rule, and he realized when he had made a solemn promise to Sarah Whiting that he had grown very fond of James indeed. Greer had not enjoyed the voyage, he had not enjoyed the unfamiliar accents of Newfoundland, and he had not enjoyed the plummeting temperatures of the Northeast that pained his fingers and slapped his cheeks.

Therefore, it was with immense relief that he arrived at his destination and caught sight of James's broad grin. The two men shook hands vigorously, and James clapped him on the back with great affection. "It's good to see you, Mr. Greer. It's like you've brought a little piece of Scotland with you." He indicated the ominous gray sky.

"Aye, that I have, lad, but things are more than a bit different here." He looked around nervously as if fearing they would be overheard. "Let's dine together, and you can tell me how things are going."

The two men enjoyed a hearty meal at James's favorite tavern and continued into the night. James had stubbornly refused to allow his mind to dwell on thoughts of home, but in Greer's company, the outlawed memories came flooding back.

Even though he had been away from his homeland for less than a year, he realized he missed his family, his old friends, and the bleak but proud history of Scotland itself. Benjamin Greer could never be mistaken for a voracious storyteller, but with a tongue loosed by alcohol, he kept James in fits of laughter, regaling him with stories of the colorful characters that worked the distillery floor.

"So have you met a nice lass over here?" Greer probed jovially.

A dark shadow crossed James' face, and he stared miserably into his nearly empty glass. "No, sir, I've been too busy with good old-fashioned hard work."

"The reason I asked," Greer began cautiously, "is that I had a visit from a girl after you left."

James had been poised to take another drink but froze midair. "What girl?" he rasped.

"A girl you used to know."

"Sarah came to see you?" he whispered, his voice hoarse with emotion. "Why?"

"Because she's in love with you, you fool," Greer said wearily. "You certainly know how to pick them. Whiting's daughter! Of all the lasses you could have chosen…" He shook his head at the folly of youth.

"What did she say?" James asked desperately.

"She's coming to see you."

"Here? To St. Pierre?"

Benjamin Greer shook his head. "She's coming to New York, and she'll be spending a day in Atlantic City."

"Atlantic City? Do you know how far that is from here?"

"I know some geography, lad," Greer replied impatiently. "What do you say to taking a trip to Rum Row?"

James was trying to connect the dots. Rum Row was a stretch between New York and Atlantic City that ran just far enough into international waters to have the advantage of evading the jurisdiction of the U.S. Coast Guard. It was a lot riskier than the operation he ran in St. Pierre, and his men had heard the rumors swirling that the Coast Guard was beefing up their operation in response to the high activity on the water. Even worse was the threat of the "go-through guys" who hijacked cargo and thought life was cheap. James shuddered as he contemplated the perils.

"Rum Row isn't an easy stretch," he told Greer, "for anything."

"Not for the others, but your crew will be under the protection of something else."

"What?"

"Elderflower wine."

Benjamin Greer proceeded to explain a plan that made his head spin. The Canadian competition had been making things a little more challenging for their regular shipping route into St. Pierre, and Whiting and others had been exerting their influence over the American political decision-makers. They believed it wouldn't be too much time until the Volstead Act was repealed, and they were carefully considering the risks and benefits of the current situation.

"Of course, he doesn't want to leave his important customers high and dry," Greer said, chuckling at his own pun, "so there's to be one final shipment. The right hands have been greased, and we'll bring her in near Atlantic City. We need you and your men there to do what you do best."

James nodded slowly, his quick mind running down all the possible scenarios. "But what does this have to do with Sarah?"

"She'll be there. It's an opportunity for a photograph to showcase the honest and quality import business of Whitings."

James snorted at the statement but could see the audacious plan might have merit. "Hide in plain sight," he concluded.

"Exactly. But discretion will be the key to success."

"My men know how to keep their mouths shut," James said with conviction, "if we treat them well."

"Don't worry about that. They will be well compensated for the trip."

"What exactly did Sarah say?" James asked, unable to focus on any other matter until he had his answer.

"Did you send letters to her?"

James nodded his head morosely. "But she never responded."

Benjamin Greer pulled a slightly creased envelope from his breast pocket. "She has now." He passed the paper to James, who took it with slightly shaking hands.

"Go on with you, then." Benjamin Greer waved him toward the door. "I'm heading to my bed anyway."

James practically ran out of the tavern and sprinted to a lone rock close to the coastline that would afford a semblance of protection from the wind. He ripped open the envelope.

*My darling James,*

*You have been gone for almost three months now, and my heart is broken. I cannot sleep, and I cannot eat; nothing matters anymore except you.*

*My father found out about us, and I tried to protect you by ending things between us. It did no good. You are in danger and must leave. Benjamin Greer is a good man, and we can trust him. If you still want us to be together, you must tell him. He will know what to do.*

*With all my love,*

*Sarah.*

James reread the letter several times and unconsciously wiped his face, only just realizing it was streaked with tears. There was no doubt in his mind of what would come next.

Chapter Fourteen

"We're dining with the Campbells this evening," her aunt's voice broke into her reverie.

"That's nice," Sarah replied absentmindedly.

"You don't seem very interested in your future husband." Kitty was watching her with a suspicious look.

"I am. Of course I am. I wasn't expecting him to be aboard the same ship, though. We had planned to meet in New York. Will his mother be there too?"

"Yes, there will be another small party joining us too. The Dahlbergs, I think she said." Sarah feigned a look of enthusiasm which didn't convince her aunt, who continued to shoot her looks as they walked arm in arm along the deck of the floating city.

The *RMS Aquitania* was aptly nicknamed "the ship beautiful" and justified her place as one of the crowning jewels in the Cunard line. The rooms were more spacious and opulent than some of the sleeker designs in current use, and Sarah had been impressed when a fellow passenger had told her that the interior had been fashioned by the same revered designer responsible for the Ritz in London. She was looking forward to dining in the first-class saloon with Kitty later that evening. When her father told her she would be accompanied on her "little excursion," she had been momentarily furious but, on reflection, would much prefer her aunt than her father's irritating manservant. She was also very fond of

Kitty and had missed her greatly during her time in Scotland. She took a deep breath of the salty air and felt her trepidation recede as the shape of land disappeared into the distance.

Sarah appraised herself in the large mirror in her quarters. Her black beaded evening gown fit her like a glove, and she applauded the seamstress as she whirled around to better see her reflection. The sequined pattern and flowing capped sleeves made what could have been a boring dress into something quite exquisite. She completed the look with long black silken gloves, a string of pearls, and a feathered hairband that accentuated her red hair perfectly. Entirely too fashionable would have been her father's disapproving opinion, and she was glad he was not there to chastise her. She paused in the mirror a moment longer, struck by the thought that it might be a considerable time before she saw him again.

"You look quite a vision," Kitty complimented her as they made their way to the upper deck for pre-dinner cocktails. Sarah returned the compliment and squeezed her arm affectionately. Kitty did look well in a powder-blue gown, and Sarah thought, not for the first time, that given the relatively small age difference, their relationship was more like that of two sisters than an aunt and her niece.

They paused as the steward showed them into the ballroom. Kitty spotted Archie and his mother immediately and nudged Sarah toward their corner of the room. The beleaguered girl stepped in their direction, and Kitty, sensing her reluctance, grabbed a couple of champagne cocktails as the waiter glided past. She handed a flute to Sarah, who took a large gulp as she neared her future husband and mother-in-law.

"Sarah, dear, you look divine," said Winnie Campbell, greeting her with an insincere embrace. "You have such an eye for these dramatic new styles."

"Thank you," Sarah responded sweetly, not acknowledging the veiled insult. She turned her attention to Archie and bestowed him with the full weight of her charm. "It's wonderful to see you again." She took another smaller sip of the cocktail and tried to appear engaged.

"The pleasure is decidedly all mine." He looked at her with a mixture of admiration and amusement, and Sarah got the uncomfortable impression of a fox surveying its prey before it went in for the kill. Her previous fleeting impression of him had been over a year ago, and this was clearly not the meek and pliable young man she had been expecting.

They passed a few minutes of inconsequential small talk until they were interrupted by the arrival of John and Ida Dahlberg and John's younger brother, Robert. As the group exchanged introductions, Sarah made sure to address them each one on one. A careful compliment here, a quick smile there, her social graces were the envy of any finishing school. She had a natural talent for ingratiating herself with people and was always a companion in much demand.

As they sat down to dinner, Sarah noticed the younger Dahlberg was paying particular attention to her aunt, who was giggling like a schoolgirl. Sarah saw Robert skillfully position himself next to Kitty and hold out the chair for her with unnecessary ceremony. She was paying more attention to them than anything else and was almost surprised to hear Archie's voice from the chair next to her.

"Are you enjoying the *Aquitania*?"

"Yes, of course. It's a delightful ship."

"What are your favorite diversions?"

"Cards, reading, anything really," she responded, uninterested.

"There are not many passengers of our age," Archie remarked, "although I don't suppose that would affect the number of people undressing you with their eyes."

Sarah was jolted back to attention and thought she must have misheard. "Pardon me, Archie, what did you just say?"

He gave a humorless laugh and lowered his voice. "You don't need to pretend with me. I've heard things about you from friends in London. You have a lot of opinions and a spirit that could get you into trouble. Look at you now, playing up to get the attention of all the men in the room. Enjoy it while you can, my dear."

"What is that supposed to mean?"

"When we're married," Archie continued loftily, "things will most likely change. Certainly, in terms of your behavior. At least in public. I'm rather an admirer of some spirit in more private places." He leaned in a little closer, and she instinctively recoiled in disgust. Sarah then felt his hand graze her thigh as he continued to swig his champagne with arrogant confidence.

"You seem to be under the mistaken impression that we're already engaged," she spat, not trying to disguise the disdain in her voice, and pushed his hand away from her roughly.

"Your father, my father… It's not like either of us gets a say in it. However, I'm not complaining. I'm looking forward to us getting to know each other better as only a husband and wife can."

He set down his champagne flute and sat back in his chair wearing a look of self-conceited smugness. Seized by anger and with a swift motion, Sarah knocked the glass back onto his lap, where the liquid pooled onto his tuxedo. He jumped up and spluttered in anger. A nearby waiter rushed over to assist and tried to mop the mess, but Archie rudely waved him away.

"Oh, my goodness, I'm so sorry, Archie! Please allow me to apologize as profusely as one can," Sarah crowed loudly, a distraught expression on her face that was already soliciting looks of sympathy from the other parties at the table, including Archie's mother.

His face reddened by anger, he sat back down slowly and turned to Sarah. Matching her loud voice, he bestowed what could pass as a kindly grimace. "It's quite all right. These things do happen. It's of no consequence." He received a nod of satisfaction from his mother, and the hum of conversation resumed around the table.

"You fool," Archie whispered to Sarah once more. "You think you can behave like that toward *me*?"

"Hush, Archie darling, you're making people stare at us. I'm already so upset at that little incident. Who knows what could happen next?" Sarah gave him a sweet smile and tipped her glass at Archie's mother, who was still watching them with a look of approval.

"Don't play with me," he said nastily. "I could make things very unpleasant for you."

"No, Archie," she responded, her tone hardening. "You shouldn't play with *me*. London is littered with corpses of little boys who underestimated me. Now, if you'll excuse me…" Sarah stood up, joined by the other gentlemen, who matched her with a slight bow. Archie, his face the color of crimson, gaped as she sashayed in the direction of the powder room.

Sarah stared at herself in the powder room mirror and breathed deeply. Her heart raced in her chest, and she leaned heavily against the wall to steady herself and control her anger. The encounter with her future fiancé had strengthened her resolve. Freedom would be hers. She smoothed down her hair and straightened the feathered headband. She would miss some of the finer things, but it was a small price to pay to be free of this prison.

She was headed back to rejoin the group when a concerned Kitty accosted her. "Are you well?"

"Everything is fine," Sarah assured her and motioned for Kitty to follow her back. En route, they were stalled by a photographer from the *Sunday Herald*. Sarah fixed the photographer with a smoldering glance and struck a dramatic pose. The photographer, who had managed to capture the deck behind her with Kitty's figure in the background, seemed delighted with what he assured her would be one of the finest photographs taken of the voyage. The photograph would later be published in the newspaper and regarded with enquiring eyes down the centuries.

****

"He's just so accomplished in so many ways," Kitty gushed later that night as they sat in their nightgowns to dissect the evening's events.

"And handsome too," Sarah teased, smiling at her aunt. Kitty was completely smitten with the younger Robert Dahlberg and had spent the remainder of the evening either in his company or watching him with barely disguised adoration. Sarah had studiously avoided Archie after their unpleasant dinner exploits and effortlessly worked the room, already a favorite of some of the more distinguished guests. Sarah had a carefully studied knack of subtly charming the married gentlemen while bestowing much of her attention on their wives, or in some cases mistresses, to position herself not as a threat but an attractive future friend and confidante. Sarah knew friends were often more loose-lipped than anyone, and she knew it would be to her detriment to earn any type of reputation with someone else's man, however undeserved. It was due to this careful reluctance that she had been so surprised by Archie's comments to her. The dreadful man, she thought again, then sighed audibly as she realized she would have to keep him at bay for at least the duration of their voyage.

"Sarah?" Kitty was looking at her in surprise, alerted to the fact that she had not been following her effusive conversation about the charming and witty Robert Dahlberg.

"I'm sorry. You have my complete attention." Sarah smiled at her encouragingly, and Kitty, not needing further persuading, continued her chatter. Sarah was happy for her aunt. Indeed, she had never seen her so taken with anyone in all their time together in London. There was something about Robert Dahlberg that didn't fully put her at ease, although she was loath to form a negative opinion of someone she had just met based on an unsubstantiated feeling. She probably let her dislike of Archie transfer onto Robert, she thought wryly. Either that or jealousy that her aunt had the company of someone whom she at least liked. Regardless, the distraction was a welcome one, as Kitty had no clue of her intense dislike of Archie Campbell.

They readied themselves for bed, and as Kitty settled down, Sarah quietly reached for her trunk. She rummaged around until she found what she was looking for and pulled it out surreptitiously. A man's plain white shirt made of inexpensive material. She brought it to her face and inhaled deeply. She closed her eyes and thought of James.

****

Sarah walked through the first-class lounge the next morning, her light footsteps almost bouncing on the plush floor coverings. She greeted some of the stewards by name and headed to the library. She earned herself a few glances from the male passengers as she pulled out a couple of volumes of the business guide and a refresher on letter-writing etiquette. She looked around for a quiet spot to hide and heard a shrill voice call out her name. She looked around in trepidation for the owner of the voice and was dismayed to see Winnie Campbell perched on the edge of one of the club chairs. "Come and join us!" She motioned to one of the unoccupied seats.

Sarah reluctantly sat down, trying to conceal her books, but Archie's mother's sharp eye missed nothing. "What odd reading material you have, dear. Could you not find the novels?"

"No. But I shall have another look for them right now," Sarah responded, seeing an avenue of escape.

"Sit with me for a moment. I feel we should get to know each other better," Winnie commanded and began to drone on endlessly about the fashions of the other passengers on the *Aquitania*. Her monologue required little input from Sarah, who nodded at appropriate intervals and allowed her mind to wander far away from the petty gossip.

Respite only came when a steward interrupted to tell Winnie that her presence had been requested in the writing room. Sarah insisted that she go and reassured her there would be many other opportunities for them to become better acquainted. Sarah watched her go with relief and was about to get up from her chair when a figure slightly farther away put down his newspaper and announced, "Thank goodness for that. I thought she was never going to stop."

Sarah looked at the face of Robert Dahlberg with amusement. "Do you not enjoy hearing about fringe wraps and cocoon fur coats?" she asked.

"I think I enjoy it as much as you do," he replied, and they both laughed.

"I saw you talking to my Aunt Kitty a lot at dinner." Sarah cut straight to the chase.

"Your aunt is very good company—she has a good mind. As you seem to." He nodded at the business volumes in her lap. "I approve of your reading tastes."

"You don't think I should be reading fashion magazines?" Sarah baited him.

"Heavens, no. I'm not sure the world could cope with any more Winnie Campbells." They laughed again. "Or her son, either." His voice had taken on a more serious tone.

"Is it wise to say such things to Archibald's future fiancée?" she asked guardedly.

"Perhaps not, although I imagine that both you and Kitty can make up your minds. My comment is meant as a suggestion to look into your fiancé a little more, perhaps. I intend no ill will toward anyone."

"Thank you, Mr. Dahlberg. I will take your

comment under advisement."

"I would like to take the opportunity to get to know your aunt better. Do I have your permission to spend some time with her?"

Sarah laughed again. "My permission? I think you're confusing me with my father."

"You are Kitty's nearest relative onboard, and I'd like to assure you that I will take the greatest care of her."

Sarah surveyed the man in front of her and saw only sincerity. "Of course you have my permission." She bestowed a smile on Robert Dahlberg as she walked away and hoped she had not misread the man. Kitty deserved someone who would treat her like a queen and nothing less.

****

Days later, she was on her way back to their stateroom, preferring to read in privacy, when she stopped abruptly at the entrance to the music salon. She recognized Archie's voice and then heard a female voice respond softly. She checked behind her and then pressed her eye to the crack in the door to the salon. She immediately stepped back and put a hand over her mouth in disbelief. Footsteps indicated fellow passengers heading in her direction, and she hurried to the safety of her rooms.

Kitty was sitting on the bed and looked up quizzically as Sarah closed the door behind her and looked at her aunt with eyes as wide as saucers. "What is it?" Kitty asked in alarm.

Sarah shook her head mutely, still scarcely believing the scene she had witnessed in the salon. "It's Archie," she whispered.

"Has he done something to you?"

"No, not me. It's Ida Dahlberg."

Kitty's face creased in a mask of confusion. "Robert's sister-in-law? What do you mean?"

"Archie had his hand up her skirts, and she was doing the same," Sarah blanched.

Kitty looked at her niece sympathetically but without any surprise. "Are you upset?"

"Upset?" Sarah exclaimed. "She's married to John Dahlberg!"

"I mean, are you upset about Archie?"

"I couldn't care less about Archie or what he does."

"Ida Dahlberg has a reputation for this, and her tastes are often...younger," Kitty concluded.

"Is this common knowledge?" Sarah asked incredulously.

Kitty gave her niece another look of sympathy. For all her spirit and pert opinions, she really was an innocent in the world sometimes, she reflected. "It has been said a time or two. Archie is just the latest in a long line of young men. I'm sure it won't last very long."

"What about her husband, John? Imagine if he found out."

"I think he knows. I believe he has his own line of *interests*," Kitty said meaningfully.

Sarah sat down hard on the edge of the bed. "So many secrets," she murmured.

"Are there any that you would like to share?" Kitty asked her gently.

Sarah opened her mouth to respond, but they were interrupted by the clanging of a bell and the footsteps of a steward running by the door. Kitty wrenched the door open and stuck her head out to hear the commotion. "The captain thinks about four hours, and we'll be there,"

Kitty told Sarah excitedly. "Are you all packed up?"

"Yes, I'm just finishing up the trunks, and I think the bottle that Father had made for the Campbells will be delivered directly to the Grammercy."

"Bottle? Of what?"

"The gift of the whisky. I thought I'd told you about it."

"Sarah, we are entering America. You know how the Americans feel about alcohol right now."

Sarah waved away the comment. "Don't worry, Father had it recorded as an artwork, which it is, I suppose."

"I don't want us to get into any trouble with the legal authorities," Kitty continued to worry.

"Of course we won't," Sarah scoffed. "Besides, we're empty-headed women." Her voice dripped with sarcasm. "Obviously, we don't know any better."

"Well, if the worst comes to the worst, I have a medical certificate," Kitty informed her. Sarah gave a delighted laugh. Her aunt appeared so timid sometimes yet was well versed in the ways of the world.

Four hours. They were almost there. Sarah forced herself to focus on packing her trunks and assured the anxious maid that it had always been her preference to do that herself. The chore was a welcome one as it left less time for her to contemplate the future.

Sarah and Kitty joined the other passengers on the deck as the skyline of New York finally came into view. There was joy and hope in the air as the passengers of the *Aquitania* saw their destination. The faint outline against a misty sky would be their reality in a short time. Was she ready? Sarah took a deep breath and gripped the railing to steady herself. Here and now would be the beginning of a new life, whatever that might bring.

Chapter Fifteen

Disembarkation was noisy and chaotic, and it was a considerable time before Sarah and Kitty finally cleared the customs area and the luggage was brought to their waiting carriage. "We have a suite at the Grammercy," Kitty directed the driver. "I'm exhausted," she said to her niece, but Sarah wasn't listening. She was transfixed by the mess and bustle that was New York City and stared out the window, not wanting to miss a moment of the commotion.

There was an excitement in the air that even London didn't possess, but Sarah was also struck by the contrast of the "haves" and "have nots" of the people she passed, and she imagined life must be very hard for some of the city's inhabitants. She felt a nervous flutter in her chest as she contemplated the thought that, soon, she might not be so wholly under the protections that money could buy.

Sarah and Kitty's assumptions about New York being unfashionable or uncivilized were dispelled on arrival at the Grammercy Hotel. The awe-inspiring lobby, with its art deco furnishings and unmistakable elegance, exceeded their expectations. "Father has not been tight with the purse strings," Sarah commented.

"We're going to have a superb time," Kitty told her with glee but noted she seemed preoccupied with other thoughts. "What are you going to do about Archie?"

Sarah was saved from responding by the arrival of

an impeccably dressed waiter. "I'll have a Dubonnet," she told the hovering man.

"Sarah," Kitty admonished her niece, "are you forgetting the Volstead Act?"

"Goodness me, I was!" Her hand flew up to cover her mouth. "I do apologize," she told the uncomfortable waiter. "Perhaps an orange juice?"

Kitty excused herself to the powder room as the waiter returned with the glass of orange juice. "Here you go, miss," he said in unfamiliar New York vowels. He then cleared his throat and looked around furtively. "There is also this." He thrust a small piece of paper discreetly from its concealment in the palm of his hand. Sarah took the note with a word of thanks and put it quickly into her satin purse, where she felt it burning a hole. Who knew she was there? As soon as Kitty returned, she feigned a headache and went directly to her room, where she ripped open the note and scanned the contents.

To her extreme surprise, she saw that it had been authored by none other than her father's manager, Benjamin Greer himself.

*Dear Miss Whiting,* the neat script began, *I have a matter of which I must speak with you most urgently. The matter is confidential, and I wish for us to meet. I act in this matter as a liaison and confident of another of your father's employees whom I hold in high esteem. Please send word via the hotel employee Ed O'Brien, who may be found serving in the lobby of the hotel. I will be in the vicinity for the next two days only. Yours truly, Benjamin Greer.*

Another of her father's employees? She swallowed nervously. Did she dare to hope? Who else could it be but James? Then why had Greer not mentioned his name? Perhaps he was worried the note would be intercepted by someone else. Her head was swirling with questions when she heard a frantic knock on the door. She stuffed the note back into her purse and opened the door.

Kitty burst into the room excitedly. "Are you feeling better?"

"I'm fine," Sarah responded with a smile at Kitty's undisguised excitement. "What were you going to tell me?"

"Guess who else is staying in our same hotel?" Kitty demanded triumphantly.

"Who?"

"The Dahlbergs!"

"Or more specifically, Robert Dahlberg," Sarah said slyly and saw her aunt redden slightly at the mention of his name.

"I just thought they were pleasant company on the *Aquitania*," Kitty said a little huffily.

"Indeed, they were. I have no objection to getting to know them better. Perhaps we could have dinner together tomorrow?"

"It won't be difficult with Ida Dahlberg after the Archie situation?" Kitty asked delicately.

"Not at all," Sarah reassured her.

Kitty beamed, and Sarah shuffled her back outside the room to make the arrangements. Sarah needed to get a message to Benjamin Greer's go-between in the hotel's lobby as soon as possible. Greer had said he would be in town for only two days—there wasn't time to lose. She quickly reapplied her cosmetics and arranged her fur stole. She stepped out in the direction of the grand staircase and realized, a little shamefully, that she couldn't remember the face of the waiter O'Brien.

"Miss Whiting," came a voice from behind her. She whirled around and came face to face with her betrothed.

"Archie! What, what are you doing here?"

"We are staying at the Grammercy. Your father thought it might be prudent for us to spend a little time together before the wedding," he said.

Sarah looked at him with intense dislike. "After your behavior on the ship, you should consider yourself fortunate we are even on speaking terms."

"You forget who I am," he cautioned and took hold of her upper arm and squeezed tightly. Sarah tried to pull away, but he tightened his grip to the point that she gasped in pain. "Don't play with me," he said, teeth gritted as he repeated the warning he'd made aboard the *Aquitania*, and she had a flashback to the time her father had used exactly the same words.

"Let go of me," she hissed, "or I shall scream and make a scene, and everyone shall know what kind of man Archibald Campbell is. Ida Dahlberg?" She left the name hanging in the air, knowing he would interpret her meaning.

He smiled nastily and released his grip. "Until next time, Lady Whiting." He gave a mock bow. "It won't be long until we have all the time in the world to get to know each other."

Sarah was shaken but continued to the lobby, more determined than ever to get a message to Benjamin Greer. It was worth the risk if there was even a chance he could be her conduit to James. She surveyed the smartly dressed patrons, looking for O'Brien's uniform, but instead saw the portly figure of Benjamin Greer himself intently studying a menu card.

"Mr. Greer?" Sarah said, and he looked up, startled.

"Yes, can you meet me outside in a few minutes?" He looked around furtively. "There are too many prying eyes in here."

After a few minutes, Sarah followed him outside at a respectable distance. He beckoned her to pursue him down the street and turned a corner. She quickened her pace to avoid losing him on the busy street. The clanging of the streetcar and shouts of the newsies jostled for her attention, and it took all her concentration to keep his figure in view as well-dressed pedestrians weaved between them.

Sarah kept her eyes raised upward on Benjamin Greer. As if by design, a man's foot appeared in her path. She stumbled and almost tripped, but a strong arm grabbed her elbow and pulled her into an alcove. A man clamped a hand over her mouth, and she struggled furiously against her assailant. She abandoned the effort when she looked up and saw the face of the man she loved.

"James!" As she said his name, tears poured down her face, and she kissed him with such force he almost lost his balance.

"Oh, my lass!" He blinked himself to keep emotions in check as he held her face in his hands and pulled her into his arms. She smelled his scent, and, wrapped in his strong embrace, her body heaved with great sobs of relief.

"I thought I'd lost you, I thought…my father…did you get my letter?" Her words spilled over each other as she tried to make sense of the situation and how it could be possible he was there.

"It's going to be all right now," he soothed, brushing a tendril of red hair from her beautiful face.

Benjamin Greer's stern voice interrupted the reunion. "Macleary, this isn't a good place. Make the arrangements."

"Have you changed your mind? Do you still want to be with me?" James asked nervously. "You know there will be no going back." There was not a single doubt in Sarah's mind as she looked into his eyes.

James Macleary, Sarah Whiting, and Benjamin Greer spoke with urgency in an alcove on the street around the corner from the Grammercy Hotel for almost an hour. They planned an event that would change the course of all their lives—indefinitely.

****

"The Coco Chanel," Sarah told Kitty for the second time. They had dinner reservations with the Campbells and the Dahlbergs that evening, and Kitty, clearly besotted with Robert and eager to make an outstanding impression, was showcasing a parade of gowns to her niece.

"But what about the Madeleine Vionnet?" Kitty began to rummage once more through the closet.

"The Coco Chanel," Sarah repeated firmly and excused herself before her aunt could change her mind again.

Back in the confines of her room, she threw herself down on her bed and willed herself to relax. Her head was a jumble of emotions, and it took every ounce of her self-control to keep them in check. James. James loved her, and James was here. She had kissed him just the day before, although it seemed like an eternity and her body already ached to hold him again. Any misgivings she had experienced in their time apart had disappeared once she set eyes on him. Her recent dealings with Archie Campbell had given her a steely resolve that she would share the life she wanted with the man she loved.

She swung her legs off the bed and pulled out her trunks. Only two, Benjamin Greer had instructed. It was already risky, and they couldn't take the chance of O'Brien having to make more than one trip through the servants' entrance, as it would arouse too much suspicion. Only two. Cramming all her worldly possessions into two trunks provided a stark realization of how much her life would change. She had begun to lay out her gowns on the bed when she heard a knock at the door.

Kitty was probably having second thoughts about her dress for the evening, again, thought Sarah with a sigh of exasperation. She shoved her gowns unceremoniously back into the closet and opened the door. The figure of Archie Campbell stood ominously in the doorway.

"I believe we have some unfinished business," he sneered nastily.

"How dare you come to my private bedchamber," Sarah thundered, but Archie shoved her forcefully back into the room and clamped a hand over her mouth. He pushed the door closed with his other hand and forced her arm roughly behind her back to prevent her from moving. Sarah struggled in vain against his superior strength, and he pulled her arm up so hard she thought it would break. Her screams of pain were muffled by his hand, and Sarah's panicked mind thought perhaps he was going to kill her.

Archie pushed his fiancée down onto the bed, face

first and with such force that she was unable to breathe, her airways stifled by the bedding. He pressed the full weight of his body onto hers and tried to force her legs open. Sarah writhed with all her strength to take a breath and break free of his monstrous grip, but he held her too tightly. "It will be better for you if you calm down," Archie gasped in the effort to control her.

"Never," Sarah cried, but her voice was barely discernible as he pushed her head back down into the bed. He was still grabbing at her legs, trying to force himself in, when Sarah suddenly felt his body go limp and his full weight collapsed onto her slim frame.

She heard a whimper behind her and her name being uttered frantically by her Aunt Kitty. She finally pulled her shoulder free of Archie's weight and moved her head enough to be heard. "Kitty!" She gulped for air. "Kitty, help me."

"I'm going to try and roll him off." Kitty struggled with his bulk but finally dislodged the body, and it rolled and hit the floor with a thud. Kitty screamed.

"He's dead!"

Now free of her captor, Sarah looked at the motionless body on the floor. "What did you do?" she asked, eyes wide as saucers.

"I hit him," Kitty whispered, shaking like a leaf, "with that…" She pointed to a heavy lead crystal vase now abandoned on the floor. "I came in… I saw him… Oh, my!" She covered her face with her hands and began to sob hysterically.

Sarah slammed the door shut lest they should attract any attention, then knelt beside Archie's body. "Pass me that powder mirror," she pointed to the cosmetics.

"Sarah! How can you think about that at a time like

this?" Kitty was horrified.

Sarah grabbed the mirror herself and held it in front of Archie's mouth. "You didn't kill him—he's still breathing. He's probably just passed out."

"Oh, my God, what do we do? What do we do?" Kitty wailed uncontrollably.

"Stay here," Sarah commanded, and covering herself with a thin coat, she ran to the lobby.

Luck was with her, and she spotted O'Brien immediately. He came as soon as he saw her, and she relayed the situation. His face changed momentarily to shock, then resumed his mask of stoic calm. He nodded, then instructed Sarah to go back to her room. She ran back upstairs, where she tried in vain to comfort the quivering Kitty. Moments later, there was a knock on the door, and they were joined by O'Brien and another muscled man wearing the uniform of a bellhop. "Good afternoon, misses," he said, raising his cap to Sarah and Kitty.

O'Brien threw a blanket over the unconscious Archie and indicated to his helper to carry the other side. "Where will you take him?" Sarah asked.

"Back to his own room where he probably should have stayed," responded O'Brien cheerfully.

"Perhaps he won't underestimate you ladies in future." The bellhop grinned.

"Will he be all right?" Kitty said shakily.

"Most likely. It isn't the first time something like this has happened." They shuffled out of the room with the body of Archie Campbell between them and closed the door.

Kitty and Sarah looked at each other with shocked faces. "I can't believe I hit him." Kitty was still shaking her head in disbelief.

"Well, I'm glad you did. You know what he would have done to me, don't you?"

Kitty nodded mutely. "But now we have to see them at dinner!" Her voice had reached a new height of panic as she recalled their dinner reservation with the Campbell and Dahlberg families. "Do you think Archie will say anything? I mean, if he's even conscious."

"What exactly could he say?" Sarah said in disgust. "That he tried to assault Samuel Whiting's daughter and she resisted? And in front of his mother? No. He won't say anything."

Despite her reassurances to Kitty, Sarah dressed for dinner with a feeling of foreboding. What if Archie *did* say something? What if he tried to turn things around to make it her fault? That was exactly the kind of thing someone as low as Archie would do. How would he put a spin on their engagement? She shuddered as she imagined her father's response to the recent events.

Together they made their way to the dining room with a deep sense of trepidation. Kitty's face lit up when she caught sight of Robert Dahlberg and his party, but Sarah was firmly focused on searching for the Campbells. She finally caught sight of Archie's mother, Winnie, who wore an expression of disapproval, and steeled herself for the unpleasant scenes to come. Winnie made a beeline for Sarah, and to her surprise, Winnie's face changed to one of sympathy. "Sarah dear, there you are. You look radiant as always." She seemed flustered, and the remark was delivered with none of her usual sarcastic undertones. "Unfortunately, Archie is unable to join us this evening."

"Oh?"

"It's quite a terrible business. He was attacked outside the hotel. He went to take some air and enjoy a cigarette and some of these…" She lowered her voice. "These *uncouth Americans* decided to accost him. It is such a dreadful thing to have occurred. And Archie is such a gentleman." She looked at Sarah as if seeking affirmation, which Sarah supplied in the form of a sympathetic nod. "He didn't even want to summon the constabulary."

"Really? How odd," Sarah remarked drily.

"Well, we must let the poor boy recover in peace and try to salvage the evening."

As the group made their way into the dining room, Sarah intercepted Kitty from the crowd and pulled her aside. "Archie's fine," she hissed. "He told his mother some cock-and-bull story about being attacked in front of the hotel." Kitty looked relieved, then opened her mouth to say something more, but Sarah interrupted sternly, "Archie's fine, now carry on talking to Robert Dahlberg."

The evening passed at a snail's pace for Sarah. She listened respectfully and smiled dutifully at her dinner companions, but her mind was entirely elsewhere. Two days. In two days, she would inspect her father's cargo off the coast of Atlantic City. It was all arranged. Benjamin Greer, his most trusted advisor, had understood her desire to become more involved with the family business to pave the way for her future husband. She would take this opportunity to have a photograph taken with the Whiting company's import of Elderflower Wine, nonalcoholic of course. She was the perfect ambassador for the Whiting company. Nothing could go wrong.

Chapter Sixteen

Kitty brushed her hair at the large gilded mirror and watched her niece covertly in the reflection. "You have something on your mind," she stated. "Is it Archie?"

Sarah's face broke into a scowl. "That despicable creature doesn't deserve any thought."

"That 'despicable creature,' as you put it, was going to be your future husband and probably still will be if your father has anything to do with it."

Sarah didn't respond but gave a deep sigh, and Kitty saw the defeat etched on her face. "I'm going to talk to my brother about Archie. I'm sure he wouldn't want him to be your betrothed when he finds out what kind of man he is."

"Really?" Sarah spat sarcastically. "You think he would care?"

"I'm sure he wants the best for you," Kitty faltered. "I know he can be—"

"A cold, heartless creature," Sarah finished.

"Sarah! I'm sure it's not as bad as all that. I'm going to try and talk to him."

Sarah felt contrite as she saw her aunt's anxious expression. "I'm sorry." She put her arms around Kitty's shoulders. "I know you always try to look after me."

"Do you want to tell me what's going on?" Kitty whispered.

Sarah now felt the tears welling up behind her own

eyes and realized she would most likely never see her aunt again if everything went to plan. "I'm fine," she stammered, and Kitty drew her close and kissed the top of her head.

"What's the matter? You can tell me. I will do everything I can to help you." Kitty was on the verge of tears herself, seeing her niece in such distress.

"I know you would." Sarah gulped. "I just can't tell you, though."

"I understand," Kitty said, her voice hardening. "I've lived with your father longer even than you have. He controls you. He controls us both, and sometimes I think…I think he might be…*evil*. The last word was whispered, and Kitty looked around irrationally, afraid someone might hear them despite the privacy of their rooms.

Sarah pulled away and searched her aunt's face, finding no trace of insincerity but instead an odd mix of despair and determination. "I can't. I can't live like this forever."

"And if you marry Archie Campbell, you will be doing just that."

Sarah looked at Kitty in bewilderment. "Do you know?"

"Know what? That my beloved niece is in love with another man?"

"How?" she whispered incredulously.

"I'm not blind, dear. And I know you think of me as your boring old aunt, but I'm not quite so unaware of what happens under my own nose."

"I don't think that at all," Sarah responded seriously. "I think that about myself sometimes. I had no clue of what was happening between Archie and Ida Dahlberg, but you knew about it."

"Don't inflate listening to gossip as a substitute for knowledge. You have a spirit, my darling, a spirit that I don't want the world to extinguish, and I fear, if you stay here and marry that repulsive creature, that's precisely what will happen."

"I'm not going to," Sarah told her levelly. "I'm not going to stay."

"Who is he?"

"His name is James, and he's the best man I've ever met in my life."

"You can't just run away!" Kitty exclaimed, horrified at the thought. "The world out there is not a kind one."

"I'm not going to run away."

"Then what? You can't stay here in America!" Kitty's voice had become panicked and shrill.

"If I am to succeed, I need level heads," Sarah chastised her, "and soon."

"Then tell me how I can help you, my darling."

\*\*\*\*

The motor proceeded slowly to the dock with Sarah and Kitty huddled closely together in the back. The trip to Atlantic City had not been a particularly pleasant one, and both women had stared wide-eyed at the things they had seen along the way. America was certainly a new world. They finally crawled to a stop at their destination, and the driver jumped out to assist them. Sarah climbed out and was hit by the force of the unrelenting wind and the slap of cold on her face. She was a vision, in a blush-rose floor-length coat and black pearls. Immaculate makeup showcased her beauty, and she commanded the eyes of everyone in the vicinity.

The group assembled on the dock was larger than Sarah had expected. It seemed that professional publicity required a large cast to execute it properly. Sarah exchanged a smile with the photographer she recognized as the man who had traveled on the *Aquitania*. She cast around for the familiar face of Benjamin Greer but couldn't place him in the commotion. A drop of rain landed on her cheek, and she wiped it away impatiently and shivered slightly. "How cold is the water?" she asked one of the sailors within earshot.

"Very cold, mademoiselle," answered Jacques Bisset. "It is not a good day to go swimming."

Sarah finally caught sight of Benjamin Greer, and she made her way toward him. "Mr. Greer, what a pleasure to see you this side of the Atlantic," she crowed in a loud voice.

"Lady Sarah, the pleasure is distinctly my own," he responded, and the two exchanged a look. Greer proffered his arm and escorted her to the boat, which would be used as the backdrop for the photographs. "Are you sure you still want to do this?" he whispered in her ear.

"Yes, Mr. Greer, I am sure. Where is he?"

"He's around the back. Where is the other motorcar?"

"It followed us. It should be here very soon."

"I'll tell the boys to move the trunks as soon as it arrives. And your aunt?" Greer had noticed Kitty hovering nearby, wearing a worried look.

Sarah pulled away from him and addressed her aunt. "Kitty, you need to stay here," Sarah instructed. "Now, remember what I told you…and keep calm." She emphasized the last two words and squeezed her hand.

"Yes, I will," Kitty responded. "Now, you will do two things for me. First, always remember that I love you very much…" She swallowed but then continued determinedly, "And second, you must take this." She pushed a small purse into Sarah's gloved hands.

"What is this? I can't—"

"Take it," Kitty hissed. "Now, go."

With the assistance of several burly sailors, Sarah was up on the ship's deck. A large wooden crate proudly bearing the Whiting name was positioned front and center. The photographer was shouting commands to position the group, but his words were lost to the ferocious wind. Sarah snaked her fingers around the knot of her neck scarf and clenched her fist tightly. Patience had never been her strong suit, but she knew their success would depend on all the players waiting for the right moment. She walked to the stern and peered down into the dark water below. She tasted the salt in the air and shivered again as she saw the mocking waves lap impatiently against the ship. She looked back at the dock again, where she saw that the second motor had arrived, and a man she hadn't seen before was unloading her trunk. The pieces were falling into place. She scanned the crowd again, looking desperately for the one man she needed to see, but she could not find his face among them.

People were working everywhere, loading crates, unloading crates, hoisting barrels and boxes. The constant movement of caps bobbing in the crowd as the regular hum of work at the docks continued. So much movement and so much commotion, she could see why James had chosen this place. She felt an arm push the small of her back to guide her toward the front of the boat. Greer was holding her arm a little too tightly and asked again, "Everything is in place. Are you sure this is what you want?"

"Where's James?" Sarah felt momentary panic. "I thought I would see him here."

"Turn back around and pretend I'm pointing at a seagull," Greer replied. She turned and saw the broad figure of her lover. As if her gaze had physically touched him, he looked over his shoulder and winked, then, quick as a thief in the night, he was gone.

"Thank you, Mr. Greer," Sarah told him with a faint smile. She steadied her breathing and straightened her gown. "I think we may proceed to the business."

The players took their places, and the photographers readied their equipment. Not an easy task with the challenging wind. "Bello!" came a booming voice, followed by the clang of a large pipe hitting the dock. A woman screamed, and all heads swiveled instinctively in the direction of the noise.

"The oil lock! Watch out!" came another voice from the opposite direction, and a loud bang was heard, followed by a plume of black smoke that engulfed the front of the ship. Sarah and Benjamin Greer, standing like statues poised for the photograph, jumped in fright. Screams arose from the crowd as they tried to retreat as one, away from the formidable heat.

Kitty stood near the front of the crowd and felt someone pull her back, away from the suffocating smoke. Where was Sarah? She couldn't see her. Kitty looked around desperately, but the smoke and heat invaded her eyes, and she could see nothing through the smog. "Move back! Move back!" a man was shouting, and the crowd pulled and pushed in every direction.

Flames leaped up beyond the haze of the smoke, and more voices yelled for water.

Kitty and the other observers watched in horror as a fireboat descended on the scene. The men who worked on the docks had jumped to action, guided by instinct, and all the available hoses had rained down on the ship. Less than fifteen minutes had passed since the explosion, and a half-hearted cheer arose from the workers. They had reigned victorious, and the flames had been extinguished. However, there was no celebration as they surveyed the ravaged remains of the ship. She was still afloat, and her hull was intact, but there was extensive damage to the decking and stern. Two others were helping a small, portly man as great coughs wracked his body, and they half-carried him to the safety of land. "Mr. Greer!" Kitty exclaimed as she recognized him through the dirt encrusted on his face. "Sarah? Where is she? What happened?" She grabbed desperately at him as he tried to speak through unrelenting fits of coughing.

"She fell," he gasped, "overboard."

Kitty let out a wail and fell to her knees. "Find her!" she screamed.

A small crew was dispatched immediately to find any people who had jumped overboard to flee the flames, and to retrieve any of the cargo that was still intact. An entire platform of Whiting's goods was being transferred to the wharf at the moment the explosion occurred, and a great number of crates had crashed into the ocean.

While the explosion and fire had lasted only minutes, the aftermath would take a lot longer to subside. Confusion and panic reigned supreme, and it was a challenge for the newly arrived authorities to make sense of the situation. Kitty had been there hours and hours, wringing her hands as she waited for news of Sarah. The comforting and familiar figure of Benjamin Greer had waited with her, his smoke-streaked face a weary picture of sadness. The hours slowly passed, and the faces of the patrollers grew more and more resigned. Finally, the head of the Coast Guard, a man who introduced himself only as Bobby, carefully approached the two and removed his hat in a gesture of respect.

"Miss Whiting?" He cleared his throat. "I'm very sorry, ma'am. We haven't been able to find your niece."

Kitty threw herself into the arms of the flabbergasted Benjamin Greer, who muttered, "Please, please keep looking."

Not many things had the power to touch the heart of the corrupt coast guardsman, and the early death of a spoiled little rich girl was no exception. But he had felt sorrow when he learned that young James Macleary had also been lost in the blaze. He had been a good lad, an honest one, and goodness knows they were hard to come by in these waters. Macleary's second in command, the Irishman O'Brien, had given Bobby a couple of bottles of top-shelf Madeira wine. "Say a toast for him. He'd want that. And leave his body to the sea where it can be at peace. He always said that's how he'd like to go."

****

Benjamin Greer had a lot of things to check off his list before he returned to his native Scotland. He had taken inventory to see how severe the losses were and had found the damage to be very severe indeed. He was finishing up his task, relieved to be finally able to leave the damp warehouse, when he was approached by another of Samuel Whiting's employees, this one a little more off the books.

"What will happen now?" O'Brien asked him. "I can't imagine it will be business as usual."

Greer affixed him with an odd look. "Mr. Whiting is not going to be very happy with the loss of an entire shipment, but I think the disappointment might pale in comparison to the news that his only daughter is dead."

O'Brien removed his cap and clutched it to his chest. "Of course, sir, but she's not the only one," he whispered. "I mean no disrespect, sir, but we are all just feeling the loss of Macleary, too, and some of us need to return home." He looked at the older man meaningfully.

"Of course. It's a very unpredictable time. Let's try to ease the tensions. Can you gather all your men around?"

O'Brien rounded up the remains of James's trusted crew. A few men were already gone, seeing the writing on the wall after James's demise and the loss of Mr. Whiting's whisky or supposed elderflower wine. Benjamin Greer was unaccustomed to being the center of attention and cleared his throat nervously before announcing, "Mr. Whiting is very grateful for your services and thanks you for your hard work. However, in light of recent events, your services will not be required henceforth. As a gesture of his gratitude, he has decided to give parting pay to everyone."

"You mean we are to receive payment even though there is no work to do?" Jacques questioned.

"Mr. Whiting is a man of considerable means, and he appreciates all that you have done for the Whiting company. He asks in return that you do not broadcast the details of your employment."

Jacques and several other men began to study the ground to contain their amusement, although a couple of titters escaped, and Benjamin Greer looked at O'Brien quizzically. "In this line of work, sir, we are not usually loose-lipped," he said by way of explanation. "But," he added quickly, "Mr. Whiting's generosity is much appreciated."

Greer handed a stack of envelopes to O'Brien, who passed them out to the crew. "Remember," he warned in a low tone, "they are not to advertise this, not even to anyone who might let it reach the ears of Mr. Whiting himself. Do they understand?" O'Brien nodded and gave him a reassuring squeeze on the shoulder.

Greer allowed himself a little smile as he heard the amazed exclamations of James's men as they eyed the sizable stack of money in the envelopes. He then hailed the motor to take him back to his hotel.

"O'Brien, can I have a word in private?" Jacques Bisset accosted his friend. "There is something strange about this business."

"Strange how?"

"Something doesn't feel right."

O'Brien clapped his friend on the back and laughed. "Let's have a toast to James Macleary and be thankful we're still here and we made some money today. Trust me." O'Brien gave Jacques a cryptic look. "Macleary is in a good place."

A few days later, O'Brien would meet his younger brother, another O'Brien, who worked as a waiter at the Grammercy Hotel, and he would give him some money, buy him a drink, and the brothers would agree they had done a very good deed.

Chapter Seventeen

*Present Day, Montana, USA*

"Are you busy right now?"

Marcus looked every inch the cowboy, leaning on the doorframe. His sleeves were rolled up over his arms, and his weathered Tony Llamas peeked out from under jeans that were held up with a large belt buckle. He would have looked completely out of place in the corporate world of the East Coast, but here he looked perfect.

"I am busy. My current employer works me very hard," I responded playfully, "and it has been said he can be a little grumpy if things don't go his way."

"I think your employer sounds like a great guy. And grumpy is a good counterbalance to feisty."

"Feisty?"

"It's been said, little lady." He gave me that look again, and I gave a little shudder as it brought to mind all his many talents. *Focus on the job.*

"I know I'm missing something important," I told him, turning the subject back to the present.

"I think that's a sign you should take a break."

"Is that the universe sending a sign or Marcus McClean?"

"I've heard Marcus McClean is a pretty grumpy guy, so you probably don't want to cross him." He held out his hand to help me up from my chair. I looked guiltily back at the table, where the piles of papers seemed to mock my lack of progress.

"What do you want to do?" I noticed he had not let go of my hand, and I didn't want him to.

"Now, that's a question I'm not sure I should answer," he said in his low voice, and our heads moved together, then stopped abruptly as Betty banged loudly on the glass.

"I found the extra waders," she shouted through the window.

"Thanks," Marcus shouted back, and we both giggled, caught in the act.

"What are waders?" I asked, and he looked at me with undisguised amusement.

"They're for you. And judging by that question, this is going to be a lot of fun."

An hour later, I found myself standing waist-high in freezing cold water as I tried to master a fly-fishing pole without success. Marcus stood a short distance away, clearly enjoying the view.

"Aren't you glad Betty found those waders?" he asked cheerfully, shouting over the torrent of rushing water.

"You're enjoying this, aren't you?" I shouted back at him.

"Yes, ma'am. Although I'm not sure how full we're going to be if we're relying on you to catch our dinner."

"Hey, don't underestimate the power of me in this camo," I indicated the cap and overalls that a gleeful Betty had outfitted me in.

"It's a good look for you."

A couple of hours passed in a euphoric blur. I was

an unskilled but willing student, and after overcoming the initial shock of the icy-cold stream, I was hooked. Marcus was a patient teacher, his demeanor so completely at odds with my first impression of him. Here, in the great outdoors, he was a different person. I sneaked a look at him as he tutored me in the use of a tippet. I reflected that it was a shame he didn't have any children, as he would have made a great dad to some lucky kid.

Finally victorious, I caught my first fish. Marcus announced it was time to celebrate, and I gratefully climbed out of the water, lost my footing for the hundredth time that day, and splashed into the cold water with a sense of elation. Marcus pulled me up from the muddy riverbed and gave me a funny look. "You're enjoying this, aren't you?"

"What's not to enjoy? Hours in an ice-cold river, I'm soaked to the bone, my arms are throbbing, and all I can show for my effort is a tiny minnow that wouldn't satisfy a kitten." I laughed again. "But yes, I am having a great time. I had no idea that fly fishing was going to be such fun. I think I'm addicted."

Marcus had come prepared. He handed me a towel for my face as we settled under the portable shelter. "Is this what they call glamping?" I was surprised at how comfortable the shelter was as I settled back into a reclining camp chair as Marcus prepped something that looked to be a coffeemaker.

"Just essentials." He smiled. I indulged myself by watching him work, not tiring of seeing his well-toned frame move supplies out of the truck. He bent down and leaned over the stove. It was definitely the best view in Montana. I soon smelled the welcome aroma of freshly brewed coffee and thought how much better it smelled in the cold, damp air of the riverbank than in the muss of Boston's crowded coffeeshops. Marcus passed me a large campfire mug, and I cradled it in my hands, enjoying the warmth. He settled in the chair beside me, and we sat in companionable silence, blissfully sipping the hot liquid.

"So how was your first time?"

"I think I might be an angler for life now." I laughed. "I bet you come out here all the time. I would if I lived here."

He shook his head a little sadly. "I don't much anymore. I'm pretty occupied with the business, probably more than I should be."

He didn't need to explain that to me. After my world had fallen apart, I had held onto my work as a drowning person would to a lifeboat, giving it outsized importance over everything else. Work was certain, and work was routine, and work wasn't going to cheat on me with my best friend.

"I used to come out here a lot when I was married to Justine," Marcus reflected, studying the moving river intently.

"It's a nice thing for a couple to do together."

He gave a loud laugh. "Oh, no, we never came together. I used to come to escape from her."

"Oh." I couldn't think of anything to say, and we looked at each other and then started to laugh.

"She hated all this kind of stuff. She was all about the show, was Justine."

"She was very beautiful, though," I said, remembering the photograph of the stunning blonde.

Marcus nodded his head. "She was, is still. We

weren't compatible, though. I should never have married her."

"Hindsight is 20-20," I responded, thinking how I had almost made the same mistake with Leo. "Don't be too hard on yourself. At least you realized while you have so much time left."

"But I didn't realize it." Marcus rubbed his eyes resignedly. "I caught her cheating on me with my business partner."

"Wow."

"Yeah. Pretty much made all the headlines in the Montana gossip circles."

"I know how you feel. I caught my ex-fiancé sleeping with my best friend."

It was his turn to say wow. "I'm sorry." His hand touched mine. "He didn't know what he had."

"Oh, he knew. He had multiple women and was probably having the time of his life." I started laughing again, finding the whole situation oddly humorous for the first time. "The bastard," I concluded cheerfully.

"The bitch," said Marcus and chinked our coffee mugs together. "It seems we have quite a lot in common. We should start our own lonely-hearts club."

We sat and talked and laughed until the sun began to sink lower in the sky, and the dropping temperature made me shiver. "Time to go," he concluded reluctantly, noticing my discomfort.

"That's a shame." I matched his regret. "I've had an amazing day."

"Me too. Maybe we can come again some time."

I gave him a sad smile. We both knew that whatever happened with the Whiting Whisky, my time in Montana would soon be at an end, and our lives would resume as if our paths had never crossed.

"Don't hesitate to call me if you discover another priceless bottle of whisky," I joked pathetically.

"I might just have to plant one," he responded gruffly.

We drove along the bumpy track back to the main house, and it suddenly occurred to me how vast Marcus's lands were. He slowed the truck to a crawl as he talked and told me about the types of trees that grew here, the animals that lived on the land, and the delicate balance of all the ecosystems.

"It sounds like you're a conservationist," I surmised.

He shrugged. "I don't understand why everyone isn't. Besides, I don't see it as 'my land.' I'm just here as a shepherd. People don't last forever, but the forests and the rivers should."

We finally arrived back, and I walked toward the house with a tinge of regret that our beautiful day together was at an end. Marcus grabbed my hand and pulled me into his arms. My breath quickened as I looked up into his eyes. He leaned in to kiss me, and we shared the perfect moment to end our perfect day.

We walked to the deck, and I spotted Betty and Ron sitting on the rockers together, sharing a joke. I pointed them out to Marcus and remarked what a perfectly suited couple they were.

Marcus smiled fondly. "As much in love as anyone I've ever seen. Why don't you head down and join them? I'll grab some hot cider and blankets, and we can sit out for a bit longer."

Marcus was balancing some cups and a large jug of cider when the doorbell chimed, and he set them down again in annoyance. He walked to the door and threw it open.

"Leo Dahlberg," the visitor introduced himself and offered a weak hand to Marcus, who shook it awkwardly.

"What do you want?" Marcus asked bluntly.

"I have been informed that the Whiting Whisky has been discovered."

"Isn't that just a myth?" Marcus wore a look of puzzlement which was almost convincing.

"Has there been a discovery that is linked to Whiting?" Leo pressed impatiently.

"I don't think anything found on my property is your business," Marcus said, slightly menacingly.

"I don't want us to get off on the wrong foot." Leo smiled insincerely and handed Marcus his business card. "I am a certified authenticator of Scotch whisky, and I am just offering my services. If such a remarkable discovery has been made, it would be my pleasure and privilege to help you."

"We already have all the help we need," Marcus replied curtly and tried to close the door, but Leo put his hand out to prevent it.

"I hope you haven't employed Angus Balfour. I would hate to see anyone else fall victim to his exploitation."

"Exploitation?"

Leo cleared his throat and shook his head as if pondering the poor fates of the victims. "Angus Balfour is a dishonest person. He's not a reputable businessman. He has a terrible reputation in London, which is probably why he tried to expand his business here, where people don't know who he is."

"When I researched who to employ, I was told that his company was the best." Marcus looked down at Leo, arms folded.

"He does a very good job of self-promotion," Leo said contritely. "I just feel a responsibility, as someone in the business who knows about these things, to warn the public."

"What does he do that's so unethical?"

"He will approve any passable bottle without doing any due diligence. So his opinion isn't trusted by anyone, and even worse—" Leo's voice got a bit louder, warming to his theme, "—He has also been known to relieve people of the genuine article by declaring it a fake or claiming there is a saturated market."

I chose that moment to join Marcus in the kitchen, and I heard the low murmur of voices at the front door. I stepped forward and stopped in horror when I recognized Leo's pinched voice. I continued to creep toward the entryway, straining to hear what they were saying. I felt a wave of nausea engulf me as I realized Leo could conceivably ruin everything for me again. Right then, the whisky wasn't my main concern. My feelings for Marcus had become much more than a business relationship, and the moment of reckoning would soon be upon us. Marcus was silent for a long moment, and unconsciously I found myself leaning toward them.

He finally spoke. "Get out."

"Excuse me?" Leo dared to appear offended.

"Get out," Marcus said again in flat tones.

Leo spluttered but had the sense to move in the direction of the car. "You're making a mistake. Especially with Angus and Emily." He pointed a jabbing finger in the general direction of the house and wrenched open the door to his car. Marcus closed the front door, and the room was silent. I moved back to the kitchen, so he wouldn't realize I had overheard the conversation, and muttered a four-letter word under my breath.

"Do you need some help with these?" I asked a bit too loudly as he came back to the kitchen.

He gave me a funny look and passed me the glasses. "Can you take these out to Betty and Ron? I'll be there in a minute."

I walked back out onto the deck, holding the glasses tightly, aware that my hands had been shaking slightly. I had to tell Marcus about Leo. It would ruin everything if he found out from someone else.

"So, tell us, Emily, have you found out anything more?" Ron engaged me as I joined them on the deck.

"The pieces of the puzzle are beginning to fall into place. We have confirmation that Samuel Whiting paid the artist John Duncan a large sum for his services in 1921. They were described in the ledger as etched on glass, so it's not too much of a stretch to say that links the bottle we found with Samuel Whiting." I leaned back in the comfortable rocking chair and sighed despondently.

"You don't look so happy about it," remarked Ron.

"Well, it's good news that our researcher Danny is dating everything and verifying the materials. I assume everything on that end will match up. It's good news that we have the link to Whiting, so we can certainly market this as the Whiting Whisky if Marcus decides to sell. That one bottle alone will fetch an enormous amount at auction."

Betty shielded her eyes against the last vestiges of the sinking sun and squinted in my direction. "What's the problem, then, hon?"

"The problem is that we don't have a good

explanation that places the Whiting Whisky here in Montana."

Marcus chose that moment to join the group and caught the end of the conversation. "And you think that's the point, don't you?"

We shared an intimate smile as he knew his observation was spot on. "There's something we're missing. I've felt that I'm close several times, but then it seems to elude me. I don't consider that I've done my job if we don't know the story."

"Maybe some things are just better left in the past," Betty responded.

We all sat mulling Betty's words of wisdom. A part of me agreed with her. Things like broken hearts and those steep learning curves to love probably should be put to rest. But perhaps the pain and the lessons were all part of the future and had to be lived first before we could understand the important things. I sneaked a look at Marcus, who was sharing an account of my first-day fishing, to Betty and Ron's amused delight, and wondered if Marcus was my destination or just another lesson to be learned on the long and winding road of life's mistakes. I sipped my cider, feeling very philosophical in the waning sun.

****

I held the black-and-white photograph up again but couldn't explain why I felt such a draw to it. It was undeniable that the woman was striking, but there was something else that kept nagging at me. As beautiful as she had been wealthy, Sarah Whiting met with a tragic fate, either consumed by flames or overtaken by the might of the Atlantic Ocean. No bodies had ever been found, although a local sailor claimed to have seen two flaming cadavers he thought were a man and woman, so the local authorities concluded that the corpses had just been lost to the sea. They wouldn't be the first, and they wouldn't be the last.

So what did we have? No bodies. And no whisky. Everything disappeared without a trace. What were we missing?

I looked up from my futile efforts and saw Betty in the garden below. She waved at me with a green-gloved hand. "Just picking some of my herbs," she shouted.

"Let me join you." I moved lithely down the steps from the deck, eager to embrace a distraction. "What are you picking?"

"Smell," she commanded, raising a sprig to my face.

"Rosemary! I love that smell."

"What about this one?" She pulled another from the earth.

"You can smell that mint a mile away."

"Okay, then, what about this?" She selected a leaf from the cuttings she had collected.

"Lemongrass, and that one is strong. You're making this too easy."

"Ah, I see. Miss Emily thinks she knows about what grows here in Montana," she teased me affectionately. "Wait here." She walked a few steps across the neat rows of plants in Marcus's garden, and I sniffed the air appreciatively, enjoying the mix of aromas. "This one will stump you." She proffered another sprig, and I took it and sniffed suspiciously.

"Aha, nice try, Betty. You want me to say mint again, but I'm going to say stevia. You better bring it inside in the winter."

She threw up her hands in mock surrender. "You

win. How do you know so much about herbs?"

"It's my job," I told her, a little surprised at the question.

"What? I thought you traded in liquor."

I laughed. "What do you think goes into a lot of liquor?"

"I never really thought about that. Well, any more news to share on the whisky front?"

"Not really. I think I've probably done all I can do here."

"You're not leaving already!" Betty exclaimed with a horrified look.

"I don't think there's much else I can do." I shrugged.

"Well, you can advise us what to do about that horrible man from the Whiting company. Did Marcus tell you he came and knocked on the door? Can you believe it? What a snake!"

"There's something I have to tell you, Betty." I looked at her kindhearted face and knew the time had arrived to come clean. We perched on the edge of the rock wall, and I explained about Leo—that the man I had once been engaged to was the same man who was trying to get his hands on Marcus's whisky. When I reached the part about him showing up out of the blue, her eyes widened, and she put a hand over her mouth.

"You have to tell Marcus," she whispered.

My shoulders slumped, and I willed the situation to be less unappealing than it actually was. "I don't think Marcus is going to be very happy about this."

"You're right about that," Betty exclaimed, "but better coming from you."

"What if it ruins everything?" I whispered, no longer

sure if I was talking about my business woes or my complicated relationships.

"I've seen you together," Betty said, gently squeezing my arm. "He's not been like this with anyone else. But you must be honest with him. After Justine, if he feels someone isn't being honest…" She trailed off.

"I know." And I did know. I knew exactly how he had felt. We were two of a kind. "But what if he thinks I knew about Leo from the beginning?" My voice had become panicked as I finally confronted the possibilities of how Marcus would react. "If only I could prove without a doubt that the Whiting Whisky belongs to Marcus and him alone."

"And would that solve everything?"

"Yes," I answered with grim determination. I realized that if Marcus was the rightful owner and I had been the one able to answer that question, he might not be so quick to think I had a conflict of interest. Not to mention the high stakes I was gambling with when it came to Angus and the business, which would likely fold if there was no resolution with the whisky. *Think*, I willed myself, *think*.

Betty was watching me and shook her head. "Oh, what tangled webs we weave."

Chapter Eighteen

*1921, Atlantic Ocean*

Sarah exhaled as the schooner completed its
navigation around the headland and began to pick up
speed. She didn't realize she had been holding her breath
and shuddered a few times despite the protection from
the woolen blanket that engulfed her. They were not free
yet. Indeed, neither of them would breathe easily until
the schooner was destroyed and they began the next
stage of their journey, far from the East Coast and, most
importantly, from her father's reach. She looked at her
lover and, despite the circumstances, felt her heart sing.

James was focused and alert. It had taken all his
seafaring skills to navigate the schooner successfully
under cover of darkness, and he knew that one wrong
move would cost them dearly. However, he had planned
well and made a dry run of the route in advance to see
the potential dangers of the terrain. He did not take his
eyes off the horizon. For now, the schooner and its
contents were his life, and he meant to bring them all to
safety.

They continued at a low speed for some time. Sarah
watched James intently, trying to make out his profile
against the black sky. Finally, she saw his shoulders
relax, and he flicked a switch to turn on some low lights.
She felt the craft pick up speed, and she rose to join him

at the helm. He put a strong arm around her waist and pulled her close. She rested her head on his shoulder, and together they looked to the distance where the horizon revealed faint specks of light as land came into sight.

"Where are we exactly?" she asked.

"Close to Ocean City, but we're heading farther inland. There's a better point of disembarkation where we can destroy the schooner."

"And that's where the motor will be?"

"I hope so." James grimaced. "That's what Greer said."

"I still can't believe he betrayed Father like that. He's worked for him for so long."

"Every man has his breaking point. He wouldn't be the first to change his mind about your father. He hasn't become so successful without making enemies, and I imagine he has more than his fair share," he said, his face hardening.

"Like you," Sarah stated.

"It tends to happen when someone wants to kill you."

Sarah didn't respond but squeezed him more tightly. He was right. Despite being her only remaining parent, Samuel Whiting had never been a focus of Sarah's love or affection, and he had never treated her with anything more than mild detachment. He had never been abusive toward her physically or verbally, but his complete disinterest in her had in some ways been worse. Sarah's childhood of intolerable loneliness in the care of a never-ending series of governesses had made her resentful and bitter but also entirely self-reliant. She realized that without her father's neglect, she would probably have never had the determination to be standing next to James at that very moment.

She suddenly remembered the purse Kitty had given her so insistently. She opened the clasp and felt around the silk lining. Kitty's ruby necklace, her most prized possession, was nestled in the bottom. Sarah touched the red jewel and felt a wave of emotion wash over her. She dropped it back in its secure pouch, and her hand felt the touch of paper. She pulled out a hastily folded note and read the words:

*My darling,*

*You will always be with me even though we may never see each other again.*

*This ruby will help with expenses.*

*My cherished child forever, luck be with you, my beloved niece.*

*Kitty*

She folded the note again and brought the paper to her lips. Her kind and loving Aunt Kitty, who had filled the void of love and companionship as her father was incapable of doing. She looked up at the dark sky and squinted until she could see the prick of a bright star in the dark canvas. She made a wish then, not for herself but for her aunt, that she would find her happy ending. The ruby necklace had been gifted as currency, but she knew she would never part with it and would hand it down to her children as a reminder of the most gentle and kind lady she had ever known.

Sarah shivered again as she recalled her narrow escape. James and O'Brien had timed their arrival perfectly, waiting until Sarah and Greer had a full diversion. The two men had each steered a dinghy to quietly rest at the back of the ship. They unloaded crates of whisky, fortified Madeiras, and a small box that housed a wedding gift of a one-of-a-kind bottle intended for a wealthy couple.

Setting the fire had been the easy part, with more care employed to stage the deaths of Sarah and himself. She had acted the part beautifully and added to the terror and confusion with a flawless display of blood-curdling screams, which she had later confessed were mostly authentic. The water was too cold for any of them to be in for long, and the most dangerous part was pulling Sarah from the icy waves in time. O'Brien pulled her into the dingy as soon as she hit the water and maneuvered expertly to the waiting schooner, not even pausing to check whether James was in pursuit. O'Brien helped Sarah, shivering and frantic, onto the boat, and she stripped immediately to change into warm, dry clothes and hide from view under an enormous woolen blanket. He began loading the cargo from the dinghy and let out a sigh of relief when the shivering figure of James rounded the bend and came into view. The two men worked vigorously to move the remaining crates, and when finished, they clasped each other's arms.

"You are a brother to me," James told his friend sincerely.

"No time," replied O'Brien. "I have to get back in time to see your bodies float away, and you have to get out of here before the Coast Guard arrives."

James scrambled onto the boat, and they hoisted the dinghy up behind him. O'Brien wasted no time heading back to the wreckage, now engulfed in flames. He turned for a split second and saluted his friend.

\*\*\*\*

Against grim odds, the plan had succeeded, and this part of their journey was almost over, he thought with relief as they finally disembarked. James let out a euphoric exclamation when he saw the waiting motor exactly as Greer had described. He sent up a whispered thank-you to his former superior and grinned as he thought of him delivering the bad news to his master.

James quickly moved the crates, bottles, and trunks into the vehicle, stopping only to wipe sweat from his brow. The physical exertion made his body cry out for respite, but he carried on. There would be time to rest when they were free. Finally finished, he poured gas over the schooner, feeling an illogical loss at destroying the craft that had served him so well. "I thought we were going to travel lightly?" he asked Sarah with a smile.

"I did, my darling, only my most treasured possessions." Sarah rummaged in one of the trunks and pulled out a leather wrapping. She undid the binding with care and showed the contents to James. His mouth dropped open as he beheld the score of glittering diamonds and precious stones. "My mother's jewels and a few of my own. These should help with travel."

"We have to be careful," James cautioned. "We're heading to the untamed west, and we won't find things the same as at home. We have alcohol, jewels, and fortunately this." He indicated a double-barreled shotgun nestled on the seat. "Greer didn't let us down."

"Did we get the bottle I wanted?"

"I think so." James looked at the crates and located the smallest one. "I don't understand what's so special about this one."

"It's a one-of-a-kind. My father said it could be valuable."

"You don't want to open it to celebrate?" James grinned and held up the bottle so Sarah could see the artful caricature drawn by John Duncan's hand. "Your father's treat."

She shook her head. "I want to keep it. As a memento."

"Of what you've lost?"

"Of what I've escaped."

"It's certainly beautiful." James was examining the bottle with wonder. "Why did your father have it commissioned?"

"It's a wedding present," Sarah said, her lip curling into an unpleasant smile, "for me."

"There will be tough times ahead for us."

"It's the life I want, James. I want to be free. And I want to be with you."

\*\*\*\*

Back across that same vast ocean, Samuel Whiting would receive several visitors over the week, upending his ordered existence even more. He was sitting behind his mahogany desk when his second in command was shown into the office. "How goes it, Greer?" he asked tiredly. "I won't ask if you had a successful trip."

"Allow me to say how sorry I am about your daughter, sir. I was a great admirer of hers. Very tragic loss." Greer shook his head mournfully.

"Yes, thank you. What about the other business?" he barked, clearly unmoved by his subordinate's platitudes.

"Ah, well, that is also a little unfortunate."

"Indeed. What a shame that such a fate should also befall that Macleary chap," he commented nastily. "I must admit, I wasn't sure you would have the mettle to arrange that."

"Certainly, sir," Greer replied with a lowered head, "although the situation is a little more complicated than that."

"How so?"

Greer fussed with the clasp on his leather bag and began to rummage through a pile of messy papers, much to Samuel Whiting's increasing annoyance. He finally pulled out a thin bundle and handed it across the desk. Whiting scanned the pages, and his grip tightened on the paper.

"How did you get this? Is this the original?"

"Oh, this is a copy." Benjamin Greer blinked at Samuel Whiting. "I have the original, along with a notarized statement from the captain. It's unfortunate that James Macleary implicated you in the illegal sales of alcohol and unethical business practices so thoroughly before he died, but there you have it."

Whiting looked as though he was going to vault over the table and strangle Greer on the spot, but suddenly the fury disappeared behind the mask, and he asked calmly, "What do you want?"

"I see no reason to broadcast any of this. The boy is dead, so any repercussions can be pinned on him. I have been offered another post in Edinburgh and will leave at the end of the month." Whiting cocked an eyebrow, knowing the man wasn't finished. "I appreciate the generous parting salary that you have seen fit to give me."

"How generous have I been, exactly?" Whiting knew he was cornered but could still not back down without a negotiation.

"Two years of my annual salary," Greer replied loftily. "I doubt you will miss it very much."

As unimpressed as Samuel Whiting was with the extortion by his formerly meek employee, the price was far less than it might have been. "Fine. I expect not to lay eyes on you again."

"I can assure you of that. Of course, if anything were to happen to me, the price would be very great indeed."

"We have an understanding," Whiting sneered. "Now get out of my house at once."

"With pleasure, sir." Benjamin Greer tipped his hat in a final insolent gesture to his former master and left Baliforth House for the last time. He had a new spring in his step and realized that, with his share from the American operation, he would embark on his career in Edinburgh a rather wealthy man.

Samuel Whiting's mood did not improve when he received yet another unwelcome visitor, as his secretary informed him in hushed tones that Master Archibald Campbell had arrived. "Show him in," Whiting barked.

Archie walked into Samuel Whiting's office with some trepidation. He had met him on a couple of previous occasions, but his reputation and his own father's warnings made him lower his eyes in an expression of deference. "Allow me to say, sir, how very sorry I am for the loss of Sar-, your daughter, sir. She was a magnificent young woman." Archie kept downcast eyes, which he hoped could pass for sorrow.

"You saw her on the *Aquitania*?"

"I did. We had a marvelous conversation about the possibilities for the future."

"Of the business?"

"Business?" Archie was confused. "No, sir, I was talking to Sarah."

"How did you find her? Meek? Suitable wife material?"

"She would have made an excellent and respectable

wife," Archie answered dutifully.

"Then you either didn't speak to her or you are lying," Whiting countered nastily, banging his fist down loudly on the desk.

The young man reddened and began to stammer, "I, I can't, I don't imagine…"

"Stop that blustering," Whiting shouted. "Did you even speak to her on the *Aquitania*?"

"Actually, yes." Archie bristled. "She did not have a mild temperament, and I had concerns she might be too spirited to carry out certain matrimonial duties successfully."

"That would have been your job, man! You're supposed to quell that type of behavior."

"Sir, with respect, this didn't appear to be the case when she was under your guidance."

Whiting suddenly felt very weary. The Campbell boy was correct. If he had failed to raise his daughter as a respectable and obedient young woman, how could he expect it from anyone else?

"Give my regards to your father." Whiting opened the door, indicating the end of the meeting. "I look forward to seeing him at the club next time I am in Edinburgh."

****

Kitty thought of her niece as she checked her reflection in the mirror. She wished she could tell her of her forthcoming engagement and have her there for moral support when Robert was introduced to her brother. She applied more powder to her face and tilted her chin in an expression of defiance. If Sarah could have the courage to change her life, then she could have the courage to tell her brother he would no longer be dictating hers.

Samuel Whiting also looked at his reflection in another part of the house as his manservant attended him to dress for the evening. He was expecting the company of his sister Kitty's new fiancé Robert Dahlberg, along with two other members of the Dahlberg family. He was not looking forward to the evening, as Kitty had been extremely close to Sarah in her caretaking role and would likely be tearful and full of feminine emotions, he thought distastefully. It was very unfortunate that Kitty had been there in person to witness the whole episode, likely contributing to a fragile state. Whiting sighed. Was it possible they could conclude the evening without discussing the topic?

He himself felt only anger as he thought about the events on the other side of the Atlantic. His hand formed into a fist when he remembered Benjamin Greer, an ungrateful little snake who had blackmailed him with help from that lowlife James Macleary.

His manservant held out his dinner jacket, and he unfurled his fist. He relaxed as he recalled that Macleary was also dead and had got what was coming to him. He straightened his collar as the manservant lined up his bowtie. At least some order had been restored to the civilized world. The distinction of classes needed to be upheld, and renegades like Macleary had to be dealt with for everyone's sake.

His musings returned to his daughter. He had thought of Sarah only a few times since her death, to reflect on the oddity of the circumstances surrounding her demise. When he had instructed the servants to clear Sarah's belongings from her rooms at Baliforth House, he was perplexed to be told they had found nothing of value whatsoever, and it appeared that his daughter had taken all her mother's jewels with her halfway across the world.

As the evening progressed, his mood improved. He had been pleasantly surprised by the demeanor of his future brother-in-law. He had given the impression of a sharp-witted and levelheaded fellow and had offered due deference to Whiting when asking for Kitty's hand in marriage. The whole event had been quite a relief, as he had been resigned to the idea of his sister as a future spinster who would need his financial support. He had met with his attorney earlier in the week to instruct the changes to his will. With his sole heir now gone, he had changed ownership for the company to pass to his sister Kitty in the unlikely event of his death. Having met her future husband, he felt a little better about the prospect. His attorney had remarked that future changes could be made if he were to father another child, preferably a son, of course. He had not given any previous thought to having another child, but the idea was intriguing. He would need a wife, of course…perhaps his mistress Belle? He frowned. Perhaps not.

After the Dahlbergs departed, he summoned Kitty and congratulated her on such an advantageous match. He had drunk a lot more than was his customary habit, basking in the company of the Dahlbergs and the compliments of Ida in particular, and felt a little unsteady when Kitty walked toward him.

"You are very kind, dear brother. I believe I will be very happy."

"At least something good came from the voyage." Whiting cleared his throat. "I know you were very fond of Sarah, and I'm glad to see you're taking it so well." It was challenging for him to finish the sentence, as his breathing had become labored, and his chest was starting to hurt. He suddenly staggered dramatically toward a chair, his legs unable to support his weight.

"What is the matter, Samuel?" Kitty looked at him in alarm.

"My chest," Whiting choked through gasps of air. "Go get the servant."

Kitty ran off and returned with the manservant, who immediately left to fetch the doctor. Whiting clutched the chair, but his hand missed its mark, and his tall body slid to the floor.

Kitty looked down at her brother and watched his face turn puce as his heart failed. He reached, grasping for her hand, and she bent down next to him on the polished floorboards. "I'm leaving the company," he wheezed with immense effort, "to you and Dahlberg." He concluded his labor, and Kitty could see the life slipping from his face.

"Oh, Samuel," she said gently through her tears.

"Sarah," he whispered, his final word.

"Is alive," Kitty told him and saw his eyes widen for a split second as the brightness disappeared, and she held his hand until it moved no more.

****

"This is the spot," Sarah concluded, shielding her eyes against the sun. After so many months of travel, she was used to the rugged landscape, but nothing prepared her for the beauty and the vastness of America's western states. After almost a year of the greatest adventure of their lives, the time had come to find a home.

They had headed first to Philadelphia for supplies

and then joined the Lincoln Highway, bound west. Even though she was an ocean away from her father, Sarah knew he had influence and connections that could find her on the East Coast, even if she was a ghost. Their last risky stop had been in Chicago, where they had exchanged some jewels for bonds to begin their new life. Omaha, Nebraska, was where they became husband and wife, at James' insistence.

"Why would we formalize it?" Sarah laughed at him. "We've already been telling people we are Mr. and Mrs."

"But I want it to be true in every sense."

Sarah used her middle name, Rose, to avoid any suspicion, despite James' protestations. "We must leave the past behind. We can be anybody we want here—it's time for a clean start."

When the registrar in Omaha asked James for his surname, he grinned at Sarah and responded, "MacClean." The registrar handed him the piece of paper, and that day it was recorded by a misspelling that the marriage of James and Rose McClean had taken place.

At Cheyenne, they finally peeled off north to the rugged beyond until they arrived in the small town of Billings. "It's mighty pretty up here in Wyoming," James remarked to the storekeeper.

The man laughed. "You've headed farther than you think, son. This is Montana."

And Montana is where they would stay. Sarah had felt the beginnings of the new life inside her and finally revealed it to a euphoric James. "This seems like a perfect place for it," he determined, and Sarah looked at the breathtaking mountain range and agreed.

"This is where we shall build our house."

"Probably more like a cabin, to start," James warned.

"That will be less cleaning for the servants," Sarah responded and broke into laughter at her husband's face. "You might have to teach me some things."

"I can certainly do that." He embraced his wife. "We have a lot of things we don't want the lawmen to find. We need to be careful."

"Maybe we can have a hidden wing, like the old castles," Sarah joked.

James looked thoughtful. "A false wall wouldn't be a bad idea."

James' first step was to figure out who the land's rightful owner was. He had assumed it was the Cheyenne tribe but had been told by a fur trader with a sad shake of his head that it was not. He pointed him back in the direction of the town, where he had met Liam Farley, a wheeler and dealer James liked immediately, even if he didn't trust the man for a moment.

"So how much land do you want to buy?" asked Liam.

"Depends how much of an honest price you can give me, Mr. Farley."

"Call me Liam if we're going to be neighbors." He pretended to consult a map and then made a show of doing some complex arithmetic on his ledger. He finally turned the paper around so James could see the amount.

"That's mighty funny, Liam. I enjoy a good joke, but I'm eager to settle down, and I don't have time to spare. Can you tell me who has the adjoining parcel of land, and I'll speak with them?"

"Settle down, son. What do you think is a fair

price?"

"That depends if you can throw in building supplies or not."

"Suppose I can."

"And also, how do we pay for the deed?"

"Are you wasting *my* time?" growled Liam Farley. "I don't take wooden nickels."

"How about diamonds and whisky?"

Chapter Nineteen

*Present Day, Montana, USA*

Betty, Marcus, and I were in the sunny kitchen once again when Ron appeared with an unusually somber look on his face. "This just arrived." He held up a FedEx envelope.

Marcus snatched the envelope and ripped it open. He scanned the contents and shrugged. "It's what we expected. There's a bunch of laws cited here… replevin…acilian…" His brow furrowed at the unfamiliar legal terms. "That asshole Dahlberg wants the whisky and thinks he has the right to take it."

"Are you going to contest?"

Marcus looked at me and registered my pained expression. He shook his head a little sadly. "It was fun while it lasted. I'm just sorry we were never able to figure out the mystery. My ancestors somehow got hold of the Whiting Whisky and stashed it. My great-grandmother had an expensive necklace, which also doesn't fit with her poor beginnings, so perhaps we just conclude that they were thieves or something."

We all looked despondent as the inevitable defeat settled on the room. Betty sighed heavily and walked over to the piles of papers and photographs we had laid out. She picked up a stack, and my eye caught a familiar picture on the top as she put it in the cardboard box. My hand shot out to stop her, and she looked at me in sympathy. "Hon, I think you just need to let it go now."

"No, wait. I think I saw something." I snatched up the picture and let out a gasp of amazement. It was the photograph of the drowned socialite, Sarah Whiting, standing aboard what looked to be an ocean liner. I had studied the picture intently before, but all my attention had been on the main event. This time, I was struck by a secondary figure in the background. "Who's this?" I jabbed my finger at the image of a shorter woman in an elegant gown. "Look what she's wearing around her neck."

Betty looked at the photograph in astonishment. "I mean, it looks the same shape and everything"—she was doubtful—"but it's really too blurred to tell."

Ron suddenly appeared at my elbow, scrutinizing the image, and he made an odd, "Aha."

"What are you doing?" Betty snapped at her husband.

"I know who that is." Ron pushed his reading glasses farther back on the bridge of his nose. "That's Catherine Dahlberg."

We all stared at him in surprise. "How do you know?" I asked.

He was leafing through one of the boxes but turned and looked at Betty accusingly. "You've mixed up all the piles. Where was the one I had?"

"We're finished. Why are you starting to make all this mess again?"

"I just want to find the article I read about the origins of the Whiting-Dahlberg company," he said patiently, as if talking to a child. They rummaged around for a while, with Betty muttering under her breath, until Ron seized one of the papers. "Here, listen. 'Until the mid-1920s, the distillery was solely owned by Samuel Whiting, businessman,' blah, blah… 'Upon his untimely death, the company passed to his brother-in-law, Robert Dahlberg, and his sister, Catherine "Kitty" Dahlberg nee Whiting.' Look at Catherine Dahlberg here." He pointed to another formal photograph of a stern-looking couple in front of a large building. "She looks almost identical to that one." Again, he indicated the figure standing behind Sarah Whiting.

"But why would Rose McClean have her necklace?" I wondered.

"Maybe she was on the ship with Catherine Dahlberg and stole the necklace or something," Betty offered.

"And stole the Whiting Whisky at the same time," Ron concluded.

"It's possible, or maybe it wasn't her, maybe it was your great-grandfather, or both of them together," I said to Marcus.

"It's starting to look like I came from worse than just humble beginnings." He gave a bitter laugh.

"We're missing something," I said desperately. "There's something… I just can't put my finger on it."

"Well, we gave it our best shot," said Betty starting to tidy away the papers again, but I placed my hand on her arm for a second time. "Wait. There's something. I've seen something." I closed my eyes and willed my brain to remember. "She wasn't the only one to drown during the fire," I muttered. I shut out the room to concentrate. I mentally sifted through the photographs we had looked at. Bingo. My eyes snapped open.

"When did your ancestors come to Montana?" I

asked Marcus.

"Early or mid-1920s, I think." He shrugged. "I mean, there's no mystery to that. Jim McClean, and his wife's name was Rose."

"Rose," I repeated.

"That was her real name, but my Grandpa said she always went by her middle name—Sarah."

"Oh, my goodness!"

"What is it?" Marcus looked at me in alarm.

"Jim and Sarah. James and Sarah." They were all looking at me with quizzical faces.

"Show me that picture of Sarah Whiting again," I instructed.

"Who?" Marcus was looking more bewildered than ever.

"The picture!" I screeched, snatching up the newspaper article again. "This is Sarah Whiting, daughter of Samuel Whiting, who, according to newspapers and other accounts of the time, died escaping a fire on a boat off the East Coast." I checked their faces for confirmation and was met with some unconvinced nodding. "Now, where is the picture of your ancestors?"

Together we scrambled through the mass of papers on the coffee table. Betty, who had been trying to keep them neatly cataloged, made an exasperated sound. "Just calm down and stop messing everything up," she chastised. "Now, when would this photo have been taken? I've tried to keep things organized by decade."

"1920s," I answered breathlessly, "the time the McCleans first came to Montana."

"They've all got mixed up now." She indicated the jumble that had once been in neatly stacked arrangements.

"Does everyone have time to take a pile?" I asked, and they nodded expectantly. My excitement was infectious. I divided the sizable stack into roughly four and handed them out to Ron, Betty, and Marcus.

"What exactly are we looking for, hon?" asked Betty.

"The McCleans right here." I pointed out the window. "Right when the cabin was being built."

"What do they look like?"

"He was handsome," I remembered.

"What about her? Was she a looker?" Ron joked.

"Yes. Yes, she was," I answered sincerely.

We all began working through our respective piles. The only sound was the shuffle of paper as we worked. After a few minutes, I plopped down on the oversized couch, and Marcus sat down beside me. I was momentarily distracted by the faint odor of cologne and his close proximity. *Keep focused.*

"Is this what you're looking for?" Marcus turned to me, and our knees touched. I swallowed and took the photo album he was holding out. He had found it.

"What's this got to do with the Whiting Whisky?" Betty asked again.

"Indulge me. I think we may have found our connection." Marcus rewarded me a sexy half-smile. I motioned for us to gather around the coffee table. "Hand me those other photographs," I instructed, "and the note. Where's the note with the blanks, that Danny found in the Whiting crate?"

"Here's your version with the fill-in-the-blanks." Ron passed me the notepad where I had transcribed the words found by Danny.

I gathered the little pile close to my chest and took a

deep breath. Very slowly, I put down the first image. "This is a photograph of Sarah Whiting, the daughter of Samuel Whiting. She was killed in the fire that destroyed the Whiting Whisky."

"But it wasn't destroyed. It was in the cabin," Betty stated with a hint of impatience.

"So this is a picture of a dead rich girl." Ron brought us back to the matter in hand.

"No. Well, yes, I mean, she's dead now," I corrected, "but I don't think she died then."

Next, I put down the photo album opened to the page that showed the grainy image of Marcus's great-grandparents, Jim and Rose McClean. "Look at this picture," I instructed. We all studied the image. Then Marcus turned to me with a shrug. I raised an eyebrow and allowed myself a cryptic smile. "Now then…" I put down the picture of Sarah Whiting next to the image. "Notice anything?"

The three of them studied it for a long moment. "Is it…? It looks like the same person." Betty sounded doubtful. "Were they related or something?"

I shook my head, still smiling. "One more photo." I placed the image of another ghost alongside. "This is a photo of James Macleary in the first world war. Incidentally, he was employed by Samuel Whiting and died in the same fire as Sarah Whiting."

We all peered at the collection on the table. Betty drew in a sharp breath. "He's the same person, too…" She trailed off.

"How can they be the same people?" Marcus sounded unconvinced. "These two died in the fire."

"Did they?" I challenged him. "What were *their* names?" I tapped the photo of his ancestors again.

"Jim and Rose McClean."

"Exactly. Jim. As in short for James. Rose. *But* you just said that she always went by her middle name, Sarah. I bet that wasn't her middle name at all. It was the name she'd gone by all her life. And do you think they were humorous when they used the surname McClean? Clean start or something?"

"That explains the necklace and the note." Ron was nodding at me in agreement.

"Does it?" Betty looked at her husband incredulously.

"Niece. It says, 'niece.' "

"Of course!" I exclaimed.

"I am completely lost," Betty said.

We all pored over the note. "So it's *to* a niece from this 'K' person." I looked at Ron for affirmation.

"K is for Kitty, Catherine Dahlberg, who was Whiting's sister. She went by the name Kitty, so Whiting's daughter Sarah—or Rose McClean, if we're right—would have been her niece."

Marcus stood frowning intently, processing the information. "So they faked their deaths and stole Whiting's Whisky?"

"But why?" Betty interjected. "If she was his daughter, wouldn't she inherit everything anyway? And some jewels and whisky wouldn't measure up to all the rest of his money."

"Probably the oldest reason of them all," Ron said, beaming at Betty. "Love."

"What are you blabbering about?" she scolded affectionately.

"She was engaged to someone else. It was in one of the newspaper articles Angus sent over. An engagement notice." We all looked at Ron in surprise for the second time. "What? I can read," he answered a touch defensively. He started to rummage in the boxes again.

"Perhaps she was already in love with this James person," Betty mused. "If he worked for her father, it makes sense their paths might have crossed at some point."

"I can't imagine Whiting senior would have been thrilled about his daughter falling in love with a regular guy like this one." Marcus tapped the photo of James Macleary again.

Betty was looking at Marcus with an odd look on her face. "Goodness me, I can't believe I didn't notice it before." She picked up the photograph and held it up alongside Marcus. Ron laughed raucously.

"There's quite a resemblance."

Marcus snatched the photo from Betty and studied it more intently. "Nah, I don't see it."

"I do." We were all staring at Marcus now. "So she gave it all up for him," I concluded.

"Well, I'd trade a little liquor for him." Betty laughed.

"Don't you think that's strange, though?" Marcus questioned. "A lot of people marry *for* money and not the other way around."

"I can't imagine anything stranger than *that*. I could never be with someone I wasn't in love with just to have a comfortable life. Money seems to make things more difficult. At least if you both have nothing, there's never any question about it."

"That's how you feel, isn't it?" Marcus was looking at me with an odd expression I couldn't decipher.

The moment was interrupted by the doorbell. Betty

left to answer it and returned a moment later, followed by an unwelcome visitor. The moment of reckoning was here.

"Leo Dahlberg." He offered his weak hand to Marcus, who shook it reluctantly. "I'm sure we will be seeing more of each other as the business is concluded." He then turned his sharp eyes on me. "Emily, are you finished here yet?"

"Do you two know each other?" Marcus looked at me with narrowed eyes.

"We certainly do," Leo said smugly, ignoring my look of anger. "Emily is my fiancée."

"Was," I corrected.

"Is this true?" Marcus demanded.

"We were engaged," I began, but he walked out of the room and out the front door before I could say anything else.

"Did I miss something?" Leo looked confused. "I'm here to talk about the whisky."

I shot him a look of pure venom and ran out of the house after Marcus. He was climbing up into his truck, and I tried to grab his hand, but he shook me off. "Don't touch me," he growled.

"Wait, please, just let me explain," I begged.

"I think I've finally caught up, Emily. You and your 'fiancé' were working together to make some money. I get it; it's business. Although I prefer to do business with people who aren't damn liars."

"I didn't lie about anything," I cried desperately. "I know I should have told you about my connection to the Dahlberg company, but it's over. I was focused on trying to do my job, and now we've finally found out the truth."

"You wouldn't know the truth if it bit you in the ass,

Emily," he spat at me and, finally shaking me off, climbed up into the truck cab and drove away in a cloud of dust.

I stood in the drive and struggled not to let emotion overwhelm me. "Are you okay?" came Leo's sotto voice behind me. "That McClean guy seems like a real piece of work."

"I don't want to talk about it, Leo. Especially with you."

He held up his hands. "Got it, I understand. Can I drive you back to the hotel?" I looked back at the ranch and realized that if I didn't take him up on his offer, I would have to go back to the house and ask Betty or Ron for a ride.

We drove in silence, and I stared out the window, trying in vain to figure out how I had got everything so wrong. When we arrived back at the hotel, Leo took my hand gently. "I'm sorry you're upset. I understand if you need some time alone, but you also have to eat." He gave me a sympathetic smile, and I remembered how charming he could be. "I'm available for dinner or a drink if you want. Just send a text."

I retreated to the sanctuary of my room and stared at my hollow reflection in the mirror. I would likely never see Marcus again, and he would forever think of me as a scheming liar. The thought overwhelmed me, and I threw myself down on the bed and sobbed uncontrollably until I had no tears left to cry. When my body stopped convulsing, I wiped my sore cheeks dry. I wanted someone to comfort me, and there was only one person who could do the job.

"I'm on a date, Emily," Angus whispered as the call connected.

"What's his name?" Despite myself, he still made me smile.

I heard him mumble an excuse to his companion, followed by footsteps as he retreated, presumably to find somewhere more private. "Casper. Danish. Wanted to buy a rare Glenlivet. He's very nice, Emily." The last sentence was said very earnestly, and I smiled again. Angus sounded smitten.

"Well, I won't keep you from your date, but I just wanted to give you the bad news before you heard it from anyone else in the Scotch circles."

"It's not the Whiting Whisky?"

"Oh no, it's certainly the Whiting Whisky, and the Dahlberg company has sent a legal request. Marcus found out that Leo was my fiancé, so he thinks I'm a liar, hates me, and never wants to see me again."

"Will you still get credit for the authentication?"

"Oh. I don't know. I haven't thought about it."

"I see."

"What do you mean 'I see'?" I asked in annoyance.

"This discovery could save the company and push you into the limelight as *the* authority on the subject. *But* you're more worried about what Marcus thinks about you. So it's not too much of a stretch for me to conclude there's something more between you and Marcus than you've been letting on."

"It doesn't matter now anyway, because he hates me, and Leo's won again." I sniffed.

"Only if you let him, Emily, only if you let him."

I released Angus back to his date, only just realizing that it was already midnight in London. I looked at my phone again, unrealistically hopeful Marcus might have sent a message, but there was only a text from Leo with the word "dinner?"

We met in the lobby, and he asked me where I wanted to go. I shrugged uncaringly. "There looks to be a nice restaurant on the main street, an old hotel or something. We could—"

"No. Not there," I cut him off, thinking of my dinner with Marcus, which had only been a few days before but seemed like a lifetime. We ended up at a passable Italian restaurant, and Leo ordered a carafe of wine and some calamari while we looked over the enormous menu cards.

"I've missed this," he whispered.

I took a large mouthful of wine. "Leo, we're not getting back together."

"I know, I know, I just miss your company." I didn't respond and turned my attention back to the menu when he asked slyly, "How's Angus?"

"He's fine," I responded coldly. Angus had always been a source of contention between us, as he had never disguised his dislike of Leo, which was a sentiment entirely reciprocated. The two men could not have been more different. Angus was loud, unpolished, and had the biggest heart of anyone I had ever met. On the other hand, Leo was charming and slippery, and you never really knew where his allegiances lay, I realized for the first time.

"Good. I had just heard something different."

"What have you heard?"

"Only that he had some business woes. Or should I say you both do?"

"I imagine that's one of the reasons you came here so quickly." I finally saw the situation for what it was. "Two birds with one stone. You get your hands on the

Whiting Whisky and get Angus out of the way at the same time."

"I thought perhaps you would see the error of your ways and do it for me," he said.

"Do what? Ruin Angus and the business he worked his whole life to build?"

He shrugged as if it was of no consequence and speared a piece of calamari with his fork. I watched him with an amazed detachment. How could I ever have wanted to be with this man? Leo would always be handsome, but at that moment, he reminded me of a cold, slithering snake. He had been born with wealth and privilege but had never felt any responsibility for those not as high on the food chain. I had a lurch of self-revulsion as I now saw I had been so blinded to his faults that I had even once agreed to marry him.

"It doesn't matter now anyway. You can authenticate the Whisky, and I'll take ownership of it. The Dahlberg company will credit you and Angus with the discovery, and his business can fold on a high note."

"I'm not following…"

Leo gave me a patronizing smile and opened his mouth to continue, but I put up a hand to stop him. "What I don't understand is why you believe you would take ownership of the Whiting Whisky."

He was confused but astute enough to realize there was something more to the story. "What have you found in your 'investigation'?" he asked, using his fingers for air quotes.

"It's going well," I responded cautiously. "Doing these things properly always takes time."

"It is strange that this McClean guy called you and Angus to authenticate his amazing discovery. But it probably makes sense if he's trying to bypass the rightful owner."

"We don't know that you *are* the rightful owner, Leo. You seem to be forgetting that it was discovered in Marcus's house."

"Oh, *Marcus* is it now?" he said sarcastically.

"I'm here to do a job. If the bottle is genuine, we will further investigate the origins."

"Do you take me for a fool, Emily?" I said nothing, instead raising my eyebrows to indicate that was exactly what I thought of him.

"You've already concluded that the bottles are genuine, which means that you and your *Marcus* are trying to either claim that it's not the Whiting Whisky so he can sell it privately or concoct some story to make him the rightful owner."

"That's a lot of assumptions, Leo, without any facts to stand up in court."

"As you know, Emily, this business is built on reputation."

I laughed in his face unpleasantly. "Then I'm at a loss to understand why you're still in business," I shot back.

"Be careful," he warned. "Angus's reputation may be a little more fragile than you realize. Not everyone in the world of high-end Scotch is as liberal-minded as you think."

"What's that supposed to mean?" I snarled back at him. "You're threatening to 'out' him? You're disgusting and pathetic. Angus has never tried to hide who he is from anyone."

"I've never understood why you worship him so much. You're like a pathetic little puppy." I stared at him in shock.

"Look, I'm sorry, I shouldn't have said that." He tried hastily to recover. "This whole thing has just got us all acting a bit crazy. Trust me, everything can still work out fine. Suppose you conclude that the whisky was once the property of Whiting holdings. In that case, you can maintain your high ethical standards and recommend that Mr. McClean return it to the rightful heir." He pushed his business card into my hands. "It would be nice if you could keep me informed. In the spirit of cooperation, I will be sure to eradicate any unpleasant gossip about your employer."

"You're never getting that whisky, Leo. I'll make sure of it."

"Be careful," he spat. "I could make things very difficult for you." The words rang in the air, and I had a strange feeling they had been spoken a long time ago by another threatening man.

"You won't win this time, Leo." I grabbed my purse and walked out of the restaurant into the clear Montana air.

Chapter Twenty

"I'll miss you," I told Ron sincerely as we hugged tightly. "I've begun to feel quite at home here."

"Montana suits you," he said with a smile. "I'm happy to take her to the airport…" This last was addressed to Betty, who dismissed him with a shake of her head.

"I want to take her, but you can carry her stuff to the truck."

"I'll send a full report when I've written everything up, but we have a compelling case."

"You solved the mystery, just like I knew you would." She smiled at me affectionately. "Okay, time to go, then."

I followed her out of the house and paused for a moment as I passed the bottles on the mantelpiece. "Do you think Marcus is going to leave them there?"

"Probably not." She gave me a meaningful look. "They would make him think of you."

I swallowed but didn't reply. I couldn't blame him for hating me, but I wished he had given me a chance to explain. I climbed up into the cab and took my last look at the beautiful ranch. It hadn't been many days since I had first arrived, but I was a completely different person. One with Leo finally relegated to my past. Marcus, too, would soon be a person of my past, although that thought was a much less welcome one.

"Is Marcus…?"

Betty looked at me sympathetically. "He's made himself difficult to find until you leave."

I nodded morosely, resigned to the fact that I had made a huge mess of things. It had taken me a long time to see Marcus for what he was, a man of principles and values, and one I had fallen for, head over heels. I hoped Misty knew what a good man she had.

"Ready?" Betty hopped into the driver's seat and started the engine. "Bet you're going to miss this place," she said as we started down the drive.

"I am. The view is so beautiful."

"I'm not talking about the view," she snapped.

"What then?"

"I'm talking about Marcus."

"What about Marcus?"

"Lord knows what I'm supposed to do with the pair of you," she said in exasperation. "Perfect for each other, and you can't see what's right in front of your nose."

"Betty, right now, he can't stand the sight of me and is probably in love with Misty. Whatever happened between us was nothing more than a passing fling."

"Misty! Are you out of your mind? I already told you you've got the wrong idea."

"I heard them," I said quietly, "on the phone. Marcus said that love had everything to do with it, and he didn't want things to get ugly."

"Oh, you silly girl. He wasn't talking about the love of a person. He's talking about the love of the land."

"What?"

"Misty Farley is hard up for money. She's selling a chunk of her land to a developer who wants to build some wilderness resort thing, bring a bunch of idiots up from the city and charge them ten dollars for a glass of iced tea. Well, they'll give her a good price, but they want an access road, a direct one, and that would cut through Marcus's land. He won't grant her permission, so she's not very happy about it. He even offered to buy the land from her to help with her money troubles, but the developer offered more."

"Oh."

"Yes, *oh*." Betty gave me a look of annoyance and focused on the road once more.

"Well, you said they had a connection and always would," I persisted, "and it sounds like Marcus has a soft spot for her, at least if he's willing to go to these lengths trying to help her, even if she is ungrateful."

"Of course they have a connection. She was his sister-in-law."

"Sister-in-law?" I was dumbstruck.

"Yes, she's Justine's sister, Marcus's ex-wife. I thought you knew that. And they're the Farleys. They used to own pretty much the whole state until the McClean clan and a couple of others came along."

I shook my head mutely. It appeared Betty had been right, I *had* got the wrong end of the stick, and now it was too late.

"And what about you and Mister-thinks-he's-all-that Dahlberg?"

"You know exactly what," I told her grimly. "It's been over a long time, but thanks to our trip down here, I finally got the closure I needed. Thanks in part to you," I added quietly.

"So you told him to leave you alone?" she asked, refusing to look at me.

"Yes, not just me, but Marcus too. I said I was going

to do my very best to make sure Marcus retained ownership of the Whiting Whisky." I gave a humorless laugh. "He wasn't exactly happy, and I have a feeling he's going to make things as difficult as possible."

"I see. And was Marcus right to think you were working together?"

"Working together!" I exclaimed. "It's the exact opposite. Leo is trying to ruin the business Angus and I have built up, and he's likely to succeed. Also"—I was working myself up now—"Marcus was the one who called *me*. I didn't mention *anything* to Leo, because I hadn't spoken to him in months and months, *and* he was the absolute last person I would ever want to show up here." I sat back in my seat, fuming, and Betty gave me a look of amusement.

When we arrived at the airport, she practically kicked me out to the curb. "I hate goodbyes like this," she concluded, then dropped my bag on the ground, and the truck was gone, leaving me standing, dejected, on the sidewalk. Betty had got me here very early for my flight, considering that the airport comprised a single building, and I would be lucky if there was a vending machine.

I was also more than a little hurt by the abrupt way she had just left me. What did I expect? Her employer contracted me, and that contract was now at an end. I felt tears welling up in my eyes and chastised myself for my stupidity. If my dealings with Leo had taught me anything, it was not to rely too heavily on other people. It had felt so different, though, with Betty and Ron; they had treated me with affection and a sense of belonging. And Marcus… I plopped down onto one of the hard plastic chairs. Marcus wasn't my problem anymore.

\*\*\*\*

The speedometer was hovering at least fifteen miles over the limit, but Betty didn't lift her foot from the gas pedal; there was no time. She pulled into the McClean ranch in a cloud of dust and left the engine idling as she stomped in through the front door.

"You!" she shouted, pointing at the unsuspecting figure with downcast eyes at the breakfast bar. "You are coming with me."

"Give it up," Marcus said resignedly. "We were all wrong about Emily, and now she's gone. Let it go."

"You're not fooling anyone," Betty shouted. "I know you fell for that girl, and you're too scared of getting hurt again, so you're just looking for excuses."

"Betty, it's none of your—"

"It *is* my business," she thundered, and both Marcus and Ron looked at her in fear; neither dared to contradict the statement.

"She made her choice, and she's gone," Marcus said quietly and cupped his coffee mug protectively.

"Only because she thought *you* were in love with Misty."

"Misty!" Marcus spat out a mouthful of coffee and looked at Betty as if she was deranged. "Why would she ever think that?"

"Because you're an idiot who won't say what's on your mind, and it's probably cost you the one girl who could make you happy."

Marcus seemed to crumple before her eyes, and then he whispered, "She's the one who ran after that asshole Leo Dahlberg. It's obvious there's unfinished business there."

"Not anymore," Betty crowed triumphantly. "She told him to get lost and leave her and your whisky alone."

Marcus looked like he'd just been slapped. "Get in the truck," said Betty.

\*\*\*\*

I climbed the rickety steps and took my seat. I looked out the tiny window at the Montana landscape and saw a hundred missed opportunities. I had no reason to come back. My business with the Whiting Whisky was over, and with it, my association with Marcus McClean. Whatever it was that had been between us, it was over.

\*\*\*\*

"I can't go any faster," Betty admonished an impatient Marcus.

"I don't know why you didn't let me drive," he growled.

"Because you would have been reckless and either got a ticket or got us both killed."

After what seemed like an eternity, Betty finally pulled up to Fairview's airport. Marcus sprang out of the truck before Betty had the chance to come to a complete stop and sprinted into the terminal. He cursed as he saw the regional jet taxiing to the runway.

"Evening, Mr. McClean," said one of the junior employees. "Can I help you with something?"

"I want to stop that plane."

The young man looked stricken and began to stammer, "I don't think we're allowed…" He was saved by the sound of a crackling voice down the radio line he was wearing. He gave Marcus a nervous shrug and answered.

"Does Mr. McClean need something, Bobby?" came the voice again. Marcus looked up and saw the familiar face of a more seasoned man looking out of the glass tower. He grabbed the radio, still attached to the

252

bewildered young man's shirt, and spoke.

"Good to see you, Sam. Can you radio the plane for me? I want a passenger removed. Then everyone can get on their way."

"Do you have a good reason?" Sam's voice crackled back.

"Yes."

Moments later, the airplane slowed to a halt, and an unfortunate young man struggled to get the steps into position for disembarkation.

****

"What do you mean I have to get off the plane? I have a boarding pass." I was not in the mood for this right now. It was as though fate was mocking me; the last thing I wanted to do was spend more time in the close proximity of a man who hated my guts. I opened my mouth to argue again, but the pilot silenced me with a stern warning that he would prefer to do this the easy way, but the choice was mine. I glared at him and muttered some choice words under my breath. I gathered my laptop and bag and climbed down the uneven steps. I took the last step to greet the ground too fast and stumbled on the tarmac, but a strong arm grabbed my waist. I looked up into the face of a man I'd thought I would never lay eyes on again.

"Marcus! What are you doing here?"

"I'm afraid you didn't keep to your side of the bargain."

"What?" We were both shouting now over the sound of the plane, which had resumed its slow taxi to the runway. The wind whipped my hair, and I struggled to pull it out of my face.

"You," he shouted, pointing to me.

"What?" I shouted again. I pointed to my ears and shook my head.

"Screw it." Marcus gave up trying to make himself heard over the noise of the engine and cupped my face in his hands.

It was the kind of kiss that you remember for a lifetime. There was nowhere else in the world I wanted to be than exactly where I was at that moment. When we finally pulled away from each other, we began to laugh, and he put his arm around me as we made our way to the exit.

"Did you get what you needed, Mr. McClean?" asked the young man who had been staring openmouthed at the scene.

"I did," Marcus replied curtly. "Do you have Miss Clemonte's luggage, son?"

"Oh, yes, yes," he stuttered and ran off to retrieve my suitcase from where it had been hastily pulled off the plane.

"What did you mean when you said I didn't keep my side of the bargain?"

"You were supposed to teach me about Scotch."

"I tried. You just weren't a very good student."

He laughed. "I think I'm just a bourbon man, but that doesn't mean I can't appreciate Scotch, and perhaps I'd like to have it around…for a long time."

I knew we weren't talking about whisky anymore. "Do you think maybe Scotch and bourbon are too different?" I asked lightly, swallowing down the dread I felt, in case he answered yes, but knowing I had to ask the question all the same.

"They are very different," he responded, his eyes never leaving my face, "but I think they might just be exactly what the other one needs."

"And Misty?" I had to check.

"Was never anything like that." His jaw hardened slightly. "And Dahlberg?"

"Will never be anything like that again," I responded with certainty. "You know the best way to drink Scotch is with a slow sip."

"We have a lot of time to savor the moment." He squeezed me and kissed my forehead. "This isn't the first go-round for either of us, but I think we've learned some lessons on the way." We walked together arm in arm to where Betty was waiting outside.

The three of us arrived back at the ranch, and Ron greeted me with a hearty embrace. "Welcome home!"

"Let's celebrate you not leaving today with some iced tea on the deck." Betty started to shuffle us outside, but the doorbell rang. Moments later, Ron walked back into the kitchen holding the crown jewel of the Whiting Whisky. A legend turned into a reality. Danny must have arranged for the Duncan bottle to be shipped back as soon as Marcus had requested it. We all huddled around the package, and Betty hopped from one foot to the other excitedly. "Can we look at it again? Can we open it?"

"Sure," Marcus replied. "It does belong to the McCleans. Or should I say the Maclearys?" He pulled a pocketknife off his belt and began to cut the packaging carefully. We waited in anticipation as he finally removed the last vestiges of the protective plastic.

It was beautiful. Even though I had seen it only days earlier, I still felt I was looking at it for the first time. Now we knew its story, it was as though the ghosts of the past had come back to life again. I could see the deft hand of John Duncan creating a masterpiece on a canvas of glass. I could see a beautiful young woman receiving a gift to celebrate a marriage that would never take place. I could see a handsome sailor leaving the sea behind forever for a greater love. The story of James and Sarah had echoed down the years and had finally revealed their happy ending, against all odds, in the stark beauty of Montana. Without James and Sarah, there would never have been Marcus. We looked at each other simultaneously and, in that look, said a thousand words. I didn't know what the future held, but I knew I was done with being too scared to find out.

Our moment was interrupted yet again by the unwelcome chime of the doorbell, and Betty ran to answer. "It's like grand central station in here today."

She returned stony-faced, followed by the figure of a man I once thought I loved but now despised. His eyes landed on me, and then he looked at Marcus and back again. "Oh, I see how it is," he sneered.

"It's over, Leo," I said forcefully. "It's time for you to leave."

"Get over yourself," he spat nastily. "I'm not here to see you. I'm here to see him and make the arrangements to get my whisky back."

"It's not *your* whisky, though," Betty told him delightedly.

"There is ample evidence that links Mr. McClean's family to the discovery and legitimizes him as the rightful heir," I said formally.

Leo snorted and gave me a withering look. "Oh, you're really in your element now, aren't you?"

"Yes, I am."

Betty turned to me and asked rudely, "What did you ever see in this idiot?"

"Is that it?" Leo had caught sight of the bottle, nestling in its protective case. "It's the Whiting Whisky?" His voice had taken on a tone of wonder. "How did it get here?"

I proceeded to explain the situation to Leo, feeling stronger in my conviction with every word. When I finished, he had a face like thunder and finally said, "I think you're going to find that a little hard to prove."

"We *can* prove it, though," Marcus said quietly. All heads turned to look at him expectantly.

"If my great-grandmother was Sarah Whiting, then we have her DNA."

"To compare to what?" Leo asked sarcastically. "I doubt there are any blood samples of Samuel Whiting's lying around Scotland waiting for comparison." Marcus was watching Leo and began to chuckle. I suddenly got the joke.

"He doesn't need anything from Samuel Whiting when he has his great-nephew standing right here," I said gleefully.

Leo looked as though his blood was going to boil. "I won't consent to people taking my DNA," he said haughtily. "Besides, is that even how that would work?"

"Then you'll find it hard to prove that it's your whisky over ours, won't you?' came Marcus's commanding voice.

Leo looked around the room with a furious expression, and then his face transformed into a malevolent sneer. He stalked over to the bottle, snatched it from the protective case, and smashed the neck on the side of the table.

"Noooo!" someone screamed in horror, and I realized it was me.

He slammed the bottle back down on the table and walked out the door. Marcus tried to go after him, but Betty grabbed his arm. Moments later, we heard tires on gravel as he drove away.

I have no idea how much time passed, and not a word was uttered. The four of us stood paralyzed in horror, all eyes on the now open bottle. Marcus was the first to finally move. He walked over to one of the kitchen cupboards and slowly removed four glass tumblers, one by one, which he handed to a shell-shocked Betty. He then carefully picked up the broken bottle from the table and, motioning to Ron, Betty, and myself, started to walk in the direction of the deck. "Come on." He beckoned and went outside. "It's the perfect time of evening to have a slow sip of Scotch whisky."

He poured the liquid slowly, taking care not to cut his hand on the jagged glass of the neckless bottle. He handed us each a glass, and I took mine with shaking hands. "What a waste," I muttered, still scarcely believing what Leo had done. "It was one of a kind."

"Yes, it was," Marcus concluded, "but what made it so special was its story. A story you discovered, that would otherwise have been lost forever. I now know something else about who I am." He raised his glass. "Let's make a toast."

"To the past?" I offered.

"No, this time, to the future."

**A word about the author…**

Kirsten Abel grew up in the UK, lives in the US, and loves to travel. She has always been an avid reader who loves stories about interesting people and was gratified to find that the world is full of them.

She spends most of her time doing humdrum things like working, running after her kids, and then hiding from them with a glass of wine and a good book.

*The Slow Sip* is her first novel.

Thank you for purchasing
this publication of The Wild Rose Press, Inc.

For questions or more information
contact us at
info@thewildrosepress.com.

The Wild Rose Press, Inc.

CPSIA information can be obtained
at www.ICGtesting.com
Printed in the USA
BVHW051101060323
659766BV00015B/517